I0614136

Northern Haunts

100 Terrifying New England Tales for the Campfire and the Fireplace.

EDITED BY
TIM DEAL

SP
Shroud
Publishing

A SHROUD PUBLISHING
ANTHOLOGY
WWW.SHROUDPUBLISHING.COM

NORTHERN HAUNTS

The Third Anthology From
Shroud Publishing

You are holding a limited edition small press anthology in your hands.
This book is a result of hard work and creative effort. Enjoy it and
celebrate the possibility of all things.

Designed and Printed in the USA

SP
Shroud
Publishing

First Edition
First Printing December 10, 2008
Copyright 2008 Shroud Publishing
All Rights Reserved

Cover Art by Christopher J. Zibelli
www.cjzdesign.com

Line editing by Christa M. Miller

Layout by Dale Mythito and Brian Hanson

ISBN: 978-0-9801870-5-2

Shroud Publishing LLC
121 Mason Road
Milton, NH 03851
www.shroudmagazine.com

TABLE OF CONTENTS

TABLE OF CONTENTS

TABLE OF CONTENTS

TABLE OF CONTENTS

TABLE OF CONTENTS

TABLE OF CONTENTS

To Phil Kuhlman and Joseph McGee—two talented young writers taken from the World too soon. Phil and Joe will always occupy a special place in our history. This book is for you both.

-Tim Deal, December 2008

INTRODUCTION
Tim Deal

It was a wet autumn night in Bloxham, and a thick fog had begun to fill the streets in the ancient British village. With our dampening clothes and scuffed school shoes, my brother and I rushed back from the churchyard where we had been playing in order to make it home for dinner. There, our darling gran had hot plates of sausage and Yorkshire pudding waiting for us.

After dinner, the family gathered around the fireplace for hot cups of tea and cocoa as my grandfather told us tales of apparitions and strange creatures glimpsed in the garden. The cottage was more than 300 years-old, so these stories held a special significance to my brother and I — even more so because were a couple of "yanks" accustomed to drab American navy housing and low-rent apartments.

When my father went on long cruises, my mum would pack us up and take us to England for months at a time. It was there, among the cobblestone streets, old buildings, and rolling green fields that my appreciation for stories developed. Both of my English grandparents were storytellers — my gran focused more on fairy stories, while my grandfather oscillated between stories of the Second World War and ghosts. It was a magical time for us and did much to fuel my imagination.

A number of cultures possess rich storytelling traditions, but so many of these traditions are becoming lost in the mix of technological alternatives—all competing for our attention. Despite this, there are some moments in our lives where we take a break from our laptops, MP3 players, and smartphones and simply engage with other human beings to talk, share anecdotes, or even lament and complain. It is in these quite little moments that the fertile seeds of storytelling are sown. The spirit of those moments lead me to compile 100 frightening stories set in New England from scores of different, talented authors.

My submission guidelines were simple. I wanted stories that were 700 words or less, told in first person, and featured a frightening element in one of the New England states. My intent was to put together a volume of stories that could serve as a reference for other people that relished the storytelling tradition as much as I did. I received hundreds of submissions from around the World. The stories I selected to publish resonated with me for a number of reasons. There are many stories here that I selected simply because they fit my guidelines and intent perfectly—that is, they reminded me of the traditional ghost stories that we all heard as kids. There were other stories that I selected because they were unique and original, though they perhaps did not make for the easiest tales to retell.

The bottom line is that the authors within these pages all succeeded in entertaining me. Given my specific guidelines, this was no easy task. I mandated that the stories HAD to be set in real locations in New England. This proved to be a challenge to many of the authors that submitted, because many had not been to New England, and many had never been to the United States. Why New England" You may ask? I wanted the stories to have a sense of place. I wanted the location to be as much a part of the story as the characters. I wanted the world to catch a glimpse of the only place in the United States that has rivaled my magical childhood experience in Bloxham.

I would love for this volume of stories to become a living document of sorts. I charge you, the reader, with taking these stories and modifying them to fit your personal situation. Go tell them around a campfire, or a fireplace, or during a long car ride (just don't put them in a book and publish them ;)) While, some tales will be better suited to your personal storytelling environment, all of them will tantalize, thrill or even frighten you.

—*Tim Deal, December 2008*

NORTHERN HAUNTS

100 Terrifying New England Tales for the Campfire and the Fireplace.

1. BARN AND BRIDLE
by Michael R. Colangelo

It's a pretty pony. Most ponies are. The mare is colored champagne and has bright blue eyes and a thick, ebony mane. It has sturdy bones and strong teeth.

I'm standing in the middle of a muddy field with my daughter's tiny hand holding my wrist. I'm still in my work clothes – a pin-striped banker's suit and a pair of black wingtips.

The farmer grips the suspenders of his coveralls and spits tobacco into the long grass at his feet.

"Pretty, yeah." He agrees with my daughter's observation. "She sure is that."

"How much do you want for it?" I ask, glancing at my daughter's face momentarily.

But the farmer shakes his head.

"She ain't for sale," he drawls.

I feel the grip on my hand slacken and fall away. I hear tiny bells of disappointment and sadness in the little girl standing beside me. Then she's off and running back across the field towards the Studebaker parked at the side of the road. She vanishes into the back seat in a spiral of rose and white: the colors on her dress.

The farmer watches her go with hard green eyes, and I work hard to keep the smile pasted to my face.

After a moment: "I'd like to see your barn, too. If we're not intruding."

"I can show you that, too."

Later, I'm undertaking the long drive back to our house in the suburbs. The girl sits in the back seat and the pony sits beside her.

The animal looks funny, sitting upright as if it were an over sized person that I'd stuffed into the back seat of the car.

I watch both of them in the rear view mirror. I watch their eyes, mostly. I steer the car with my right hand. The left, bloodied as it is, I keep hidden away from view beneath my seat.

The eyes of the pony have changed from pale blue to brilliant green. I keep my mouth shut for the sake of my child.

I ignore the fact that the pony might be watching me back.

◇◇◇◇◇◇◇◇◇◇◇◇◇◇◇◇◇◇◇◇◇

2. OFF THE BEATEN PATH

by Nathaniel Lambert

They were both from the research institute near Saranac Lake. Wanted to hire a local to bring 'em near the Adirondacks to radio-tag a small pack of eastern coyotes. They also needed to do some blood work. There was a whole mess of science talk about a new virus decimating wildlife across the northeast. Whatever. I'd let them worry about saving the canine world. My job was to clear a path and hump in the equipment. I said yes before a dollar amount was even mentioned. It was summer break at U of V and in this dried up town, opportunity was about as rare as a white buffalo. Shit, I grew up in those woods. How hard could it be?

Looking back, I should've asked for the money upfront.

And brought a lot more ammunition.

On the third day, we cornered the pack up against a cliff. We set up camp a good two hundred yards away. The plan was to sit back, use a tranquilizer to take the coyotes out, draw blood and snap a collar on. I offered to be the triggerman; them being the thick, coke-bottle glasses type. With one of the doctors pulling the trigger, I probably would've ended up taking a long nap.

The three of us went in with nothing more than a handful of glorified Nyquil darts... I was the only one to come out.

I used the scope to sight in on a flank shot, took a breath and readied my shot. Something was off. I thought maybe the lens was dirty. I used my shirt sleeve to clean both ends and then brought the rifle back up to the ready. Nope. I'd seen right the first time.

Have you ever nuked a hot dog for too long? The skin starts to pulse, like it's breathing. A blister forms and then, POP! The inside of your microwave becomes the set of a forgotten Lloyd Kaufman film.

Those coyotes looked the same way, like someone had put them in the microwave for just a few seconds too long. All the fur had fallen out in matted clumps. The skin underneath was riddled with giant, saucepan-size blisters. I winced and gagged as one burst and spewed forth a caseous muck.

The hell? I remember saying that. The hell?

I handed the rifle over to a labcoat for a look. His reaction was different than mine. He grinned and frantically licked his lip while calling for his colleague. I heard him mumble something about similar symptoms as before.

Symptoms? A runny nose and fever are symptoms. Melting flesh that erupts in a geyser of gore is something entirely different.

What are you waiting for, Boy? Take the shot. Slow, controlled breathing. Inhale. Exhale. Right before you feel the heart's drum-drumming in your throat, pull the trigger.

There were eight total and I didn't miss once. The tranqs pierced the flesh as easy as through rotten apples. They all dropped—way too fast for the sedative to start working—and the carcasses ruptured into puddles, splashing against the hard ground.

My employers told me to stay put. Who was I to argue? They both sprinted towards the cliff. I sighted back in and watched them come up on what was left of the pack. One bent down to take a sample and suddenly jumped backwards. Just then the ground around them began to boil violently. Both scientists turned to run back towards me, but stopped only a few feet ahead. Something large and very alive lumbered into view behind them. Its base was a geometrical shape with too many sides for me to name. The base was balanced on top of thousands of spindly legs that came to sharp points at the ends.

That's what had stopped the two in their tracks. Those legs turned them into living pin-cushions, piercing in and out and filling my magnified vision with a fine spray of blood.

I didn't stick around long enough to see what happened next, but I can guess. That thing pumped them both full of a billion copies of itself. Right now, as we sit here, it's headed this way to infect... and spread.

◇◇◇◇◇◇◇◇◇◇◇◇◇◇◇◇◇◇◇

3. ON A LONELY STRETCH OF ROAD
by Erik Williams

Halfway between Boston and Portsmouth, my car broke down. I managed to pull off I-95 at the next exit but the only thing I found there was one gas station. All the lights were off. No other car was parked in the dirt lot.

I stopped the car under a solitary light in the dim lot, shut it off, and then got out and walked around the building. It looked old and decrepit and I wondered if the place had shut its doors years ago. One thing was for sure, though: I was the only one there.

"Damn."

I turned back to my car and saw steam rising from under the hood. A few moments later, I shined a flashlight under the hood at the radiator and saw a large tear, about three inches in length, on the top hose.

"Burst hose you got there," someone said.

I spun around and almost tripped over myself. My heart raced and I shined the light in the direction of the unexpected voice. A gaunt man in a flannel shirt tucked into blue jeans stood there. I had never heard him walk up.

"Jesus, you scared me."

The guy laughed and nodded.

"I didn't think anyone else was here," I said.

The guy motioned his head toward the building. "Just hanging around."

"Do you live near here?" I looked around again. "I didn't see any other cars."

"That's right." He pointed up the road. "Live right up there. Walking distance. Walk everyday."

I nodded. "Well, do you have any hoses I can buy off you? I can change it myself. Just need a hose."

The guy shook his head and scratched his chest. "Wish I did. Stopped carrying them. Stopped carrying most things. Don't get many customers here anymore."

Shit, I thought. "Do you have a phone?"

"Pretty lonely out here." The guy took a step closer. "Where were you heading?"

"I am heading to Portsmouth." My nerves tingled. It was quiet out there in the dark. Between words, I heard traffic on the interstate. Crickets in the woods. The dying hiss of steam. "My wife's in labor. Do you have a phone?"

The guy took another step forward and for the first time I noticed a big pipe wrench in his right hand. I wondered if he'd held it behind his back or the poor lighting had just failed to reveal it.

"Now that's a damn shame," he said. "Your wife in labor and you stuck here. With me. And no way out."

Now I heard the thudding of my heart. I backed up and hit the bumper. I shuffled sideways and the guy took another step toward me. The right side of his mouth ticked up into a smirk.

"Interesting you ended up here. With me. I was just thinking how lonely it gets out here, on this road. And then you showed up with your ruptured hose. Funny how things work out."

I sidestepped away and cleared the car. "Sure."

"So lonely." He took another step toward. Only a few feet separated me from him—and the wrench. "But now you're here. And I'm here. So now it's not lonely."

Adrenaline pumped through my chest and limbs. I turned and ran, hard, as fast as I could. I had no idea if he chased me or not. I didn't down his road but angled straight for the on-ramp.

On the interstate, I waved a trucker down. My lungs burned. My legs ached. He asked what was wrong. I told him someone tried to rob me.

Two days later, after making it to Portsmouth and explaining to my wife, as I held my newborn daughter, what had happened, I had my dad drive me down to the exit to pick up my car.

"You sure this is the right place?" my dad said.

I couldn't speak; all sound lodged in my throat. There, under the solitary light, sat my car, the hood still up. But there was no gas station. There wasn't even the skeleton of a structure. It was as if it had been erased from existence.

As if it had never existed at all.

◇◇◇◇◇◇◇◇◇◇◇◇◇◇◇◇◇◇

4. OPEN HOUSE
by Phil Kuhlman

"If you'll come down here, you'll see one of the more amazing things this house has to offer. Not only is it one of the oldest homes here in Kingsport, but it still has a functioning eighteenth century well!" I smiled as I gave my typical speech. I had sold a few homes in town, and most had the same features, but these people weren't average buyers.

Out-of-towners.

I'd have to sweeten the deal, maybe leave out a few details here and there. Like the papers I'd just found on a sticky spot on the well's edge. I figured I had a few moments before the buyers came in, just long enough for a quick read perhaps.

* * *

This is insane. I can't have long. The thing is still in the house someplace. It can't be done with me. I'm still alive. There were three of us.

Were.

We came in here during a snowstorm a few days ago. The place was abandoned and unlocked. We thought, "Good luck!" We were wrong.

A few hours later we heard noises. Sheryl said it was snow collecting, causing creaking, but it wasn't. We knew the sounds were coming from the basement. Cellar? Not sure what to call this place. We don't have these where I come from. We don't have the things that came out of the well either. Terry led the search, looking for whatever the sound was. I figured it'd be a dog or something, but it was coming from inside this well. The last thing he did was lean over it and say "Echo!" It wasn't sound that came back to the source, but the thing. It was pulpy, gray, and looked to me like it was full of broken bones and shards of the things it had attacked before us. The smell was horrific, like a crypt filled with sewage. It was so fast though. Big too. It didn't make sense for a thing that size to come out of a hole that small.

Terry screamed for a few seconds, then came the crunching slurping sounds. I grabbed Sheryl and tried to get out of the place, but she was so deep in shock she just fell down when we got up the stairs. That was when I found the outer doors were stuck. The night's snowfall had trapped us. I didn't have much time to react after that. The thing had already found us. Sheryl went quietly though. Her eyes were glossy and it looked like she was just lost in her mind when the thing covered her. It didn't have a mouth that I could see, but it shouldn't have been able to move like it did either, with all that body behind it and no legs. God, the sound. Bones and flesh being ripped apart by something inside the translucent body. There was nothing I could do for her. Have to keep telling myself that.

I ran back into the basement though. I won't have a chance to figure out why I came back down here. I'm hearing things now. I've been hearing Sheryl calling to me from outside the doors. Voices have been calling me for days. Why is it doing this? Why hasn't it just come through the door? It's gotta be strong enough to break them. Her voice sounds so sweet though. Terry is saying that it doesn't hurt, that it's a better place.

No, I have to wait for the snow to unblock the windows.

It's been three days since I last wrote. I think three. Slept three times. Snow looks to be getting thicker. Flashlight dying and I'm starving.

Just want out. Want to see Sheryl again. She'd know what to do. She does know. She's telling me to open the door. I'm going to see my friends.

* * *

The wife asked me why it wasn't taken yet as they walked in.

"Well, most of the people here are old families that have lived here forever, so open homes don't go fast. So..." I grinned as I shoved the papers into my pocket. "What can I do to get you nice folks in here?"

It goes on sale again in two weeks.

◇◇◇◇◇◇◇◇◇◇◇◇◇◇◇◇◇◇

5. PREY
by John P. Wilson

It's difficult to look someone in the face and say there is such a thing as the supernatural. I don't often tell this story because how can you say, "Yes, there are monsters. And yes, they do prey upon us."

It was 2 a.m. on a Saturday morning and impossible to see through the windshield with the heavy snow and howling wind raging against my black Lincoln Town Car.

It was sometime during that white New Hampshire night—as my vehicle gobbled Interstate 95—when I decided to stop at a rest area for a quick bite.

I parked my car near a truck and tried pushing my door open against the force of the wind. I got out and my pants legs flapped like flags as wind and snow tore into me. I pushed forward to the restrooms and snack machines and almost didn't hear the shouts.

"Hey!" His voice was just about lost in the storm. "Hey, mister!"

I turned my head and saw that the truck's door had opened. He was holding it, wearing a wool coat and a Red Sox baseball cap.

"Yeah?"

"Can I use your cell phone?"

"Don't have one!"

"What?" the man said. He started walking forward and the wind took his cap with it. He made no attempt to retrieve it. He kept walking. He stopped several yards away from me.

"I don't have a cell phone." I said.

"Everyone's got a cell phone, man."

I shrugged my shoulders. "Pay phones are over there."

"They don't work. Emergency phone's out too."

I studied him for a moment. He might have been twenty-five.

"Look, sir, I just got robbed. They took my wallet, my phone and my truck keys. I need you to help me. Please? Just take me to the next phone, so I can call the police."

I walked up to him and noticed another vehicle pulling into the rest area.

"Okay, you have an honest face," I said.

"Thank you, thank you so much."

We walked to the car, got inside, and I turned the ignition switch. The engine purred, and the vehicle glided onto the interstate, sailing north.

"I'm Doug," the man said, holding out a hand.

"Bob." I took his hand and shook it.

"I really, really appreciate this. There aren't too many people willing to pick up strangers these days."

I grinned and nodded my head. "Especially strangers who say the emergency phone is dead."

"I swear it was," he said. "Must be this weather."

"Well, you're lucky I came along."

Doug nodded. "I was just stopping to take a piss. As soon as I got out of my truck, four masked guys had surrounded me. I didn't even see them coming. Each had a gun, and I wasn't up to being a hero. I gave them what they asked for and they left."

I grinned. "Wise choice."

"So Bob, where you from?"

I turned my head and looked at him. "Colorado."

His eyes got wide; he started shaking.

"Pull over."

"Huh?"

"Just pull over, okay?" His tongue darted out of his mouth; he licked his upper lip. His hand moved toward his pants pocket.

"Doug? What's wrong?"

"Pull this damn car over!" he screamed.

I watched his hand reach inside the pocket. "Calm down. What's the problem?"

"Let me out now! Let me out!"

I looked in the rearview mirror. A piece of latex had peeled away from my face. I grinned and ripped it off.

"Please let me out!"

I turned to Doug; the coward was leaning on the passenger door. His hand went for the handle. He tried to open it, but it was childproof.

"I'm pulling over right now."

I rolled onto the side of the interstate and peeled off the rest of the latex.

Doug was screaming, doing his best to get that door open.

He glanced back at me, and I took a bite out of his head.

My friends, as we sit at this campfire, I look you in the face and say there are monsters that prey amongst you. I'll even give you a five minute head start.

◇◇◇◇◇◇◇◇◇◇◇◇◇◇◇◇◇◇◇◇

6. RUSSEL STOVER IS YOUR PAL

by April Grey

I was Its keeper, and now I'm Its hostage.

Through a truly ironic act of fate, being hit by a Sweet Pete's ice cream van as I stepped off the curb with my double-dip Ben and Jerry's Raspberry Delight and Chocolate Fudge Swirl Sundae, I was put into a coma.

I am a chubby, cheerful, harmonious spirit. Since high school, I have weighed in at close to 300 pounds and have smoked three packs of Camels a day. My friends, family, and doctors have always believed that I would keel over at any moment, a cheap price for keeping the world safe from It.

The rules of containing It were simple: feed It constantly. The richer, creamier and chocolatier, the better, and It remained complacent and lethargic. Always have a cigarette lit and ready to be puffed on; two lit was even better.

And finally…

Never think of what might have been. No romance novels, no trips to the park where happy mothers with toddlers might frolic. Never, ever, think about sex.

Indeed, my unfortunate high school love affair, and poor Jerome Ryan's untimely end, forced me to learn how to lull it to sleep.

But I digress.

During the coma, I lost nearly two thirds of my mass and was deprived of nicotine.

A luckless male nurse was the first victim. His giving my now petite body an intimate and erotic sponge bath had aroused the creature.

I awoke in time to witness It gouging out the two beautiful blue eyes of our male nurse.

I was no longer in control.

Desperately I sent images of Ben and Jerry's Heath Bar Crunch and packs of pastel-colored Nat Shermans to Its mind. It ignored me. Years of pent-up rage and pain led to one simple desire—bloody vengeance. I shuddered.

In scant minutes, Massachusetts General became an abattoir. And with each new kill, It became stronger and cleverer, and more intent on punishing this sad little world.

I promised It packs of Marlboros and bars of White Toblerone chocolate. In return, It filled my mind with images of what it planned for my family, Its next target. If only we'd been killed by that truck. If only It had never awakened.

While mourning my family, I think back to happier times.

I remember the smell of Tollhouse cookies fresh from the oven that Mom would give me to stifle my tears.

I remember the sweet, gooey delight of that two-pound box of Russell Stover Assorted that my Dad gave me on my prom night. How wonderful it was to sit there in my darkened room, shades drawn, and eat the whole box in one sitting, even the ones with cream centers.

I remember my first cigarette, an unfiltered Camel, which my brother gave me when I was nine so that I wouldn't tell what he and five members of his South Boston street gang had done to me in the vacant warehouse.

In silent horror, I watched as each family member was targeted and died. Every death and dismemberment became more creative and grisly than the last. It was cunning, and a performance artist of sorts, as it gathered greater momentum from each guignol act.

Of this I am certain: just one small Hershey's Kiss would sooth this savage beast.

The SWAT team has us holed up in this tenement in my old neighborhood. The family of five hostages is dead. They were lucky; unlike my family, they suffered little. The team outside is not aware of this. They still bargain for the hostages' release.

There is a Lucky Strike hanging out of the shirt pocket of one of the victims. If I could just get my hands on it and get it lit, there would be hope. I strain, putting every ounce of my will into regaining control, just long enough to obtain that beautiful stick of shredded tobacco — and nothing happens.

Tear gas is being lobbed through the window.

Oh, if only they would shoot Snickers bars instead....

◇◇◇◇◇◇◇◇◇◇◇◇◇◇◇◇◇◇◇

7. THE PHANTOM HIGHWAY PATROL

by Rodney J. Smith

I f you've ever been through Connecticut, you might notice some of the roads have two names: aside from their official one, they also carry the names of fallen policemen and other heroes to honor their memories.

Let me tell you why you want to pay real close attention to this if you're ever up that way.

A few years ago, we were heading down one such 'Memorial Highway' late one night on our way back from a trip to Boston. I don't remember its exact name, only that it was somewhere off the Berlin Turnpike.

There wasn't a lot of traffic, just us and a handful of cars spread thinly ahead. We were lucky not to get run right off the road when a souped-up Chevy came screaming up, tailgating until they could overtake us. There were two young guys inside, giving us the evil eye as though we were the ones in the wrong. The driver punctuated his point by flipping us off as they passed. They swerved back into our lane and did the same thing to the car ahead, which narrowly avoided an accident by getting out of their way.

Then something else blew by us. We felt no wind or force in its wake, though it moved like a rocket — a dark mass bristling with bursts of bright red and blue lights.

It was like the translucent projection of a police car, gray-scaled and incomplete. More accurately, it was a swirl of cloud and light with certain definite angles, like a car door; a hood; tires. It moved in complete silence.

The thing fell in beside the Chevy, matching its speed with ease. It glided on their wing only a second before plunging into the vehicle, the swirl of cloud and colored lights passing easily through glass and metal.

The Chevy's rear lights lit up. Its tires squealed like the hand-brake was on, kicking up thick smoke as it veered from the road. The whole thing seemed guided; it didn't hit any of the other cars before coming to a stop in the grass.

No one stopped to check on its occupants, didn't slow to rubberneck. Their own tail lights just continued on into the night.

We, however, did slow to see. As we rolled alongside, the blue and red lights re-appeared in the haze of dust and dirt. The thing emerged from within and hovered beside us.

This time it wasn't a police car. At its center was a trooper — rather, parts of one. There was no head, just sunglasses and a hat hovering above a uniformed torso at the dark cloud's center. Within the coiling mist, orbiting the trooper like a plastic bag caught in a breeze, was the driver's face. It was smaller, and all the color had been drained. His arrogant sneer was gone, his face set in an open-mouthed scream none of us could hear.

The trooper drifted across the nose of our car, turning to study us. It waved us on with an empty sleeve, before zipping away in the direction it came at the same impossible speed.

As we idled forward, we passed through the wall of smoke and were able to see the car.

The passenger was still inside. When his eyes met mine they spoke only of terror.

The driver's seat was empty.

It felt like ages before anyone spoke. Only our car mumbled as we continued to roll. My friend's hands were rigid on the steering wheel, his eyes fixed on the rearview mirror.

"Keep going," I told him. "Just like it told us. Don't stop. Keep going."

We got the hell out of there.

So if you're ever up there, pay careful attention to the signs. I can't tell you exactly which road it was, and I'm sure as hell never going back to find out. You'd best just make sure you're doing the right thing whichever one you're on.

Because somewhere, on one of those highways, its namesake is still on duty.

◇◇◇◇◇◇◇◇◇◇◇◇◇◇◇◇◇◇◇◇

8. THE TREES RAN RED

by Joel A. Sutherland

It's been over ten years since that day, and I still haven't forgotten the smell of boiling blood. Don't think I ever will.

The previous night my truck had run out of gas and I coasted home on fumes. It didn't bother me much, since I lived close to my sugar shack and I kept plenty of filled gas canisters there for the equipment, but it meant a walk to work the next morning. I set out before the sun was up, completely unaware of the horrors that awaited me in the bush.

I was a little late by the time I got there. A beat-up 1989 Ford Ranger was parked next to the sugar shack. It was Derrick's, the Irishman I had hired the month before. I poked my head in the shack but it was empty. I assumed Derrick must be out in the bush, so I set out to join him and begin the day's work.

I strolled leisurely through the black maples on my Vermont property, trailing frosty clouds of breath as my feet crunched through the snow. I stopped and inhaled deeply, reveling in the clean smells of the winter woods as my lungs burned from the frigid air. Something odd dawned on me. Other than the sound of the wind, the forest was perfectly silent. I checked my watch: 5:35. The woods should've been teemingwith animal life. My heart sped up and my breathing suddenly sounded very loud in my ears, but I shook it off and focused on my work.

I neared the section of maples Derrick and I had tapped the day before. The air smelled vaguely of copper. A chill shot through me and my skin prickled with gooseflesh. There was still no sign of life.

I removed the metal bucket from the nearest tree, turned around and dropped it with a curse. Instead of maple syrup, it was filled with blood. It coursed over the white snow, melting it with a crackle. I stepped back involuntarily and bumped into the tree. It seemed to bulge upon contact. Blood still dripped from the tap, forming a small red circle below like a pox.

Desperate to keep a grip on my sanity, I paced around the maple. Its back bore an irregular crease unlike anything I had seen before. It ran from top to bottom and looked like two lips pressed firmly together.

In a daze I prodded back to the shack, grabbed an ax, and returned to the bleeding tree.

If I had paused I think I would have lost my nerve, so I swung the ax over my head and landed it in the middle of the crease. The tree groaned with the sound of wood being split. I wrenched the ax head free and raised it again, then hesitated. Blood gushed from the cut in torrents. I don't know why, but I laughed and swung the ax again and again, spraying myself with blood and wood chips.

Flinging the ax to the ground, I stared into the gash I had made, terrified I'd see a wooden heart pumping blood through the tree. But the maple hadn't produced the blood that had filled the syrup bucket. It came from the creatures the tree had fed on. Inside the trunk were two raccoons, a rabbit and a dray of squirrels, all in various states of digestion. Blood seeped from every pore of the animals, good God, so much blood...

I checked the other buckets. They were all brimming with blood as well. The other trees had similar creases, some with fur, tails, or antlers sticking out. My head spun and I didn't know what was real anymore. I had no idea what to do.

And then I saw Derrick's hand, identifiable by the Claddagh ring on his bone-white finger, sticking out from one of the trees.

Suddenly all became clear. I knew what had to be done.

I walked to the shack as if in a dream. Picking up a gas canister in each hand, I set out back into the woods, ready to burn down my livelihood.

Ready to boil some blood.

◇◇◇◇◇◇◇◇◇◇◇◇◇◇◇◇◇◇

9. TOURIST TRAP
by Ayne Terceira

We read it off scripts when we do the Ghost Walk. Some of the tourists think we just know this stuff because we're townies. But it's all scripts. I don't know who writes them. Maybe they do research, but I don't think so. It's made up, most of it.

I've been doing the Newport Ghost Walk tour for five years, since college. A nice summer job. I think I'll quit next year. Not because of what happened, but because of the traffic. I can't afford to live in Newport anymore. Nobody can, except the tourists. It just isn't worth it.

If you've never done the Ghost Walk, here's how it works:

You pay your fifty bucks (that's what we call in the biz a R.I.P.-off), then you wait around on the wharf like an idiot. Eventually, a trolley comes by and I'm on it, or Sean, or Tiffany, or one of the other guides. We are supposed to be in "period dress" but all us guides like to Goth it up a bit, corsets and makeup and whatnot. Tiffany has her own fake raven to wear on her shoulder and Sean's got this whole Clockwork Orange thing going on. I keep it simple. I do a British accent. I'm pretty good.

The trolley takes you up to Bellevue Avenue via Touro Park. "And on your right you can see the remnants of an old Viking tower, what dark rites went on there none can say!" Then I tell the story about the Viking war hammer that keeps appearing on the front desk of the Hotel Viking and the Norse god rumored to come back some day and claim it. My mom has a better story about the Hotel Viking which involves a drunk college friend and a couple of sailors from the naval base. I don't tell that one.

Then the trolley takes you past the mansions. Honestly, you'd get a better (and cheaper) view from the Cliffwalk. But if you paid fifty bucks to sit on my trolley, I'll tell you about how Doris Duke accidentally closed her mansion gates on her chauffer, straining him like so much play-doh. Then it's up Ten Mile Drive. There was a murder there and a movie about it, but only old people have ever seen the movie. It was in black and white, I think.

At the Lost Sailors memorial, we get out and stretch our legs. Then I look out mournfully at the ocean and tell you about ghost ships. A friend of my father died kayaking off King's Beach, but he's not famous, and not in the tour. Instead, it's all pirates of old. This is where the English accent comes in handy.

The tour ends up back at the wharf. We go into the Red Parrot Inn and I tell this story about the widow who haunts the attic watching the sea, waiting for her husband to return. Then people buy drinks and I stick around to answer questions until my trolley comes back for me.

And if you tip me real well, maybe I'll tell you to meet me later for a special tour.

There's this little nineteenth century graveyard between Easton's Beach and Second Beach. People have been stealing the headstones from it. It's really sad. I wish they'd stop.

I don't use my accent here. It isn't respectful.

We grab flashlights and head up past the little iron gate. At the end of the path, I say hello to my dad's kayaking buddy. And to my mom's drunk friend, her throat still slit. And to Doris Duke's chauffer, several dead Vanderbilts, sailors, and pirates. And to the Norse god, who never says 'hello' back.

And if you don't run screaming, they will answer your questions. But do not tip them, or ask them for souvenirs. Don't take out your camera. Or laugh and think you are on vacation. They get angry. And if they do, I cannot help you.

I will walk away. That's what I'm paid to do.

It's in the script.

As I said, it's all scripts. I don't know who writes them. But it's made up. Most of it.

◇◇◇◇◇◇◇◇◇◇◇◇◇◇◇◇◇◇◇

10. ASYLUM
by Linda L. Donahue

Village Hill Northampton seemed idyllic. My terrace looked upon the hilltop. Though Northampton State Hospital had been demolished, there remained a stray stone or piece of foundation.

The hilltop and its history intrigued me. Yet when screams woke me, it terrified me. I hoped by exploring the hilltop, I could put to rest those ghosts my mind had conjured.

On a sunny day I climbed the hill, ignoring the "No Trespassing" sign. It felt timeless standing where once had stood an asylum build in the mid-nineteenth century. Knowing that had surely filled my head with the conjured spirits of tortured souls.

A leathery corner protruded from the earth. I dug out a remarkably well-preserved book. Though its cover was worn bare, the faded ink was surprisingly legible.

I felt a rush of overwhelming fortune to discover such a treasure. The first journal entry had been recorded in July of 1924.

I don't belong here. I don't know exactly how I came to be here. But I can't leave.

Every night I endure torment intended to return me to sanity. But my being here was the insanity. If only they understood. The more I tried to explain, the more extreme the treatment. Shock therapy was supposed to rid my brain of crazy thoughts. I'm told I'm delusional, that what I know to be true is mad prattling, an fantastic world in which my mind seeks refuge. My doctors say that until they can shatter that imaginary world from inside my mind, I'd never be cured

But I'm not ill

The writing grew steadily more jagged, as if in counter-argument. I skimmed descriptions of this madman's "world." What he had envisioned, while not possible in 1924, was a reality today. Perhaps the only illness this poor man suffered had been to be psychic.

Seeing a partial wall peeking above brush, I sat on what had been a window sill. No sooner had I settled down than I heard a cart's wheels squeak and footsteps against tile.

I looked for the source, but saw nothing. The auditory hallucination sent chilling ripples down my spine and wasn't helping my fear of ghosts in the least.

The squeak drew closer. Village Hill faded from view. Without moving, I suddenly sat on a padded window seat inside a fully functional, not the least bit dilapidated, hospital. A nurse in a long, striped gown with apron pushed a cart loaded with medications.

I jumped up, rubbing my eyes, wondering when I'd fallen asleep. Surely the journal had stimulated this dream.

"How'd you get out of your room?" the doctor asked.

"I'm not a patient. I live—" I pointed out the window, even then knowing my house wasn't there. The land beyond the asylum was just woods now. "How did I get here?"

"It's all right. There's no cause for alarm." The doctor waved for two orderlies to take me to the treatment room, saying he would join them later.

When the largest of the orderlies grabbed my arm, his firm grip surely real, I dropped the journal. The other picked it up.

I was strapped down. One orderly hooked me to the machine and fitted my mouth with a leather strap so I couldn't bite my tongue and choke. The other flipped through the journal.

Electricity streaked throughout me, straightening my limbs, making them so stiff I thought my joints would pop. My back arced. Sweat poured from me and I bit hard into the leather.

No sooner did my heart stop racing than another jolt shot through me. My brain burned with fire.

Then, one orderly said, "Listen here, Tom." He held the journal open to its final page. "Whosoever finds my journal, run now. Whatever you do, do not step within those confines which once defined hospital grounds. To do so is to meet the ghosts of the past. Just as the horrors that occurred here have trapped this place in time, it has trapped me."

"Utter nonsense," the heavy-set orderly said.

◇◇◇◇◇◇◇◇◇◇◇◇◇◇◇◇◇◇

II. BOGG'S ISLAND
by Barry Napier

In the past, most dogs on Bogg's Island ended up either missing or dead. The island is only six miles long and eight miles wide, but I guarantee you that at one time, the roads that run along Boggs Island had the highest rate of roadkill in New Hampshire. And of that roadkill, three quarters of the carcasses were dogs.

It took folks a while to understand what was going on, and it started with Angie Griles wrecking her car in '84. She had swerved to miss a Doberman and went right into a tree. Angie ended up getting a few stitches in her head and it was because of the whack she took in the wreck that no one believed her story.

Angie claimed that some horrible creature came out of the woods, chasing after the dog. She said the monster walked like a spider, but on four legs. It had two big red eyes and a mouth that came unhinged like a snake. It chewed the Doberman in half and pulled most of it back into the woods, where it disappeared into the dark.

The part of the story that folks leave out is that the next day, the highway department found that dog, and it had been torn in half. And Angie sure as hell didn't hit it because there were tire marks all over the road rom where she hit the brakes. For an automobile to rip an animal apart like that, you'd have to be driving a damned big truck pretty fast.

But the legend of the Bogg's Island Monster didn't really start until the next sighting. Six people saw it at dusk along the beach back in '85. The monster actually came out of the surf, as would a crab or a tortoise, and snatched up the stray mutt that everyone had gotten so friendly with at Bogg's Beach that summer.

Of course it could have all been a story used to drum up tourism; that's what everyone believed, anyway.

But then more dogs started showing up dead, or went missing. Check the newspaper archives over at Bogg's Library; there were sixteen missing dog reports in '85 and the highway department logged in nine bodies. The numbers got higher in '86 and '87, and it was then that people began to take the stories seriously.

For a period of five years, there were constant stories circling the island. Stories about a monster that walked like a spider and fed on dogs. There are pictures of doghouses splattered with blood, holes torn in the sides of chain link fences that served as kennels. Folks sent these pictures to the newspaper but they were never published.

Someone broke into Annie Ayerson's house in '90. When the police came by, they saw that her front window had been smashed. Annie had not been hurt, and the only thing missing had been her poodle, Darling. There were fluffs of Darling's fur found scattered around Annie's back yard. A few feet further into the forest there were splashes of blood and pink coils of intestine that were too small to belong to any creature other than little Darling.

Fishermen started seeing the monster slipping in and out of the ocean. Others saw it crossing the road, mainly around the swampy area near the western coastline. Bizarre footprints were seen along the beaches and in people's back yards where their dogs had once been.

This went on for years, until sometime around '95 or '96, people just gave up on having dogs. Whether or not you believed in the Bogg's Island Monster, it was clear that there was something going on. Something around the island did not like dogs. Or, to be more precise, it liked dogs just fine… for meals.

For a while, all was quiet on Bogg's Island. By the summer of '01, there wasn't a single dog on the island. But just because there were no dogs didn't mean that the monster just retreated into the sea.

No... by cutting off its food supply, islanders ensured that it simply moved on to other food.

In the spring of 2002, there was an alarmingly high number of missing children reports.

◇◇◇◇◇◇◇◇◇◇◇◇◇◇◇◇◇

12. INCIDENT ON ROUTE 44

by John Grover

There is a stretch of road between the city of Taunton, Massachusetts, and the state of Rhode Island called Route 44. Of course it doesn't end or begin there, but if I live to see another day I hope to God I never have to drive through that section of it again.

I had a friend who lived in Providence, and the easiest way for me to visit him was driving up Route 44 through Dighton, Rehoboth and Seekonk until entering Rhode Island. Once there, he was just one street away from 44. It was never a big deal to hang out with him there; we often took turns making the drive, mostly on weekends. It was about a forty-five minute drive.

Forty-five minutes. On that night forty-five minutes felt like hours. It's a long time when you're scared witless. All I wanted was to get the hell home, but the hitchhiker had other ideas.

One Saturday night I was driving home from a visit to my friend's home. It had been a late night of dinner and movies, and it was well after night sky was clear, filled with twinkling stars and a moon that was almost full. The road, stretching long and straight ahead of me, was bathed in milk-white moonlight. There was not another soul on the road, dark woods grew thick on either side of it, and I just cruised on with my radio blasting until something unbelievable happened.

A tall man with red hair darted out of the woods in front of me. He appeared to my left in the corner of my eye and quickly ran across the road. Startled, I turned to watch him disappear into the woods on the other side. I could see his big frame in the moonlight and patches of his flannel shirt.

Oh my God, was that him? I'd heard stories of a red-haired hitchhiker that haunted this road, but I never knew anyone who'd seen him. It couldn't have been. I reassured myself and even chuckled in relief. I turned my attention back to the road when he stepped right out in front of my car.

I slammed my brakes but drove right into him!

My heart leapt into my throat. Sweat poured off my face. I'd hit him, by God. I ran someone over! I put the car in Park and got out. My hands were trembling as I searched for him, someone hurt very badly on the road, but couldn't find him.

There was no one there. I looked around my car, behind it, under it, but could find no body. My car wasn't even damaged. Suddenly I heard laughter echoing in the woods. The dark, silhouetted trees were only feet away.

His laughter bellowed through the night and grew louder as footfalls resounded with snapping branches.

I ran back into my car and pulled the door shut. My hands were shaking and I was nearly out of breath. I tried to throw the car back into Drive, but the gearshift was stuck. Damn my luck! It was all I could do to stay calm and in control.

A tapping came at my window.

No, don't look…don't look but I had to. With seemingly no control of my own, I turned to look at the passenger's window. His face glared back at me. His hair was as red as flames and it radiated all around him, illuminating the tree trunks behind him. His narrow eyes, set on a bearded face, were bloodshot and filled with rage.

A scream caught in my throat but I couldn't find my voice. Finally he laughed out loud as the gear ultimately shifted into place and I sped off. As I looked back in the rearview mirror I saw nothing but empty road.

I drove in silence the entire way home with my windows rolled up.

To this day I take another route into Providence, and if you're smart you'll do the same.

◇◇◇◇◇◇◇◇◇◇◇◇◇◇◇◇◇◇

13. LET THE COLD COME

by Shadow Kain

My mother was born and raised in northern Maine. She used to say that Maine belonged to the entire country three quarters of the year, but come winter Maine was for the natives. Only someone bred in such harshness could ever come to appreciate it.

Maybe that's why I came here.

One month ago I made a mistake. I took things too far. It's a line easily crossed when your sight is blinded by desperation. There is nothing more dangerous in this world than a person who feels wronged.

I started the fire one night after having a few too many at the local pub. Living in the tri-state, a place where you live to work, when you get fired like I did, well, you either have to find something else to live for or you get started dying. I found something else to live for, found it deep inside in a place I didn't even know existed. A gallon of gasoline, alcohol to blur my conscience and numb any sense of conformity was all it took. I felt a sense of accomplishment as the office building burned. All the charts, folders and faxes that had once ruled my life, consumed by the fire, becoming nothing but ash.

When you work somewhere for as long as I did, it becomes a prison. You become an inmate to the routine. It's the same as a marriage, or a long relationship. It's not the love or the company you miss when it's gone. It's the routine.

Four people broke their routine the night I set the fire.

No one worked late on Saturday nights. They may come in on the weekend, but once the sun went down people returned to living the lives they were able to squeeze in between working hours. For fifteen years no one worked late on Saturday.

I don't know why they were in the building. I'll never know. No one will. Three men, one woman, charred so badly they had to use dental records to identify them. No one ever worked late on Saturday nights.

I'm no expert arsonist. Hell, fire was man's first creation, discovered and harnessed before the wheel. Anyone can start a fire. Not everyone can do so anonymously. I fall into that category. It was only a matter of time before they traced the fire back to me. So I came here. To the north. In the winter.

The cabin is humble. Few pieces of furniture, chairs, a wooden table, no bed. I've been sleeping on the floor. The wind howls through every nook and cranny in this place, whistling and stinging me through my three layers of clothing.

The snow started yesterday and hasn't slowed since. It covers everything, a white blanket that never brings warmth. It's not like the snow back home. There's nothing to turn it to a gray mess of slush. This is real snow, powder that weighs on the world and strips it of color.

I started a fire in the fireplace last night. That's when they came. At first I thought the whispers were just the wind, slithering through the cracks in the windows and the door, playing tricks. I checked outside, thinking maybe someone had found the cabin and was seeking refuge from the storm. But no one was there.

The licking flames called to me, screams growing louder in my head as the fire danced on the logs. Asking me why I did what I did. They are coming for me. Alone in this cabin, the brutal winter at the door, they are coming for me in the fire. I can see their faces, orange and yellow and red. The flames are hands, reaching for me, wanting me to join them in eternal dance, the beat set to crackles and snaps.

I won't dare light another fire tonight. The cold has encircled everything in the cabin, the kind of cold that makes a man wish he didn't have fingers, toes or earlobes. The cold will eventually take me, freezing me solid. But that's what I want. If I'm solid as ice, I can't dance like the fire does.

I can't light another fire.

◇◇◇◇◇◇◇◇◇◇◇◇◇◇◇◇◇◇◇◇

14. LONESOME PINE

by Catherine J. Gardner

As I carved our initials into the purple bark of the white pine, Danny hopped and complained that a needle had pierced shoe, sock, and skin.

"Stop griping, I'm nearly done." I flicked the knife closed and placed it in my pocket. "If the heart vanishes by morning we have to break up."

Danny snorted.

Two centuries' worth of graffiti and Somersworth legend rose several feet above us. Branches swayed as the gentle breeze billowed and morphed into a howling banshee. Pinecones fell like bombs and, in succession, two split against Danny's shaved head.

Blood trickled down his forehead. I clung to the tree as the wind howled along Old Wood Lane.

"Jeez, the local weatherman couldn't forecast his way out of a snow storm." Danny spat on a leaf and pressed it against his wound. "I'm going."

A horn beeped as tires skidded to a halt. Danny wrenched open the door.

"Wait."

He grinned and held out his hand as I battled the wind. The Lincoln's door slammed shut and we fell laughing into the back seat.

"What's up with you two?" Jack asked as he turned around in his seat. "Hey, watch you don't get blood on the leather, man."

I checked Danny's wound and picked out a few slices of pinecone. It looked nasty.

"We should take you to the clinic."

Jack groaned, Danny grunted and the Lincoln stalled. Jack slammed his hands against the wheel, scratched the key against the ignition and let out a stream of expletives. He got out and began kicking the tires.

"And you say I overreact." Danny winked.

Danny shuffled out. I followed. The wind rushed through the old white pine. Its branches rose up like arms, and as they shook, needles stabbed down. If a tree can hold a grudge against a person, then the old white hated Danny. Spikes poked from his arms, legs, t-shirt and cheeks. It looked as if he'd had a fight with an angry acupuncturist. Blood bubbled and gave his skin a purple tinge.

"You don't look good."

As he pressed his hand against the tree to steady his balance, he sank ankle deep into the earth.

"Oh look." I pointed. "The tree has erased my initials but not yours."

Danny whimpered. Where the needles had pierced his skin, branches were erupting. They were growing needles of their own.

◇◇◇◇◇◇◇◇◇◇◇◇◇◇◇◇◇

15. MOTHER OCEAN

by Blu Gilliand

There was a pirate named William Ward that took a liking to the New England coast. Had a ship called *The Liberator*. He was a bad man, crazy from years of sun and saltwater, and he had this patch of the Atlantic pretty much to himself.

The story goes that Ward was coming in from a long trip when he ran across *The Pelican*, captained by Jefferson Douglas. The Pelican was out for a short run, during which Douglas was to marry his true love, Emily.

Needless to say, Ward and his crew didn't take this into consideration when they swarmed *The Pelican*. They made the couple watch as they killed the wedding party. The whole time, Douglas was begging for Emily to be let go. Emily just stared a hole right through that pirate. She was a tough girl, so they said.

Ward didn't like her staring. He took his sword, stained with the blood of her family and friends, and chopped Douglas at the neck. Nearly took his head off with one swipe.

"Take a look at that," he told her.

They stuck Douglas's head on a spoke of the captain's wheel. Then Ward took Emily below and had his way with her. When he was done, the rest of the crew got a turn.

When the crew was finished, they hauled her back up top. Ward had them tie Emily to the captain's wheel, right next to her fiance's head. When everyone was back aboard *The Liberator*, they threw torches onto *The Pelican* and watched it burn.

Emily never screamed. Just stared right at Ward while the flames melted her skin.

Ward didn't stay around for long after that. *The Liberator* sailed off, and wasn't seen for more than a year. But just as people began to relax and think maybe Ward was gone for good, he rolled back in with the fog.

Now, I can't tell you if the rest of this is true, but I've heard this tale a half-dozen times, and it's always told the same way.

Right about the same patch of water where they'd burned *The Pelican*, *The Liberator* got caught in a storm. Ward had his number two crewman at the wheel while everyone else was getting drunk down below. The lightning was flashing, and in one of those flashes, that crewman spotted someone standing in front of him on the deck.

She was covered head-to-toe in twisted scar tissue. Wearing seaweed and the leftovers of a white dress. She was wearing a crown of coral on her head, and there were sea serpents slithering around her feet.

That's about all the detail the crewman got, 'cause he headed downstairs immediately, babbling for the captain. Ward stumbled topside, and right away he knew who it was. He could tell by the way she stared at him.

He was full of bravado and cheap wine, and his whole crew was peering out of the shadows, so he had no choice but to charge. He ran her through with the same sword he'd used to kill her fiancé, but when he pulled it from the wound nothing but seawater flowed out.

She stared at him, much as she'd done as *The Pelican* burned around her. Then she raised her arms, and called her children to her.

All manner of things poured out of the water and onto that boat. Stuff from the deepest parts of the ocean, where it's always dark and cold. A flood of tentacles and teeth. Ward watched these nightmares tear his crew apart and drag them into the ocean. Then Emily turned him to her, and kissed him the way she should have kissed her husband on their wedding day. He choked to death on saltwater and sand, and the whole time her cold, gray eyes stayed locked on his.

The Liberator burned, and what's left of it lies on the ocean floor. They say Emily and her children – they call her *Mother Ocean* now – are down there, too, and that she sits on a throne of William Ward's bones, making sure he'll never hurt anyone again.

◇◇◇◇◇◇◇◇◇◇◇◇◇◇◇◇◇◇

16. THE NAYJU
by Natalie L. Sin

Every summer my mom would make me go to this day camp in Everwood, Connecticut for two weeks. I hated it. The kids were jerks and so were the counselors. Say one day you didn't want to make little crosses out of popsicle sticks or sing "Jacob Row the Boat Ashore." They wouldn't let you go read a book instead, and if you still refused, they made you sit in the main house and face the corner for an hour.

The last day was the worst. That was when we all had to camp out in the woods. After roasting hot dogs and singing songs about Jesus loving the little children, the counselors would hand out old pillowcases and announce that it was time for the *Nayju* hunt. We were supposed to go in teams of three but I always got ditched, usually pretty fast too. I would find my way back by looking for the bonfire flickering in the distance or listening for counselor's voices.

Nobody ever told us what a *Nayju* monster was. Some kids said that it was a big toad that would burn the skin off your bones with its acid-slime tongue. Shelly Butcher claimed that it was really an alien like the ones in the movie and that it ran around the forest as a big spidery hand with a tail, looking for children to put its babies in. If it got you, you would wake up and not remember anything until one day your stomach would explode and a baby *Nayju* monster would run out.

I was eleven the last time I had to go on a *Nayju* hunt. That year I got teamed with Shelly and Tracy, two of the meanest girls at camp. They stayed with me for almost half an hour before saying they needed to pee and then never coming back. By then it was too far away to see the bonfire or hear anything but forest noises. I tried to be careful walking around, but it was hard to see, and before long my foot hit a rock and I went flying onto my stomach. By the time I pulled myself together and found my flashlight, I wasn't alone any more. The *Nayju* was with me.

It looked like an enormous yellow fox with blue eyes and no tail. The *Nayju's* feet were too big for its body and webbed in between like a duck's, and the toenails were jet black and sharp looking. When the *Nayju* started to talk, its whole head nearly split in half and I could see down its throat. There was something spongy and red at the bottom that quivered with each word, like it was really the part doing the talking.

"You have a choice," it said. "I can eat you now, or you can trade for two of your friends."

My mouth felt too dry to talk. All I could do was stare into the *Nayju's* eyes and pray that I was seeing things.

"Which will it be?" the *Nayju* asked impatiently.

I wish I could say I didn't mean it when I promised to bring two kids back. It was only when I found Shelly and Tracy and started to think about how their families would miss them that I changed my mind.

That night I went to sleep terrified, but when I woke up alive I started to think that it really had all been a bad dream. Until the counselors told us that three girls were missing: Shelly, Tracy, and Molly Spring. Some volunteers found Shelly and Tracy a week later—right where I had ran into them after seeing the *Nayju*. They never found Molly.

The thing with Molly was that she looked an awful lot like me. Same frizzy brown hair and freckles, even the same color eyes. The *Nayju* made a mistake, but I don't think it's going to stay fooled forever. I wonder if there are a lot of girls with frizzy hair and green eyes?

◇◇◇◇◇◇◇◇◇◇◇◇◇◇◇◇◇◇

17. PUNKIN CARVING

by Will Gorrell

I had to use my body weight to force my hand down the wet hole. Despite the faltering circulation in my forearm, I scraped the last of the congealed glop from the sides into a small mound. I surrounded the mushy pile in a cage of fingertips, bulky and clumsy from the grime gathered under the nails. The annoyance of washing up afterward made a convincing argument for wearing gloves, but I liked to feel my work.

The remaining strands of gruel detached with muffled tearing noises. The porridge-like prisoners nearly escaped between my knuckles. My fist reached the top, then stopped. "Damn, that's tight," I grumbled, louder than intended.

"No need fer foul language," Momma scolded from the next room. Momma never raised her voice. She simply used her normal warm, gentle tone that never failed to instill guilt.

"How's 'at punkin comin'? I'm almost ready fer it." She went back to carefully razoring the eyes out of the plump one I'd scooped out last night.

She always told me the keys to perfect jack o' lanterns were patience and perseverance, but I wasn't entirely sure what the latter meant.

I drew in a deep breath, then put my foot on its top. I pushed, and the small opening creaked verbal threats of splitting. Bits of goop spattered my face as my hand pulled free. I wish Momma would let me cut the hole bigger just once.

I plopped the last of pulp onto the newspapers, which as I feared, proved an inadequate choice for catching the mess. I could envision myself on my hands and knees cleaning the stains out of the old Berber carpet like so many times before.

I rested my tingly arm, knowing it would be sore tomorrow. I could feel the wet paste transforming into a crusty layer on my skin. My tattered blue jeans turned deep purple under persistent wiping, and soon, I could see the natural pink color of my skin again.

"Wha'd'ya think?" I asked, hoisting it up for Momma to see. The punkin dangled by the hair of its head, primed and ready for carving. Its fractured lower jaw hung awkwardly. At least it was quiet now.

Most punkins choked and gagged a little, sure. But this one squealed like a pig until I got my hand crammed down its throat to a point where the sound plugged off. Its limbs flailed like unmanned fire hoses until after the fourth handful. It reminded me of the time I got my arm stuck in one. I had to beat it against a tree in the back yard for a while before it stopped squirming and broke loose. We had to throw that one out. "Y'can't draw on a scribbled-up page, can y', son?" I remembered Momma asking me. Those weren't fond memories to dredge up. I hated disappointing her.

Eyeing the empty youngster, Momma nodded her approval. "That young'n'll look perfect on the porch." She went back to her work. "We'll need t'pluck another'n fer th' door; Halloween's only two days away."

I gazed down at the large, raspberry-colored heap before me, knowing the end was in sight—five down, one more to go. For whatever reason, Halloween called for three-year-olds. I'd spent countless hours staking out daycare centers for fresh punkins. Maybe Momma switched from the orange ones to the flesh-colored ones as a means of showing the Vermont city folk that they were not so high and mighty. Who knew? But I was happy as long as she was. I'll probably teach my own punkins, if I ever have any.

Decorating was hard work, but rewarding in the end, mostly because it made Momma proud. At least it wasn't December. Momma went all out for Christmas, and it was a nightmare getting a treetop up inside one of those little, bitty angels she liked so much.

◇◇◇◇◇◇◇◇◇◇◇◇◇◇◇◇◇◇◇◇◇◇

18. THE WELL OF GHOSTS

by Kurt Newton

There's an old well. You know the kind. A fat column of field stones cemented together. A nice little A-frame roof on top. A wooden bucket hanging from the middle. The kind seen in children's books about mice or rabbits. The kind used on farms in the old days.

In fact, the old well I'm talking about was once on a farm. A farm just up the road. A farm no longer there except for some grown-in fields and an old stone foundation jutting up through the grass. And the well, of course.

Some say there are voices in the well.

If you go there now, the well is nothing but a hole in the ground covered by wood planks. But once it must have been like I described. Once it must have looked inviting. Something to climb on, maybe peer down into, and drop a stone just to hear the kerplunk. Something a young boy might do. A young boy a little too curious for his own good. A boy whose father was still out working in the field, and whose mother was inside the house boiling beef and cabbage for dinner and baking an apple pie for dessert. A boy who was maybe spooked by a hornet and lost his balance, falling into the well. A boy unable to swim. A boy nobody heard or saw again until the following morning.

Some say the voices in the well sound like a little boy's voice. A little boy playing by himself, unaware of his fate. Playing forever in the cold throat of the old well.

Some say a sound like the drone of a bee precedes the voices.

Now that would the end of the story for most people. For most ghosts. Most ghosts stay put. This one didn't.

When my wife and I bought this land (land that once belonged to the farm) and built our dream home, we didn't mind a little local folklore. We had heard the stories and laughed them off. As long as the haunted well was over there and not here, we didn't see the harm.

Until we put our own well in. And heard the buzzing of the bees. And a little boy's voice echoing in the well of our empty sinks and down the cold throat of our bathtub drain. And although the sounds were just the imaginative ramblings of a child speaking his thoughts out loud, it was just too much for my wife.

You see, my wife would have loved to have had children of her own, but she was unable to conceive. I built her this beautiful home out here in the country instead, and gave her everything she wanted. Except what she wanted most. A child.

In fact, I foolishly thought the ghost child would act as a kind of substitute. Little did I know the ghostly voice of the little boy only served to reinforce her deficiency, her failure to make our family complete. I should have seen the danger, but I was just too busy working to notice. The day I came home to find my wife lying at the bottom of a bathtub full of water was the worst day of my life. I could only blame myself.

And the boy, of course.

I still hear his voice in the drain. Only now he has a playmate. They talk in the most loving and playful tones. He calls her mother.

I wonder how long I can go on hearing my wife's voice like that. How long before I too drink from the well of ghosts. How long before I take that final plunge and hear that word I never thought I'd hear.

◇◇◇◇◇◇◇◇◇◇◇◇◇◇◇◇◇◇

19. THE THING IN THE WOODS
by Bill Ward

All right, I haven't told this in about ten years and the last time I did got me a hell of a look, so just stick with me. Growing up, Dad and me used to drive up to my uncle's place in Vermont a couple times a year for turkey season and deer season and once, even, to try our hand at bear – but I'm glad to say that Uncle Ron's pickup was in such a state, he and Dad spent that weekend puttering under the hood and spared us all having to go out and kill Yogi.

I did this kind of stuff with Dad because I thought he enjoyed it; later I guessed it was so he wouldn't forget where he came from and, I suppose, it was a good way for me not to forget, too. Anyway, I'm glad we never went for black bear (though I heard Uncle Ron later got one) and I'm glad I went hunting with Dad as much as I did.

There was one thing I'd like to forget, though, and even just starting to tell this story I almost wished I kept quiet, 'cause now I can see the thick gold and orange of that November like I'd just got done dreaming about it, and that sharp snap of cold air rolling down out of the north is hitting me right in the bones.

We were an hour's or more drive away from Newport, could have been in New Hampshire for all I know. Mohican territory, Dad told me, and Uncle Ron laughed and said something about Chingachgook. That might have been the first time I was out with a really decent rifle, Dad's old one, at least that's how I remember it. The thing I shot happened upon us on the third day, sometime after we'd decided to call it quits out there.

Uncle Ron said young punks was ruining the hunting pastime for guys like him, 'cause for two nights we were hearing all kinds of sounds around us, even had a rock or two thrown into camp. Uncle Ron hollered at 'em to get off, fired his rifle in the air, but they kept at it, off and on. All that night I pictured Mohicans stalking us out beyond the lantern light, but I got more sleep than Dad or Ron I'm sure.

Next day we were up and moving soon as it was light, and I almost got the idea they were scared but that occurred to me later, so I'm not sure. It was so thick where we were, nothing but mile upon mile of rolling woods, that I didn't understand how anyone could be out there bothering us. Dad told me not to put my orange vest on over the camo, and something about the way he said it made me ask no questions. We were most of a day's good hike away from the lot where Uncle Ron had left the truck, and I had settled into a good rhythm when I noticed they were whispering, Dad and Uncle Ron saying something about us being followed.

It happened quick, and I'm glad of that because I had less time to think than they did, which is why I shot the thing while they stood there frozen. Through the trees I knew already it was huge, a thirty-pointer at least, its antlers scraping along the lowest branches. That buck came right at us, in my mind right at Dad, and I dropped it with a single, lucky shot. The three of us didn't have any words for what we saw that day, though we tried to talk around the obvious.

Thirty-some years later Cindy is home from U/Mass and I'm going through her books, like an interested father should do. Come upon this picture in an Anthropology text, called a shaman. A man with the skin of an animal on it, wearing animal horns, a picture so old it makes the pyramids seem modern. Looking at it, seeing the wild savagery in the thing, I knew it for what it was, knew I'd seen it before, knew the thing in that picture wasn't any kind of man. See, that thing I shot that day in Vermont came screaming out of the woods, right at us, on two legs.

20. BAD PLACE
by Martin Hayes

Everyone had heard the stories about something bad in the woods up by the McKenzie place. My old pal Tom Williams was going up there with his fancy new digital camera - said he was going to check the place out, shoot some moody pictures and then Photoshop them; he was trying to get a picture on the cover of some horror story anthology.

Two days later and Tom still wasn't answering his cell. It kept ringing out and going to voice mail. Nothing new; he would often disappear for days on end (some folks said that he had a mistress over in Duxbury and maybe he did) but he was so damned excited about this project and he had said that he would email me some of the pictures when he got back.

There was no sign of his truck in the car park by the picnic area. I parked up and set off eastward at about six o'clock. It was only a couple of miles to the McKenzie house; I've spent all my life around woods, so I had no qualms about going in alone. I'd been up there once before when I was a kid on a stupid dare. I didn't get closer than about four hundred yards that time before I got spooked and ran for home.

I could see the half-fallen-in roof of the house as I crested the hill and looked down across the gentle slope of trees and brambles. The house had been abandoned sometime in the eighties. A teenager had gone missing, was never found and when the police called up here to ask old McKenzie if he'd seen anything, he too was gone, vanished, although a couple of times people from the town swore that they had seen him round the back of the diner, by the bins, or out in the woods, a fleeting figure, half seen from the corner of an eye through a dusty side window.

The house had lain empty for almost thirty years. It was funny; usually an abandoned house would attract hobos and kids and vandals, but not this place. No one ever came here.

I could hear the raucous calls of crows as I crossed what had been the front yard; I scanned the tree tops but could see no sign of them.

The loose boards creaked as I made my way up the front steps. To my right a swing-chair hung crookedly from one rusted chain, something terrible about the angle that it formed with the porch. The front door was open an inch or so.

The crows called louder then, and I still could not see them.

I nudged the front door open with the toe of my boot. A wide room spread out before me, and as I crossed the threshold, the musty smell of decay filled my nose and mouth.

It was there on the carpet, no more than four paces away. I still don't know what you would call it. A talisman, perhaps? It was based around the bleached white skull of a deer. Someone had tied bunches of black crow's feathers to it, making a kind of hideous headdress, and in each of its deep hollow eyes sat the smaller skull of a rat or a bird. It was surrounded by a circle that appeared to have been smeared on the floor with lard. A convoy of cockroaches and ants scurried around the circle of grease, all of them moving clock-wise.

I stepped back out onto the porch, feeling light-headed and a little sick in my stomach. As I turned I heard the metallic creak of the swing-chair. When I looked I saw that it was new again; and sitting in the middle was old man McKenzie, smiling in his tattered dungarees, an arm around the shoulders of a thin teenage girl on his left, and on his right, my old pal Tom Williams.

Tom looked at me and sputtered the words, "Bad place." Blood ran from his mouth, and three of his front teeth fell from rotting gums into his lap as I turned on my heels and ran towards the setting sun.

◇◇◇◇◇◇◇◇◇◇◇◇◇◇◇◇

21. IN OLD WATER
by Aaron A. Polson

There was a little bait shop nestled away in the Green Mountains where old men loved to spread stories like compost on fertile young imaginations. "The water up here is full dead folk. So much history… war… disease." They laughed while we listened to the tales of those restless, lonesome souls, bobbing under the murk. "They're waiting," the old men said. Those stories pricked our courage, forced us to ride our bikes with fishing poles in hand in search of adventure.

Joel knew a place, and we rode to an old stone fence hiding at the edge of a tree line. Through a path between those trees—crooked conifers jutting to heaven with low, untrimmed branches, dying brown pines, and knobby arthritic firs—we saw the hint of a large pond. The trees encroached on the very lip of the water, leaving only two bare patches of packed dirt open for fishing. The land around the pond seemed somehow twisted, crooked, and diseased, resting as it was in the purple shadow of those foothills.

As we walked through the dense mesh of grey branches, the path vanished. Our pant legs caught on bits of jagged rocks and downed limbs, swishing and snagging through the calf-high grass in small clearings. The trees began to hoard sunlight, and the mountains seemed to fold around us. Below the sound of our tramping feet, a slight humming sound grew. "Do you hear that?" I asked Joel.

"What?"

"The buzz," I whispered to him. He stopped ahead of me and balanced his pole on the ground.

Slowly turning his head to look over his shoulder all goggle-eyed, he muttered, "Come here." Maybe his quavering voice, seeing too much white around his eyes, or the claustrophobic trees spurred my fear. I wanted to leave, climb on the bike and go. But I obeyed him against the growing storm in my stomach.

He didn't need to say anything else. Lying on the ground, jutting out from behind a low, scratchy bush, I saw two legs. Pants really, and shoes, but they had form and shape unlike they would if they were empty. The pants were black, dirty with mud, and torn in places. I thought of Grandpa's funeral and the black suit in which we buried him. The stories of the poor, unhappy dead swirled in my head.

I can't exactly explain the feeling, but the body drew me to it like some sort of obscene gravity—like a lure, a worm on a hook for a curious boy. I rounded the bush and looked on the rest of this grotesque thing. The torso was still covered by a filthy suit coat that had once been black like the pants. My eyes traced one arm to a white, bloated hand covered thickly by black flies. Corrupted by insects and water, what flesh remained shined like wax or melted fat. The hand seemed to twitch and move, curling those awful dead fingers.

Just then, Joel poked me in the ribs, shouting "Gotcha!" My body burst with terrible fire, all my nerves lit with fright. I screamed, dropped my fishing pole, wheeled, pushed the laughing Joel out of my path, and ran without thinking. I hit the stone wall and scrambled over, tearing my pants and carving a long red scratch on my leg. I toppled to the other side, rested against the rough, cold rocks, and tried to catch my breath.

Feeling a little shame at my retreat, I crawled over the wall again. I had to go back, at least to pick up my fishing pole.

That was when Joel screamed. I dodged through the trees, followed a splashing sound, and saw my friend thrashing in the middle of the pond with a white hand wrapped tightly around his throat.

I really ran then, not stopping until I reached the village and sobbed my tale to the police. They dragged the water for Joel's body, but they never found him. Officially, he became a runaway, a boy on the side of a milk carton.

I know what really happened. I'll show you the place. Maybe you'd like to bring a fishing pole or even go for a swim?

◇◇◇◇◇◇◇◇◇◇◇◇◇◇◇◇◇

22. RAVEN'S HOUSE
by Jason M. Tucker

It happened a long time ago, just a few years after I returned from the war. I remember it well, unfortunately. I can still see and smell it....

The woods seemed darker than they should have been, as though the sun, still a few hours from setting, didn't want to touch them. Something rotten hid in those trees. Cops get a sixth sense after a while; mine was kicking me in the ass.

Something about that place chilled me. Even with a shotgun in my hands, I didn't want to go down there. I stood on that hill like a fool, cold drops of sweat dripping off the tip of my nose and earlobes and then slithering down my neck like a serpent.

A tug at my belt broke the spell the dark trees held over me. I'd almost forgotten about the little girl, Greta, whom I'd found wandering on that old dirt stretch off Hollister Hill Road, between North Montpelier and Marshfield.

"Sheriff," she said, pointing toward those trees. "That's where it got my brother."

"I told you to stay in the car," I said.

"You'll get my brother?"

"You hop back in the car. There are some deputies on their way here right now. You stay in the car 'til they get here."

She went back to the patrol car, and I started down the hill across the field and into the forest. A trail led into the woods, just as the girl had said, twisting and winding inward. It was silent and darker than I had thought it would be.

The shotgun's stock was slick from my sweat, and I had to stop several times to wipe my hands on my pants. It was then that I heard a sound, a soft cry.

That cry must have given me some courage I didn't know I possessed. I hurried forward, over a small rise. Moss and white sticks covered the ground there, and then I saw the house. It was made of more white sticks, thousands of them, and of flesh, raw and dripping. Ravens sat atop the structure and picked at the meat. The sticks, I soon came to see, were bones of all shapes and sizes. It stank of death.

I felt a rise of vomit but held it back; there was no time to react to the flesh house, as the cry was becoming more insistent. I brought the shotgun to shoulder level and moved forward.

At the back of the house, I found the boy, Johann, tied to a stake in the ground. He was whimpering, but he looked unharmed. He gazed up at me.

"She'll come in the dark," he said. "Get us to the light."

I yanked the stake clear of the ground. "Can you walk?"

He nodded.

I held onto his hand as we made our way out. As soon as I could see the sunny field beyond the trees, I heard a screech that made me nearly piss.

We started running.

I heard the thing behind us, breaking through the trees. I chanced to look back once, saw the head of an elderly Native woman perched atop a gnarled body covered in coarse black feathers and moss. The legs ended in hooves and the hands in sharp talons.

"She's a witch," the boy said.

I dropped the shotgun, lifted the boy, and ran out into the bright field. My lungs were on fire and I was seeing spots; I was breathing so hard I didn't even hear my deputies come down the hill for us....

They found nothing – not my shotgun and certainly not the house made of meat, bone, and sinew. The witch, trickster, demon, or whatever it was had vanished, or was so good at hiding even bloodhounds couldn't find her.

Of course, I never told anyone what I really saw and neither did Johann and Greta. Who would believe? The deputies thought they were looking for a kidnapper. I never told them any different.

All these years later, when everything is silent and dark, I sometimes hear that screech in the distance, and then I think about what the boy said. She'll come in the dark.

◇◇◇◇◇◇◇◇◇◇◇◇◇◇◇◇◇◇◇◇

23. THE HUMAN DEER

by Kurt Newton

Teddy and I were good friends. Fresh out of high school, we didn't have a clue as to what we wanted to do with our lives. College was as unlikely as winning the lottery. Neither of us had the brains, the money, or the ambition. And, at the time, we didn't really care to think about it. We just wanted to get high.

I got a part-time job at the gas station. Teddy drove a paper route delivering a weekly ad-rag along the back roads of northeast Connecticut. Working four hours a week, he actually made more than I did putting in twenty. It gave us just enough money to put gas in our cars, weed in our lungs, and beer in our bellies.

One foggy night in April, I had nothing else better to do, so I rode shotgun on Teddy's paper route. We were half stoned, half drunk. At two in the morning the back roads are pretty empty. We didn't worry about hitting another car. What we didn't expect was a big old deer to come walking out in front of us and stop dead in its tracks.

Teddy didn't even have time to tromp on his brakes before the deer rolled onto the hood and flipped up and over the windshield. By the time we stopped, it was about ten yards behind us, trying to get up off the pavement. But its legs were broken. And there was something else on the pavement. Something smaller and barely moving.

Teddy backed up, swerving to avoid the mess, until his headlights showed us just what we'd done.

It was a mother deer. A beautiful doe. It had been pregnant. The force of the impact had ejected her unborn fawn onto the road.

I asked Teddy, "What are we gonna do? We can't just leave them like that."

The mother deer was kicking its broken legs and groaning, and the newborn was still half in its birth sac.

Teddy wasn't the brightest guy, but his heart was as big as his smile. He couldn't stand to see things suffer. I'm sure if he had had a gun he would have put both the deer out of their misery.

For a second I saw him look to the roadside. Maybe he thought about finding something to use as a club. But it was too damn foggy out. You couldn't see a damn thing. Besides, the deer was in agony. Something had to be done. And quick.

That's when Teddy walked right up and grabbed the deer around neck in what looked like a sleeper hold. He planted his knee on the deer's back and began to twist. The deer snorted and kicked, almost catching Teddy in the chin. Blood and other fluids splattered my face.

"Hold her down!" Teddy yelled.

It was like a dream. A really bad dream. But it was too late to wake up and walk away.

I was just about to sit on the deer's hindquarters when I heard the sickening snap. The deer went still.

I threw up then. Budweiser and pizza all over my Nikes.

Teddy and I dragged the dead deer off to the side of the road, the dead fawn trailing after, dragged by its umbilical cord.

Two months later, while delivering his papers, Teddy was rear-ended by a pickup truck and his car burst into flames. He died not far from where we'd hit that deer that night.

Since Teddy's death, motorists claim to have seen a naked man on all fours crossing the road where Teddy died. The naked man stops as if pinned by their headlights. He stands up and smiles. But on impact the naked man disappears.

There have yet to be any serious accidents. Just a lot of scared motorists.

They call it Dead Man's Crossing.

But I know it's Teddy taking the hit over and over again. Slowing people down late at night. Maybe saving a deer or two in the process.

Teddy wasn't the brightest guy, but his heart was a big as his smile.

◇◇◇◇◇◇◇◇◇◇◇◇◇◇◇◇◇◇◇

24. THE NATICK NASTY
by Paul Milliken

T*he Natick Nasty.*
The name caught on quickly; probably the invention of some fresh-out-of-college newspaper reporter who thought alliteration made him sound seasoned. I guess it worked. I was young, not even thirteen, but I remember hearing it everywhere; on TV, at home, at the grocery store.

In case you've never been, Natick is one of those places that's caught between being a small town and a huge suburb. On one hand, it's part of the Greater Boston area; on the other, we've only got one high school. It's full of that Colonial history that tourists come searching for each summer; the Henry Wilson Shoe Shop and Eliot Church satisfy more than a few people looking to take some snapshots of themselves in front of historical landmarks.

But that fall, everyone was focused purely on the present, and on one bizarre new tourist making all the headlines:

The Natick Nasty.

Talk about the creature was especially rampant at school, probably because it started with some kids we all knew. They were three high school boys; I can't remember their names anymore, but they were Natick Redman through-and-through, members of the champion football team and straight-A students. Word had it they'd eaten a late dinner after practice and were messing around near Bolden Lane Cemetery when they saw it.

Descriptions varied once the story spread over the next few months, but at the beginning, it was disarmingly simple. The boys were walking along Bolden Lane when they heard a clicking noise. One of the guys would say it sounded like a camera taking several quick pictures. Click-click-click-click. The boys stopped, straining their eyes in the dark to see where the noise had come from. The street wasn't well lit, but one of the teens turned toward Beaver Dam and noticed a quick flash of light moving near the ground. He whispered a quick "Hey!" and the other two turned and looked in the same direction.

Click-click-click-click. The thing made the noise again, then it lifted itself up onto its hind legs. If it hadn't been for the eyes, they might have never even seen it. But, they'd later swear, the eyes glowed. It was more than just a reflection, like a glint of light hitting a cat's eye. The eyes emitted light; two sharp yellow beams focused directly toward the road.

In the dark, they said, it was hard to get a great look, but the thing seemed to be about three feet tall when standing on its hind legs. It didn't have fur; they could tell by its outline that it was covered with slick skin, like a seal's. It seemed to watch the boys for a moment, then lowered its head to the ground.

Here's the amazing part: it didn't crawl. It slithered toward them, twisting from side to side on its belly like a fish out of water, loudly thrashing through the bed of crisp fallen leaves. As for the boys, they were off and running back toward Casey's Diner. They breathlessly told their story to the staff and other patrons; someone finally called a police officer, who apparently took a look around the area but didn't find a thing.

Once word got out, well...you already know what happened. It brought even more tourists to town. Scientists and Bigfoot Hunters and UFO fans, all with their own theories of what the Natick Nasty really was. Sightings continued for awhile; people most often reporting hearing that clicking sound or seeing the eyes. But once winter came around, burying us all in a white blanket of snow, the frenzy cooled down as quickly as the temperatures.

editing *The Boston Globe* now. I spent most of my life out West, but recently returned to my birthplace for retirement. I'd just about forgotten the Natick Nasty. But last night, as I was sitting out on my back porch puffing away on a cigar and enjoying the late-evening fall breeze, I heard it. Four quick clicks. And I knew, right then, I wasn't the only one who'd returned home.

◇◇◇◇◇◇◇◇◇◇◇◇◇◇◇◇◇◇

25. The OX-CART MAN

by Aaron A. Polson

U ntil we were twelve years old, Billy Wilson and I searched for the Ox-Cart Man during our summer vacations in New Hampshire. Our searches grew over the years, adding new technology and techniques to find the worn path where that phantom supposedly trekked home from the Portsmouth market.

That last summer was very special—we both knew it would be our last chance to find the old road and maybe catch a glimpse of the Ox-Cart Man together. Billy's dad was being transferred to California, and I would have to reconnoiter the Piscataqua River valley alone, climbing over rock and stone, through old forests, and near quietly murmuring streams for a hint of the legend. We pledged to find him that year.

Billy collected anything to do with the Ox-Cart Man—scraps of stories in old newspapers, books of regional ghost stories, pictures of lost throughways, bridges, and foundations of homes that time pushed aside. He constructed a map of the region, complete with every reported sighting.

I snuck out of my house on that last night. Both of us traveled by bicycle, dangerous in the dark, but stealthy too.

"I've learned some new stuff," he said, eyes glowing like silver embers under the moon. "Mom drove me to the library in Portsmouth today. They have a whole new local folklore section."

We slid off our bikes near an old crossroads.

"All the stories corroborate, he was shot by some highwaymen. He was on his way home from the market after bartering all his family's goods, even the ox and cart." Billy snapped on a flashlight and ducked under a sycamore branch.

"Okay, we know that bit," I said, tromping after him.

Billy stopped, turned, and smiled. "There's a part of the legend I'd never heard before. His son left looking for him after the Ox-Cart Man didn't return. The son never came home, either."

A chill breeze danced through the trees.

"They say his son is still looking for him," Billy whispered. "He was our age." He nudged me with a knobby elbow. "His name was William."

We found a spot where the old path dipped low beside a dying stream. Billy's notes indicated this might have been the location the Ox-Cart Man met his fate. I felt a little childish when fear crept in my chest; Billy needed some closure on his own childhood—he needed some verification of his beliefs.

The moon shifted back toward the morning horizon, filtering long streams of pale light through the light forest. The night smelled black: the rich smell of mud and old moss. Billy and I kept the vigil in silence. Then he arrived, shimmering like a morning fog.

The Ox-Cart Man looked more solid than I'd expected. He loped with a steady gait, a pole over his shoulder holding a black kettle. His face was drawn, long and rimmed with a reddish beard, just like the legends said. The man wore a rough cotton shirt and black coat. His feet struck the ground with no sound but the light brush of breeze.

Billy stood up. I remember the burning in my arms and legs—the tingling nerves. I wanted to stop him, but all I could do was watch as my friend walked toward the Ox-Cart Man.

The man stopped, regarding Billy. He knelt after a moment, smiling. I heard a voice—not from the specter but in my head—William? Billy nodded. The Ox-Cart Man reached inside his black kettle and pulled out a small candy, wintergreen so the stories told, and offered it to Billy.

They stood for a few minutes in silence until finally without a look back, Billy walked away with the Ox-Cart Man. I could do nothing but sit with throbbing heart as the father and son vanished into the trees, fading like the mist.

◇◇◇◇◇◇◇◇◇◇◇◇◇◇◇◇◇◇◇

26. THE SHADOW MEN

by Mark Leslie

I 'll never forget the night that changed my life forever. It happened in the woods when I was ten years old.

It was dark; the air was crispy and chilly. Curious little sounds cut through the night — small animals rustling in the nearby bushes, the haunting call of a loon on the lake, leaves rustling in the trees. And the air was charged with the smell of the still-burning embers of a recently doused campfire.

It was a night, in fact, not all that different than tonight.

I was sleeping in a four-man tent with my parents and younger brother and woke up with an overwhelming urge to head to the washroom. I crawled out of my sleeping bag, careful not to wake anyone else, slipped outside the tent, and headed down the moonlit path to where I remembered the outhouse was.

Before I took more than a dozen steps I heard a noise behind me: the crack of a branch breaking underfoot.

With my hairs standing on edge, I managed not to let out a yelp as I turned.

There on the path not three steps behind me stood my little brother, a look on his cute button-nosed face like I'd just caught him sneaking a treat from the cookie jar.

"Jimmy," I whispered. "What are you doing?"

He stood with his right leg partially crossed over the left.

"Need to pee," he said, shifting his weight from foot to foot.

"Geez, Jimmy. If you had to go that bad, why'd you wait so long?"

"Because," he said, his six-year-old eyes wide and bright in the reflected moonlight, "the *Shadow Men* might get me."

I felt a shiver run down my spine despite the fact that I knew the *Shadow Men* were something my father had conjured up that evening around the camp fire. They were the bogeymen of the New Hampshire wilderness that hid behind trees and lurked in the shadows. Their sole purpose was to trick little boys down the wrong path in the woods, deeper into the forest and far from the safety of their parents.

Even at ten, I knew my father told the story to us for fun and perhaps partially to keep us from wandering far away from them; but when Jimmy said that I still felt a chill.

"The *Shadow Men* aren't real, Jimmy."

"Are too! Listen!"

At just that moment, the haunting call of a loon echoed through the forest, delivering a deep shiver up the base of my spine.

"That's just a loon," I said, but the chill wouldn't go away.

"No. Listen, Charlie. It's a little boy. One that the *Shadow Men* tricked. He's warning us."

Frustrated with my brother — and, okay, a little frightened — I just wanted it to end; I didn't want to hear any more. So I thought I'd throw a good scare into him.

I turned and ran down the path. "Jimmy!" I called out. "Behind you! The <u>Shadow Men</u> are behind you."

He let out a cry. "Wait!"

Able to see the path clearly in the moonlight, I ran fast, took a sharp turn and ducked down behind a low brush. Jimmy ran past me, still calling ahead on the trail for me to stop, panic rising in his voice as he seemed to think I'd gotten really far ahead of him. I had to put my hands on my mouth to suppress a laugh. But I stayed silent that way, listening to the padding of his footfalls on the packed dirt path and his calls for me to wait for him receding into the distance.

His last cry was drowned out by the shrill call of a loon in the distance.

And I never saw him again.

But I hear him all the time.

Now, every time I'm out in the wilderness, out camping, I can hear my brother's voice. Somewhere, masked within the sad, mournful, unearthly half-laughing, half wailing cry of a loon, I can hear my little brother warning me that the *Shadow Men* are near.

Just listen for it and tell me what *you* hear.

◇◇◇◇◇◇◇◇◇◇◇◇◇◇◇◇◇◇

27. BROKEN CHAIN
by Craig D.B. Patton

Old places have their secrets. And sometimes, you just stumble upon them. For Karen and me, it happened when I was mowing the lawn, knocking down the meadow the previous, elderly owners had let it become.

It was on the south side of the property, a neglected, colonial-era homestead we had bought in Simsbury. I was working around the ruin of the original barn, which had burned down in 1805. All that was left was a rectangular crater rimmed by crumbling masonry. Chunks of stonework lay in the grass. I had shut down the mower and was tossing them into the shallow pit.

When I reached the place where the doors had stood, I spotted something hidden in the weeds. It was a rusted length of two-inch thick chain lying across the gap. I picked it up and discovered four equally rusted brackets fused to it. Examining them, I realized that they had been part of the door that the chain held shut. During the fire, the heat had melted the brackets before the whole, interlocked length tumbled to the ground.

When I tossed the chain into the pit, I noticed the acrid scent of charred wood and felt a sudden chill. The trees stood motionless. There was no wind to explain the change in temperature or why I could suddenly smell the remains of the barn. Puzzled, I went back to clearing the area.

I did not mention to Karen the strange experience I'd had at the old barn site, having forgotten it by that evening. We spent the evening chatting and unpacking a few more boxes before going to bed.

Just after 2:00 AM, I jerked upright. The stench of smoke filled the room. I turned on the lamp, urging Karen to wake up. She sat up, asking what was wrong. Then she smelled the smoke and her eyes widened. We had to get out of the house.

As I stood, something moved near the doorway. I saw a figure there. Not a man, though it had been once. No, what stood there had no place in my understanding of the world. It was hunched, stooped - twisted - like the melted brackets. Bits of blackened clothing hung from its frame. Its skin was charred and cracked. There was a long rent in one side of the bare skull, as though it had been struck with a blade. I heard Karen's scream, a million miles away as I gaped at the awful thing.

But the worst came last. Perhaps reacting to Karen's scream, the head wobbled up, revealing its ruined face. There was no skin, and the very bones had melted. The lower jaw sagged down, the chin extending into a nub, as though a pale, spent candle had been jammed there. The cheekbones were flattened. The eye sockets were irregular ovals. And though there was nothing but blackness within them, that impossible stare locked onto us. The pain in its expression was infinite, but what I sensed most was simple, icy malice.

It moved toward us a step, though its legs and feet remained motionless. The head twisted and bobbed as it looked at Karen, then me, then Karen again. I remember thinking it was trying to identify us.

Then the figure turned, again without using its body, and left the room. I ran forward, ignoring Karen's pleas for me to stay back, and slammed the door shut. Useless, of course, but all I wanted in that moment was to put something between us and that horrible thing.

I went to Karen and we clung to each other, hoping that it was over. We stood there, trembling, until she gasped and pointed through the window. Just visible in the moonlight-dappled front yard below, a hunched figure was moving toward the road. As it went, its speed increased, until it sped off and vanished toward the center of Simsbury.

It was off to town, looking for whatever remains of those who murdered the person it once was.

For God's sake, I hope it doesn't find them.

∞∞∞∞∞∞∞∞∞∞∞∞∞∞∞

28. HEART AND SOLE

by Allan Leverone

I hadn't always wanted to kill my wife. There was a time when we were quite the happy couple, of that I am certain, even if I can't put my finger on exactly when that was. Everything changed, though, after Debra moved in next door.

Debra Janet Morgan was her name, and she was everything Marion was not. Deb was young and beautiful, while Marion was older and plain. She was funny and outgoing and socially graceful, Marion being quiet and shy and clumsy. After starting my affair with the alluring young beauty, it became patently obvious that my wife and I no longer had a future together.

Debra was newly single, living off the support payments of her bond-trader ex-husband, who was slaving away down in Boston's financial district. She had nothing to do and wasn't one to spend her days lazing around the house; at least not by herself and not fully clothed.

After we hooked up, I began to obsess over the fantasy of arranging

Marion's permanent removal from the otherwise happy picture of Debra and me. Divorce was out of the question – my salary as a postal supervisor would not be enough to hold Debra's attention for long. It was absolutely imperative that I inherit Marion's trust fund: the one established by her rich daddy years ago that would disappear forever if I divorced his little girl.

Being cautious by nature, I considered and then discarded numerous methods of disposal before settling on the perfect plan. It was foolproof – I would be hundreds of miles away when poor unfortunate Marion took her final breath!

An avid distance runner, Debra had struck up an odd friendship with my Marion, despite our affair. They ran together constantly, a situation I was never comfortable with until I figured out how to use it to my advantage. I managed to wrangle a business trip to Philadelphia on the very day of the local 5K Fun Run, which Deb and Marion were planning on competing in together.

The morning of the race, I awoke while Marion was still sleeping and packed a bag for my two-day trip. Before walking out to the garage, I sprinkled a dose of specially customized powder lightly over the insoles of Marion's running shoes.

The mixture was composed of ordinary talcum powder laced with arsenic, which my research had informed me is water-soluble. Shortly after starting the race, Marion's entire body, including her feet, would begin to sweat in the warm weather. The perspiration would then soak through her light socks, mix with my deadly concoction, and be absorbed through her open pores into her bloodstream.

Marion would suffer greatly for a short time, unfortunately, but before rescue personnel or anyone else would be able to react, she would succumb, leaving Debra and me free to get on with our lives. I would avoid any suspicion, being nowhere near the scene of the tragedy. I congratulated myself on planning the perfect crime as I boarded the flight at Logan Airport.

Later, as the plane began its descent into Philly, I realized the starting time for the Fun Run was approaching and decided to give Marion a call. Sure, I had to eliminate her, but that didn't mean I felt good about it.

She surprised me by answering her cell on the first ring. "Hello?"

"Hello, Marion; ready for the race?"

"Oh, hi honey. Not exactly. You wouldn't believe what that silly goose Debra did!"

I checked my impatience and asked, "What did she do?" After all, this was the last time I would ever have to listen to her ramble on.

"The crazy girl drove all the way down here before realizing she had forgotten her running shoes!"

"You're kidding."

"No, but I solved the problem. I lent her mine. She was much more excited about the race than me, anyway."

My heart stuttered and I shouted, "What? Where's Debra now?" Annoyed passengers glared at me.

"I have no idea," she replied. "We got separated in the crowd, but I'll find her after the race. Enjoy your trip, honey; I'll be waiting when you get back."

◇◇◇◇◇◇◇◇◇◇◇◇◇◇◇◇◇◇◇

29. MANY COMFORTING WORDS

by J.C. Tabler

I don't read newspapers anymore, and haven't since I was a child. I don't want to be one of those old men reading a paper every morning, no matter what. That was my lesson learned from delivering papers.

Grandfather and I lived in Eastern Connecticut, among swamp Yankees and lying contests. Pop was a farmer who woke early to meet the paper, and my first job, delivering the The Chronicle from downcity in Willimantic, was his idea. I'm certain his desire for me to deliver it was so he could have one up on all of his pre-dawn, elderly brethren. It was the way Pop was, always wanting to be a step ahead, and I was his ticket to knowing everything first.

I never minded pedaling steep hills in darkness. I did mind the graveyard at the end of my route. It was a shadowed place, large enough to take in most of the county's population if needed. Tombstones sat at strange angles, worn smooth and greened with age on the outer boundaries, bright and new further back, a farm planting bodies and raising a crop of granite markers. I knew the dead couldn't hurt me, but was not so certain about those in the stone caretaker's house that sat in the cemetery's center. A million horror movie moments played in my head as I walked my bike among tombstones towards its unlit mass.

I was relieved to see an elderly man, much like Pop, open the door. At my young age, it was hard to tell where his beard ended and shirt began, and so my image of him to this day remains dark slacks, suspenders, a small black hat, and pure white hair. A nose, pleasantly reddened by drink like Pop's, jutted out from his encasing beard. He was, in short, grandfatherly.

"Toss me over here the paper, now," he said in German-accented English.

New to the job, my toss was wide, though it would be no problem. His gnarled hand made a perfect catch, and his smile made up for any lack of light. His teeth were yellowed and crooked, but gleaming in joy despite darkness. It was a smile that demanded, and received, one in return.

"Twenty years I read every morning," he lilted, "Chust work on the toss, done good now."

Every day I would be met by this kindly old man. In darkness before the dawn he would ask for his paper, and catch it with a smile. As I got better with my overhand throw he stopped speaking, preferring to nod approval. Always the same as he nodded, tipped his black cap, and shuffled off.

Collection day came fast; a month's worth of work come to fruition. After a nap I worked around Pop's farm, gaining an excuse to leave before supper and collect payments. Some weren't home, others paid with a smile and a pat on the head. In the light of a setting sun, the graveyard was not nearly as frightening. I found myself looking forward to speaking with the old man for longer than our morning exchanges.

The scrawny, shirtless man who answered the door wasn't him.

"What do ya want?" asked nasal tones, attached to eyes that considered me an obvious pest.

"I'm from the Chronicle...."

"No way, sonny," barked this skeletal man. "Been here ten years, not once have you boys ever delivered my damn paper. I'm not paying for something I don't get."

"But the old guy…" I started.

"Old guy?" interrupted this frightening visage, "Big guy, beard, suspenders, white shirt? Got a funny way of talking?"

"Yeah, that's him," I exclaimed. Finally we were making some headway.

"Sounds like Pap Besshock, but he's been here least twice as long as I have," allowed this shirtless madman, starting to close his door. "We just can't keep that man in his grave."

I don't read the newspaper anymore, and haven't since I was a child. I don't want it to become an eternal habit.

◇◇◇◇◇◇◇◇◇◇◇◇◇◇◇◇◇◇

30. METAPHORICALLY SPEAKING

by Morven Westfield

The last time I saw Amanda she hadn't been well. Hepatitis C, and then she did some God-awful treatment for nearly a year. Then she emailed me that she was ready to go camping again. So there we were.

I slapped a fat irritating mosquito on my arm. It was so full the blood spattered the sleeve of my tee shirt. I thought she'd puke. "You okay?"

"Yeah, it's just now that I've had a blood-borne illness, I can't stand the sight of blood. Good thing I'm post-menopausal."

"Can't stand the sight of blood, huh? How does that help your vampire stories?" Amanda had been trying her hand at vampire fiction ever since she got hooked on Dark Shadows. Life would interfere and she'd shelve her novel, but she had mentioned something about writing while she was sick. Maybe she was writing something else.

"Yeah, it makes it a little difficult." She played with the wax that dripped from the candle onto the picnic table. A large moth singed its wings before we could shoo it away. She wrinkled her nose at the smell of burning moth-flesh. "I think I've got it this time, though. After all, the vampire is merely a metaphor."

In the distance I could hear a rumble of thunder. I looked up at the indigo sky and noticed that it was much darker than it had been yesterday at this time. Storm. Not unusual for this campground. It was close to Monadnock and the storms that came over that mountain.

"What do you mean?"

"Well, okay, we have the story of the vampire and how he bites someone in the computer room, but the story isn't about a real vampire. It's about technology and how it can suck the life out of you."

A brisk wind tore through the trees, roaring. I didn't like that and I could see that she didn't, either. She turned around to face the field and we both searched for other signs of the impending storm. "I hate lightning storms when I'm camping," I said, getting up and walking to the edge of the campsite. "All these trees. It's like we're sitting in a field of lightning rods."

"Yeah, I know, but how long have we been coming here? It does this all the time. No one's been hit—"

"Yet," I completed her sentence, tapping the nearest tree with my knuckles. "Yet, knock on wood."

The twilight clouds tumbled and darkened in the distance. Roiled. That was the word: roiled. They roiled. Or boiled. Like the witches' brew in MacBeth. Double, double, toil and trouble... By the pricking of my thumbs...

"Anyway, it's a metaphor. It's not like I believe vampires exist. Wesley is just a metaphor."

A loud crack of thunder made us both jump. Amanda's hand knocked over the candle in its primitive empty-wine-bottle holder. The melted wax spilled, extinguishing our only light.

"You okay?" I called out. There was a short pause before she replied.

"Joe? Did you move?"

"No. Why?"

"I think I see something."

If the cold damp air didn't raise the hairs on the back of my neck, this did. It was a new moon, and dark as hell. The storm clouds blocked out even starshine.

"What?"

"Eyes."

"Raccoon?"

"No..."

"Bear?"

"Are there bears here?"

"Shit, I hope not. How far off the ground are the eyes?"

"Man-height."

The wind was up again and I could hear twigs snapping, but they were opposite the direction she had been facing at the picnic table. "Which direction are you looking in?"

"Straight ahead."

Something moved in the darkness. How we could see it, I don't know, but I know she saw it, because her last words, uttered before the lightning illuminated the site, were "It's coming—"

And then there was that moment, that single moment, when the light lit up the sky, the table, everything, and I could see him, and only him, hands reaching toward Amanda, as he spoke only these five words:

"I am NOT a metaphor."

◇◇◇◇◇◇◇◇◇◇◇◇◇◇◇◇◇◇

31. SINISTER MIRTH
by John Weagly

I write plays about the sea. Serious plays, plays that make the audience think. That's why I moved to Provincetown, Massachusetts. It was in this quaint little coastal burg that the Provincetown Players gave Eugene O'Neill, another man who wrote about the sea, his first productions. Upon arrival, I ingratiated myself with The Outsider Theatre Company. They, of course, loved my work.

It was during my second summer that I met Amanda, in Provincetown on vacation. Alabaster skin, burgundy hair and a body that was a three-act play unto itself. The minute I saw her at the Recovering Hearts Bookstore, I hit her with the best I had.

"Excuse me," I said, "Your hair is like... dusk."

She looked up from the book she was holding and smiled. "No one's ever said that before," she said. "That's really cool."

"I can do that," I said. "I'm a writer."

She accompanied me to Café Mews for coffee.

I don't think of myself as a funny person. I have a dry wit, but I'm far from a comedian. For some reason Amanda found me hilarious.

Everything I said that was mildly amusing was met with exuberant giggling. With the aid of laughter, I convinced her to come back to my apartment to sample my work.

Here's a little secret about those of us who write: we all do it to impress someone. Sometimes the public, sometimes one specific reader, sometimes ourselves. I put words on paper to impress the ladies. Every attractive woman I meet becomes my muse. After I sleep with them they become my memory.

I started Amanda off with The Misbegotten Ape. Although it is a serious work, she chuckled under her breath while reading. I was aghast! Some little Midwest bumpkin tittering at my most heart-wrenching opus! Luckily, I forgot my confusion at her reaction when I discerned that my beguiling musings worked. That night she joined me in my bed.

Our relationship progressed from there, as much as a relationship can during a two-week vacation.

And then Amanda was leaving.

"Will you write to me?" she asked. We were at Café Mews, lattes in hand, standing by her car.

"I'll do my best."

"I... I think I love you."

This caught me off guard. The liaison had been fun, but love? I didn't love her any more than any of the other vacationing women I'd dallied with.

"Look, Amanda," I said, "we had our fun, but it was a vacation fling. You'll go back to Nebraska and resume your everyday grind. You'll forget all about me."

"I'm from Indiana."

"Sorry."

"Nobody in Indiana makes me laugh like you."

For once I, the wordsmith, couldn't find the words. "Sorry," I said again.

She didn't burst into tears, I'll give her that. She calmly walked to her car and drove away.

Amanda never made it out of town. At Race Point she drove her car into the Atlantic.

I was disturbed, but I somehow managed to carry on with life.

Shortly after Amanda's death, my latest play, Extraordinary Interlude, opened. Midway through the production, while the audience was pondering what it meant to be human, a giggle arose from the house. I was in the back row and looked around to see who the offending patron was. No one was obvious.

The giggle grew to a guffaw.

From what I could see, nobody in the theater was making the horrendous noise. The guffaws grew into full blown laughter.

That was when I recognized the sound for what it was: her. Somehow Amanda was laughing at my work from beyond the grave.

The actors struggled through the rest of the performance, the laughter never ceasing.

The next night the cackles began as soon as the lights went down.

There was no third night. My brilliant, somber play closed after two laugh-filled performances.

Outsider Theater Company tried another of my plays, but the same thing happened. Then they severed their ties.

I've tried going to other theaters, places in New York, Chicago—anywhere. The result is always the same: laughter in the darkness; giggles, cackles, guffaws.

The seriousness of my plays shall never be serious again.

◇◇◇◇◇◇◇◇◇◇◇◇◇◇◇◇◇◇◇◇

32. SO FAIR AND FOUL A DAY

by David E. Chrisom

The girl who lives at the dead end of my street is a witch.

I don't care if you believe me. It's true. I can't prove it, but I don't have much time left. I want to warn you to stay away from her, if she appears.

Our street faces the harbor in Hingham, Massachusetts. Sometimes I see that girl, Orenda, by the water, hunting for frogs. I asked her once why she does that. She wouldn't tell me. She said, "My name means Magic Power." Her mother is Native American and she has hair the color of a raven, with eyes to match. I'll bet when you first saw her running to catch the school bus, or walking along the harbor, or sitting below that crooked tree in the park, you thought she looked sweet. Did she glance up at you? If she had you wouldn't feel the same. Her stare makes you cold, gives you goosebumps, like the first frost when summer fades. I think there is something behind those raven eyes of hers. Something wrong.

I tried to be her friend, when she first moved in and came to our high school. She was different from the people here, with her dark, tattered clothes and shiny, silver jewelry.

She isn't like us. "I don't trust anyone," she told me once. For a long time, I thought I was the only one who could see it. People were so polite at first, whenever she was around. No one talked about the way they felt after she left. How their palms would sweat, their eyes would tear up, their vision would blur. She smells of rotten rose petals. Ancient. Bad.

I didn't think she would really hurt someone until that day Mr. Dunn told us about Salem Village in 1692. It was the week before Halloween and he told us how the villagers turned against their own, accused people of witchcraft and put them to death.

Orenda interrupted and simply said, "Stop."

Mr. Dunn continued. Orenda stood up and left the class. Most everyone laughed, except for me. I felt sad for her back then. They were always laughing behind her back.

Mr. Dunn didn't come in the next day; he stayed home sick. I was told he was rushed to the hospital two days later. Kids stopped laughing then. They went quiet whenever Orenda passed by. They stared at her like she was a witch in Salem Village. They tossed spit balls at her hair, stuck their tongues out at the back of her head. Still, their skin turned cold and their vision blurred.

"I need your blood," she said to me one afternoon, as we walked up our street from the bus stop. "Just a drop."

The burnt orange leaves crackled under my sneaker treads. I refused to look back at Orenda. She called after me, "Just a drop. Or I can't protect you from what will happen."

I ignored her until I was safely shut inside my house.

The next day was like every other, except the food in the school cafeteria tasted different. Overly salty. Most everyone agreed. I don't remember seeing Orenda at lunch that day. By late afternoon all of us had stomach aches. Pain that stabbed our guts.

I found my best friend Nancy crying behind the stairs and asked her what was wrong. I made her tell me. "Victoria Nelson's mom is a nurse at the hospital," she said. "She was working the night they brought Mr. Dunn in. He died."

"How," I gasped.

"The hospital is keeping it a secret. He had violent stomach pains. They thought it was his appendix. They cut him open and you won't believe what they found."

"What?"

"Things that looked like spiders." She winced and clutched her stomach.

I hunted Orenda down and found her in the woods behind the parking lot. She knelt over the dead body of a plump sparrow. I asked, "Why?"

"The hurly-burly is done." She glared at me with raven eyes. "Your battle is lost."

Suddenly she vanished.

◇◇◇◇◇◇◇◇◇◇◇◇◇◇◇◇◇◇◇◇

33. THE FEAR OF INNOCENCE

by Justin Pilon

He lives beyond the farmland, out amidst the torrents of ice and snow. Some say he came from the mountains. Others claim that he crawled his way out of the bitter Atlantic. I cannot say for sure. All I know is that he is not entirely human.

The first time I saw him, I was only ten. I was making my way up the long, winding pass between my parents' farmhouse and the stables, a rusted bucket of water in hand. The wind was frigid and ripped at my clothes. My skin burned as if on fire. And yet, I had no choice. It was my job and my duty to feed the bulls.

The moon was full. It cast a silver glare across the rolling hills of snow. I stood there on the sanded path, staring out into the unknown and wondering why my parents asked this of me. Did they not understand the mind of a child? Did they not know that I was afraid of the night?

There I saw him, crouched low to the ground, out in the open field. His body was long and gangling; his flesh was paler than the surrounding snow. Had it not been for his eyes, I would not have seen him at all. They were fat with darkness — sickening things — bloated about their rims. And they watched me, forever watched me — never flinching, analyzing my every move.

My hands trembled. The bucket slipped from my grip. Icy water sprayed across my pants and boots. The wind kicked up again, filling my body with violent chills, and all the while the strange figure stood, licking his leathery lips, dreaming, perhaps, of the day he could devour me. And so I did the only thing I could think of. I ran.

In the house, chilled to the bone and trembling like a leaf, I called out to my parents. My father emerged from the cozy warmth of the living room, his pipe spewing thick wafts of smoke.

"What happened?" he asked.

I could not force a single syllable through my quivering lips. My mother wrapped her arms around me and whispered words of comfort in my ear. At the top of the stairs, my elder brother appeared.

"He's seen it," he said.

A deathly silence ensued. I closed my eyes, trying not to imagine the creature's eyes, trying to forget the despicable sight of its tongue caressing its flaky lips.

"Come down here and explain it to him," my father growled. My brother obeyed, clamoring down the stairs. His face was taught and white, his eyes as wide as ovals.

"He lives out there in the cold," he whispered, "out in the deepest waste... He feeds on men, Johnny."

My father nodded his head.

"We can't go out there," he added taking a moment to puff smoke from his mouth. "Men have tried. They brought guns and torches. They died, Johnny. It is not the way. And so we stay inside..."

"W-why do I have to go out?" I whimpered, tears welling up in my eyes.

"Because," my mother cut in, "it's afraid of you!" She gently stroked my head.

My elder brother patted me on the shoulder.

"Let me take him upstairs," he whispered. "I'll try to explain it all to him."

In the bathroom, lost in a world of steam, everything came clear to me.

"It hunts men," my brother whispered. "It eats them piece by piece.

Why do you think everyone on the island closes shop at 4 o'clock? Why do you think Mom and Dad board the windows up at night? But you know what, there's something it cannot touch."

"What?" I asked.

My brother smiled.

"It's afraid of innocence."

This knowledge comforts me, and yet still I am afraid. Every night I walk out to that barn aware that it is there, watching me. With every day, its courage grows and it gets just a little bit closer. And so I close my eyes and dream of the day when my innocence will fade, the day I can stay inside, away from its abysmal gaze.

◇◇◇◇◇◇◇◇◇◇◇◇◇◇◇◇◇◇◇◇

34. THE PREDATOR
by Douglas E. Wright

You know, Maine's minus forty-six degrees Fahrenheit feels no different than New Brunswick's Celsius. But that never mattered to me. My clothes were just as rigid in July as in December. Their deep-grounded filth made them as stiff as a rigor-mortised corpse.

I remember the sugar maples, black alders, elms and pines, each one trimmed with ice and snow. Their cold distant branches cracked while the echo of my jingly bells saturated the air. Icy threads stretched over my balaclava'd eyes like sparkly fangs. The forest welcomed me with outstretched arms.

And then everything had grown quiet. I had slung the axe over my shoulder. My feet crunched into the crystallized snow.

As I shoved a slew of frozen sumac branches away from my face, I felt their bare spines strike my frozen cheeks. It was then I knew my forest would puke up its bounty one last time.

After a while, the afternoon light diminished and a frigid north wind began to whip the tops of the trees. Not far away, I spotted a niggling creature hopping from limb to limb.

I stood mesmerized, watching it vanish into the blowing trees. And then my mind grabbed a half-forgotten time, a place and time when I really felt I had to kill.

A mental string of images danced before my eyes: scattered provisions, half-eaten vegetables, rotted meat, spilled diesel fuel, chewed electrical lines, and tufts of yellow and pink insulation pulled out of ceiling holes.

My voice came out crusty and raw. "Long time ago, you damn neared killed me. I'll be fucked if that happens again." I continued to raise my jittery tone. "Fred, I'm comin' for ya."

I moved to where I'd last seen the animal and rounded my axe. I sliced the frosty air like a whip carving a convict's spine. Snow fell from the upper tree limbs and dusted my shoulders.

Once I was home, I stood in front of the creature's jagged entryway in my short crimson robe.

It poked its nose out, only to see me: The Predator.

The animal looked behind me, where a sparkling field of moonlit window-glass caught its tiny eyes. The ticking of the grandfather clock must have brushed its ears. It stopped rubbing its matted fur against the door edges and licking the wet frost off its whiskers. It squeezed out of the hole into an unnatural world. Its ink-drop eyes darted to where the base of the tree had been hacked away.

The squirrel then spotted my puffy scarred legs. Each was crisscrossed with thick blue veins, all misshapen and coated with deathly white.

I took a whack.

A whirring purr kissed the decorated tree limbs.

Fred sprang up. I sliced the air a second time. The rodent's head spun and then tumbled into a nest of artificial snow.

I set the stained hatchet on the warped floorboards and whispered, "Figured you was still in there somewheres."

My robe's miniature bells jingled as I pinched the dead animal off one of the painted glass spheres. I tugged it through a maze of glittery tinsel and blinking blue lights.

I fingered my grimy beard and then tacked the little bastard onto the fireplace mantle. Right alongside the other eleven headless trophies I had scored that New England December.

◇◇◇◇◇◇◇◇◇◇◇◇◇◇◇◇◇◇

35. TOM VANE
by Sheldon S. Higdon

Not too far from here lies Mackworth Cemetery. Among the many tombstones that sit atop the brown grass, one reads: Here lies Tom Vane, A child of Maine. Twenty feet away sit two other markers that read: Mary Wellington and Eliza Wellington. Mother and Daughter in the afterlife. No other markers with these names stand among the granite nametags of the dead.

For many years, stories and legends have been told of the account of these three souls that lie buried beneath the ground.

Here is the story as I've heard it…

In September of 1892, a young boy named Tom Vane was caught eating an apple by Horace Wellington, a strict Puritan preacher and farmer who was well known for beating his own daughter, Eliza, if she didn't obey his orders or live under the laws of God. Some even say that Horace murdered her, as well as his wife, Mary. Others say that it was the diphtheria outbreak that swept through Maine in January of 1893 that took Eliza's life. But from Horace Wellington's own journal, he believed his daughter to be the product of the devil himself.

Nothing is known about Horace's wife. Only that her name appears in his journal and that her body lies in Mackworth Cemetery.

Folklore says that Tom Vane cried, imploring that he did nothing wrong, but wanted only to rest in the shade and eat an apple his mother had given him as a reward for his chores. Horace heard none of this as he dragged him to the barn, where it is believed that he took a girth from a horse harness and strapped the boy across the back. He continued beating him until blood had soaked through his cotton shirt. Even Eliza begged for him to stop. Sweat streaked Horace's face as he turned and scolded her for interrupting God's work. And that she'd be punished for such an intrusion. Eliza refused to leave. This angered Horace. Tom's back revealed crimson slashes as he stood on weak legs and made his way to Eliza and out the barn door.

Horace tossed the girth aside and grabbed an ax that had been hanging next to the barn door. He headed for Eliza and Tom as they made their way to the house. Horace yelled as he made quick steps toward them, ordering them to stop at once.

Some say Horace killed both Tom and Eliza right there with the ax: chopping them to pieces and stuffing their remains in Eliza's hay-filled mattress up in the loft where she slept. There are also rumors that Mary died on this day, and that she was the one who begged Horace to stop beating Tom.

The only thing that is known is that Tom Vane's body was in fact found beneath Eliza's mattress. Mutilated and left in several pieces. Apple cores scattered about.

Horace was never placed under arrest for the murder. It is said that he was in the barn chopping wood and replacing the horse's shoes during what would have been an unholy act under his sacred roof, and especially under God's watchful eye. There is no record as to whether Eliza recounted any of that day's events to the authorities. But four months later, Eliza's body was laid to rest at the Mackworth Cemetery.

Three years after Eliza's death, Horace Wellington was found dead beneath the very same apple tree that Tom Vane had been caught under those many years ago. His body was never buried at Mackworth, because his body was never found. Only his head was discovered beneath the apple tree that day.

Some say that Tom Vane came back and sought revenge on Horace. And that he chopped his body to pieces with an ax and buried him beneath the apple tree, leaving Horace's head as proof of his death. Others believe

Tom dragged Horace's body back to the mattress, where he still waits.

So when you lay in bed tonight, listen closely. That sound you hear is Tom Vane eating an apple and waiting… waiting for your arm or leg to dangle over the side.

◇◇◇◇◇◇◇◇◇◇◇◇◇◇◇◇◇◇◇◇

36. TUNNEL VISION

by Derek M. Fox

"**W**e relied on rail then," I told 'em. "I'm talkin' turn of the twentieth here, 1903 an' before. Had a humdinger of a network, lines still exist, at least their rights of way do.

"Damming the Nashua River to create Wachusett Reservoir sure changed the face o' Clinton, that there mill town in Central Massachusetts."

I'd hooked 'em all aware there'd be a point to this.

"Tunnel was bored over a thousand feet through granite, sure put a sizeable hole through Wilson Hill. Became the second largest tunnel in the state."

Eager, bet your life. They ached to know. See, I'd mentioned the name Baxter earlier. Guessin' one or two might've heard it. Rumour travels.

"All right, but I guess you know they closed the tunnel. Last train went through late fifties; demolished the old trestle mid-70s. Footings are still there, not the tracks. They went too."

I was getting to the hub of m'tale about Baxter.

"That particular night a couple o' months into '53, the engine stopped at the red light a few hundred yards south side o' Clinton. Driver was Joe Cornwall. Remember Joe? Big guy with a chip on his shoulder as big as a rail sleeper; had a temper too. So he stops the engine, eases himself up for a stretch and wants to know what's happenin'. Was puzzled 'cause there weren't no more trains due that late especially on a single track.

"Dark with a bit o' breeze, noises in the undergrowth. Spooky for one man drivin' a freight, no passengers t'speak of. With the head of the loco-motive shielding him, poor Joe didn't see the thing watching him from the tunnel's parapet."

Mmm, that sure caused a ripple amongst the listeners.

"Time eased by; light stayed red. Breeze died. Joe stepped off the foot-plate. His shift was due to finish at ten. Thing was, he didn't give a hoot. The argument to end 'em all stuck in his craw, all over his missus Eleanor wantin' Baxter to build her a porch on the house. I mean, Joe was more than able to do it. But no, she insisted that little turd build it."

It drew a few looks.

"Poor Joe was sickened by thoughts of Baxter and Eleanor together. Hit the side o' the loco' with his fist, didn't feel pain, that guy. Hadn't time. Weird scrapings fetched him around the front, nearer the tunnel. Silence that followed was like a closed crypt, except for engine noise.

"Moon was tacked to an inky sky; parapet's arc like a down-turned mouth breathin' cold air. Joe used waitin' time to dwell on Baxter. Did he really believe Eleanor when she'd insisted nothing happened 'tween her and Baxter?

"Twigs and leaves rattled like dice in a crap game, Joe's heart bounc-ing alongside 'em. Somethin' soundin' like footsteps brought him 'round in a full circle.

"What in blazes was it crouched in the tunnel's mouth, that shape thrown by the bloody glare of the light? He scooted back, aiming to hoist hisself into the cab, and felt his ankle grabbed so hard his boot leather creaked.

"Panicked, he kicked out, reliving every damned second of what he'd done, said, the reality of it. See, he'd used Baxter's own hammer to beat the life out of him, every hit dotted by a scream from Eleanor.

"The locomotive roared . . . warning light flared . . . and the shape behind Joe ranted.

"To hell with the light, Joe thought, and sent the locomotive into the tunnel. Heard the steam whistle warning too late. Single track, shame there was no room for two.

"The noise of the impact eventually died. It left Joe Cornwall's fear laughing like crazy between the tracks, bloody hammer raised, all soaked in red. Its name was Baxter."

That shut 'em up. Could've heard a pin drop . . . or a hammer.

I glimpsed at a guy who hadn't spoken all evenin'.

See, Joe Cornwall never did speak after that night. He'd lived, but never said a word.

I make sure he don't. I still carry the hammer.

◇◇◇◇◇◇◇◇◇◇◇◇◇◇◇◇◇◇◇

37. BIG JIM CAN WAIT

by J.C. Tabler

Some folks say snakes aren't smart, just do what comes natural. I don't believe that. It has nothing to do with a strict Catholic upbringing, believing that Adam ate the apple because Eve listened to a snake. It isn't because a lady at the zoo once made me pet a python, which hissed at me back when I wasn't so good at making it to the bathroom in time even when I wasn't scared. I know snakes are smart because of Big Jim and Randy Baylor.

Randy and I grew up together in the Maine backwoods. Our town wasn't even unincorporated, being just a collection of trailers set back near a state road. Our dads worked together, both of them loggers for a pulp company, so when we ran into each other on a worksite, we became fast friends. A lot of evenings were spent together playing, right up until the day I came over and Randy was playing with Big Jim.

To be fair, Big Jim was actually a little on the small side for a timber rattler. The first time I saw him, though, I knew I wanted nothing to do with it. He was pressed up against the glass in an aquarium, trying to get out. When I came in those black eyes stared me down, shining with blame as he rattled away.

"Dad caught him out on the site," Randy exclaimed, flush with that glow all boys get right after they start noticing girls but before puberty explodes "Said it sure didn't like being put in a bag, kept trying to get at him through it."

"That's a rattlesnake," I answered right before Big Jim made a noise of dried peas shaking in an empty can.

"Thank you, Captain Obvious," said Randy.

Big Jim looked mad, angry enough to rise up when I came near his tank. Curled up in a little ball, tasting the air, focusing on two boys who held him captive. That snake, I told my friend as he slid off the cover, looked mad enough to kill.

"Big baby," Randy teased right before Big Jim did what snakes do.

That rattler must have taken ten or fifteen good strikes at Randy while I climbed, screaming, up onto the kitchen counter. Persistent, making sure Randy was good and dead before slithering back and forth on the floor below me. Every now and again it would rise up, trying to reach my leg, then curl back up and wait with its wagging tail. Big Jim could wait forever, and when he went out the door after Randy's dad's truck crunched into the drive, I breathed a sigh of relief.

Snakes aren't supposed to have long lives. Humans are supposed to be the only creatures that practice revenge. Those are outright lies.

After I got married I moved back to the old homestead, now a suburban development that stood on land my dad's trailer once occupied. Quiet little place, with a picket fence and a dog that yapped all night and day. Except the other day, when I came home and the dog wasn't yapping. Must have been about ten or fifteen marks on that tiny little thing, and as I stood there staring at the bloated body I heard it again. My wife says it might have just been wind on dead leaves, but you don't ever forget the sound of a rattler.

I've got a son now, and he's got a swing set in the yard he likes to play on, but I don't think I'll let him anymore. See, last night my wife was in the kitchen, right by our big glass door looking out back when she yelled for me. She said our son must have gotten ahold of his baby toys and been playing with a rattle, cause there was this noise that was just driving her crazy. I laughed it off, but when she went to bed I looked outside and I swear I saw eyes gleaming in my porch light. Big Jim can wait forever,

◇◇◇◇◇◇◇◇◇◇◇◇◇◇◇◇◇◇◇

38. FISH TALE
by Jim Ehmann

For the first time in a couple years, I had the family up at Lake Champlain – my wife Suzanne, daughter Melissa, and my son Jake. Melissa's friend Crystal was there too. We stayed on the Vermont side and had the pontoon boat on Malletts Bay.

Suzanne liked the antique shops more than the boat, so that afternoon the rest of us went out on the water. I managed to get the kids into some nice perch and crappie, but they got tired of fishing pretty quick. They tied their inner tubes to the back of the boat and pushed off, floating around in the sunshine.

I fished, read, and had a few beers while the kids played. Eventually I had more than enough panfish for dinner, so for sport I switched rods, trying for bigger game. The area looked good. The noise from the kids didn't help, but oh well.

Pretty soon I had a little foot-long pike, but I was hoping for something three times that long. About fifteen minutes later I got my wish. The fish hit at the end of a long cast and felt like a submarine. I couldn't turn him and just watched the line peel off the reel. I needed luck to bring this one in by myself – the kids were too far out, having fun.

I carefully let the fish wear down and eventually started bringing it to the boat. This would be a new record for me, by the feel of it. Finally I saw it, like a green torpedo nearing the boat, every bit of a yard long.

I held the net with one hand and got ready to land the pike. What I saw next makes me freeze deep down, even now. I was focused on the fish, maybe eight feet from the boat, when this shadow appeared and a great mouth snapped open. I can't forget that eye, like one of those old Magic 8-Ball toys. Teeth flashed like knives, and the big pike was gone, snipped clean off. Something huge thrashed the surface, spraying me with water, waves rocking the boat. I saw the black body for a second before it went under. My hands shook so hard I just dropped my rod and grabbed the railing. I heard Jake calling from way off the other end, asking me if I fell in.

I couldn't even talk. Later I just explained that I had a big fish on. I didn't need them to roll their eyes and accuse me of being an old drunk with a fish tale. And I'm not the type who wants to be on the evening news, talking about monsters.

The next day I said I wasn't feeling well enough to take the boat out. Later they all went to town for shopping and pizza while I stayed at the cabin. There was a good reclining chair down by the dock, so I brought my cooler down and listened to the ball game on the radio.

The lake was almost completely flat, the way it only gets near sunset. The boats were all in by now, but far away I spotted a kayak moving peacefully across the bay. I opened a brew and took in the beautiful scene, my head still haunted by that huge eye.

That's when the kayak tipped over. I saw some splashing and the man somehow got it back up. But instead of paddling, he slapped down at the water with his paddle. Like watching a movie, I saw the black shape rise, knocking the kayak over again. There were big swirls in the water, and then it all just settled down. The man was gone.

I called 911 right away and said I saw a kayaker in trouble. They got a boat there in about ten minutes. When they found the empty kayak, they called in another boat for search and rescue. They looked for the body all night. We left the next day, but later I heard they never found him. I never went back and never will.

◇◇◇◇◇◇◇◇◇◇◇◇◇◇◇◇◇◇◇

39. LURES: A FISH STORY

by Jason M. Tucker

L et me tell you 'bout the last time I ever went fishing.
You might remember a few years back when all of those severed feet and hands began washing up along Otter Creek. It was all over the papers. The national media got hold and ran with that story, making it seem like we had a gang of Satanists running around the woods of Vermont, hacking folks up and tossing their feet in the damn creek.

Well, I can tell you that it weren't a bunch of devil worshippers. No, it was something else out there...something else entirely.

I had just got off work and was heading out to my fishing hole, hoping I might snag a couple of trout for dinner and make the missus happy. The sun weren't quite down yet – just enough that the dark started easing out over the creek.

Well, I got down to my hole, took a seat on the bank, and dropped in my line with a fat nightcrawler wriggling on the hook. I remember that afternoon being near perfect. It was nice and cool... quiet too.

I sat there for a while without so much as a nibble, and decided to tie on one of my favorite lures. No sooner had I reeled in my line did I see something out of the corner of my eye, something like a glint of light.

I looked up the creek where I had seen the flash. The sun was still on its way down, so I figured it was reflecting off an old bottle or something of that sort. I saw the light again, only this time it seemed to be coming from further upstream.

To this day, I can't tell you why I chased after that flash of light, but I did. I got up, grabbed my pole and tackle box, and then went stomping after it like a damned fool. Folks ain't shitting you when they say it was curiosity killed the cat.

I trekked up the Otter for 'bout a quarter mile, maybe less, when the scents of fresh fish, rotten eggs, and something I couldn't quite figure hit me like a fist to the nose. Those smells pulled me, a fool on a string, yanking me onward and over a little hummock where my feet hit something slick. I fell on my ass, snapped my best fishing pole in two, and then slid into a muddy little hollow off the side of the creek.

Didn't have long to feel like a fool though. When I sat up I saw some shit I ain't ever going to forget, and I don't give a rat's ass if you believe me or not. Bodies, all those folks whose feet and hands had been washing up on shore, were partly buried in the mud. Their eyes were missing and their chests were open, gutted, filleted. Some were more rotted than others were, but all looked like something had been chewing on them.

That something gurgled at me from across the hollow.

It was a bony thing, hairless, gray and naked, squatted in the mud. It held a piece of shiny glass in its sharp claws. Shiny mucus covered its skin. The thing's mouth was wide and filled with rows of tiny needle-teeth. The eyes were the worst, dead and dark like a fish's. It didn't give a shit what I was. It lured me, wanted to gut me, tear off my useless parts and eat me just like it did the others. I was food.

The thing inched toward me. I gripped my tackle box and swung it in a wide arc toward the thing's head. The box broke when it connected, sending my tackle into the mud. That gave me a chance to scramble up out of the hollow and back to the woods. I ran to my truck and didn't turn around once to see if it was following.

I can still feel that thing's dead eyes on me; doesn't matter if I'm awake or sleeping. That's why I don't go fishing anymore, why I don't set foot down near those creeks, and why I don't go swimming in Lake Champlain. I know what's down there.

◇◇◇◇◇◇◇◇◇◇◇◇◇◇◇◇◇◇

40. PLAY TIME
by Ginger Nielsen

I didn't like the room after I rented it. I was driving through New Hampshire after visiting relatives, and I'd stopped in the town of Hooksett since I was ahead of my return schedule. I passed an old farmhouse turned bed and breakfast, which boasted a gorgeous view of the Merrimack River, and I was sold.

After settling into my room, however, I began hearing noises: soft scratching sounds. It could have been mice, but there was something about the room that unnerved me. As the night wore on, the noises seemed to get closer, more distinct. There was a plastic-sounding jangle, then the sound of something falling to the floor. The sounds were coming from the closet, I realized, though I really wasn't up for night-time investigating. After awhile I turned my back to the room, clicking on the clock-radio for its white noise.

The first thing I did the next morning was look inside the closet, half-expecting to see the source of the noises. But the closet was bare aside from my luggage leaning against the wall. I looked up, shielding my eyes from the stark white light bulb that hung from the ceiling, looking for a possible shelf. There was a single plank of wood, but that seemed to be bare as well.

I was about to close the door when something caught my eye: a dull gleam on the side of the closet wall. I leaned closer and saw that it was a tiny doorknob, below that, a keyhole. Framing this was a small, primitively shaped door, slanted on top to accommodate the stairs under which the closet was partially built. I gingerly touched the doorknob, turning it back and forth, but it was locked. With a sudden thought, I grabbed a wooden chair from my room. Standing on it, I could see the entire shelf inside the closet now, and pushed furthest away from the shelf's edge, was a brass key.

Now unlocked, the dwarf door gave way. It was a cramped little room, smelling stagnant, of dust and age. I saw old wallpaper that had begun to peel away, along with writing on the walls and on the undersides of the stairs. After getting a lighter from my bag, I held the flame near the markings, trying to read them. It was a child's rudimentary hand-writing, and some of the words I could make out were: "Alexander", "cat" or "car", "1943", and "mom", along with simple drawings of things like trees and animals.

I tried to see further back, where the stairs lowered more into the confined room, and saw something small and white amidst the shadows. I tentatively reached for it, uncomfortable with putting my hand in an area I could barely see. Finally my fingers connected with the object and I pulled it towards me, then ducked out of the small room, feeling spooked. Standing outside the closet, I looked down at what I'd obtained.

It was a plastic ring of keys for a baby or small child. I heard the sound in my mind, the jangle from the night before. I tossed the keys into the closet, and after a quick glance at the crude little door, I shut the closet door, feeling apprehensive. I didn't know why a child would spend time in such a dismal little room; I didn't know why the room existed at all. It seemed wrong and somehow malignant.

After awhile, I decided I was silly to react in such a way. Still, I planned on leaving promptly in the morning, and I settled into bed with unease.

Sometime during the night, muffled sounds woke me. There was something moving inside the closet, sliding along the walls. I sat up in bed, listening, trying to see in the darkness. As my eyes adjusted, the closet door opened, revealing a child's withered hand. It was followed by a disembodied voice: "Mommy!"

◇◇◇◇◇◇◇◇◇◇◇◇◇◇◇◇◇◇

41. SHOES
by Brandon Layng

I will never wear another man's shoes again. Not after I walked a mile in a dead man's memories.

* * *

I walked the trails at Presque Isle; summer was in full swing. School was finished, my friends were partying until university days started, and I was figuring out how I was going to pay my way. I had been accepted to the University of Maine, but my scholarship application was rejected. Any man or woman looking at my beat up sneakers with the flapping lips and the ragged tongues could see I was a young man in need of cash.
A bug flew up my nose.. Glancing around, I tried to pick it out.

That's when I saw them. Black and white. Wingtips. The kind of shoe a man going places would wear.

My feet killed, and slipping off the battered Nikes, I picked up those high-polished wingtips. I could swear that the leather shivered with pleasure between my fingertips. They swallowed my feet. The irony of them being my size never crossed my mind – at the time.

I put one foot forward...

* * *

After a mile I was at my car and driving back down the road. A rumble from my stomach told me I wouldn't make it home in time, so I pulled into a gas station outside of the Mi'kmaq reserve. My class ring dug into my finger from white-knuckling the wheel.

The bathroom key hung from a wooden paddle and when I opened the door, I was surprised to hear a loud fart from the second stall. Flies buzzed the lights. The pain was worse than my disgust and I hurried into the first stall. Pants down, I quickly covered the seat in a layer of toilet paper and sat down. Then nothing. I pushed and still nothing.

The other guy spoke and scared the shit out of me. Literally.

"What?" I asked.

"I said, 'It's hard to go in public, isn't it?'" he said and grunted.

"Yeah, sure." Needless to say, I felt very uncomfortable.

"Can't go very well anymore," he said and I wanted him to shut up, more than anything. "Not since the bowel cancer plugged me up. They took out whole sections of my gut."

I wanted to be done but my body had other ideas.

"That sucks," I said.

"Sure does."

There was a cockroach skittering by my feet and I stamped a wingtip on it, bringing my foot close to the divider wall.

"Nice shoes."

"Thanks." Pulled my legs in together and leaned forward to give a hard push to hurry the process up.

"I use to live around here," he said between sounds of effort. "Before I went off to school and got a good job, that is."

"Good for you, man."

"Not really. It was the job that gave me the cancer. The stresses made me smoke all the time, all those carcinogens going down in my spit, filling my stomach, giving me the Big C." His voice was thick with regret. "I should have stayed in town and took a bank job. I could have been there when my parents died."

"Sorry to hear that," I said. "I can't wait to get out of this dump."

"Sorry to hear that," he said and started to chuckle. "I think you mean;

'You can't wait to get this dump out.'"

Even I started laughing and then we were in a fit, both going with belly laughs accented by flatulence. He ended it with a grunt of pain and slammed into the divider.

His feet slid under and I could see one fleshy cheek poking out. Blood was splattered over it and dribbled onto the dirty tiles. Something metal tinged and rolled out into the bathroom. He wasn't moving and I was off that seat without wiping as I stared down at the black and white wingtips on his feet. I nearly slipped on the blood. The door was open and I was standing there in horror staring at the ruby red class ring resting by the sinks. My own initials visible on the band.

I left the shoes in the trash on my way out.

∞∞∞∞∞∞∞∞∞∞∞∞∞∞∞

42. THE CAVES
OF GOOSE ROCK
BEACH
by Alex Moisi

"Don't be a chicken, Jimmy. It's just an old cave. Are you scared of rocks?" We laughed, pushing poor, terrified Jimmy towards Goose Rock beach. He protested when we picked him up from school, and he even struggled a bit when we stopped the car next to the deserted Maine coastline, but now he was just sniffling silently.

"Come on, man, we gave you a ride, now do us a favor." One of us grinned.

We all laughed as Jimmy started walking on the wet sand. It was early in the year and the beach was still closed, but that just made it more interesting. Since Jack got his driver's license, we stopped by the beach every evening. There were dozens of caves to explore around Goose Rock, and without tourists, the whole place was ours. It was one of these caves that we were pushing Jimmy towards.

"Please, guys," he whined, but we only laughed harder.

"Just go inside for five minutes and that's it," I promised, feeling bad.

Jimmy looked at me with wide, hopeful eyes and started down the beach. Seeing him slowly walk towards the dark cave, I felt a sliver of shame. He wasn't a bad kid, just a little odd. Someone pushed me and we started joking again. It was just an abandoned cave. Jimmy would be fine, and after that we'd give him a ride home like we promised.

A scream pierced the darkness and we all froze in shock. We were still staring at each other when the second scream came, carried by the wind. In my mind I could see Jimmy's brown eyes looking at me with silent sadness. That accusing gaze made me rush towards the cave before fear could lock my feet.

The light of Jack's headlights disappeared before I could reach the dark entrance into the cliff-side, leaving me to advance in the pale moon shine. Jagged pieces of rock dotted the ground and my feet sank in the soft mud. I could hear my own heart beat and I prayed poor Jimmy was fine.

In the shadows I stumbled over his collapsed body. He was face down in a pool of shallow water, looking tiny and defenseless. Guilt overwhelmed me. I had known Jimmy since 3rd grade. I shouldn't have let the others tease him.

I carried Jimmy's unconscious body outside, and we all placed him on the back seat of Jack's car. He looked pale, his lips trembled, and there was a large gash on his shoulder. Under his ripped T-shirt we could see blood slowly drip from a deep wound about twice the size of a quarter. We drove towards the hospital in silence, crowded around Jimmy's shivering body.

I was holding his head, and I was the first to hear the sound coming from his half-open mouth. I leaned over, trying to understand what he was trying to say, when someone next to me screamed. I looked up just in time to see a red spider the size of my thumb crawling out of Jimmy's mouth. Suddenly I understood what caused the wound on his back.

The spider rushed across his shivering body, jumping in the direction of the scream. From Jimmy's mouth another spider followed and another. They were pouring out with sickening speed, his whole body dissolving into a wriggling mass of red legs and hungry mouths.

Jack screeched to a stop as red spiders covered his neck and swarmed down his back. I didn't wait for the car to stop before I jumped out, crawling away from the cacophony of screams behind me. It was all over in a few seconds, deep silence setting over the now empty car.

Slowly a reddish figure about Jimmy's size formed out of the many spiders. It looked at me with brown eyes and smiled before disappearing in the dark. Somehow I knew I was forgiven and after a few minutes, still shivering, I started towards the nearest town.

◇◇◇◇◇◇◇◇◇◇◇◇◇◇◇◇

43. THE DECOY
by Patrick Rutigliano

"People used to call them goatsuckers, you know."

"And what on earth was the reasoning for that?" I asked Frank as I swerved around yet another feathered body camouflaged amongst the leaves.

"They thought the birds stole milk from livestock. They also thought that they hovered near the dying and tried to catch the souls on their way to the next world."

"Charming. I'll keep all that flattering folklore in mind in case I accidentally step on one. Now can we get on with it already?"

Frank shrugged off my impatience as he continued to lead the way through the woods.

I knew it was my duty to investigate the plume of smoke I had seen rising above the trees, but my patience was already worn thin, thanks to the out-of-towners and their antics. Even Frank's normally cool demeanor had not prevented his eyes from rolling at the news. Halloween séances and parties in the woods were an annual aggravation in Salem, to which the Parks Department had forced itself to become accustomed. Perhaps it wouldn't have been so irritating if we had not broken up such a gathering the previous night, or if we had not been preparing to go home at the time I spotted the wisp of vapor, but as things were, I wished I had just kept my mouth shut.

It was nearly dusk by the time we managed to make our way to a clearing through the ranks of naked birch trees clustered off the path, and by then neither one of us was pleased with the results our search had yielded. The trail of smoke that had thinned at our approach was now altogether from the scene, as was any sign of the trespassers.

They had picked an ugly spot, to be sure. Even the stunted trees that bordered the area refused to take root in the soil beneath the legions of dead leaves, and the few visible patches of grass appeared as though they had been the victim of a blazing summer sun. The eyes of a whippoorwill flock flashed red in the illumination of my flashlight as I scanned the ground for a campsite.

"Why can't these kids just celebrate the holiday with costumes and jack-o'-lanterns like everybody else?" I groaned as I lowered my beam.

"Perhaps our reputation as firemen precedes us?"

"Maybe," I growled. "At any rate, we better look around for any embers that those idiots forgot to extinguish. They certainly left something burning out here when they left."

With the exception of a few restless birds, the place was silent as we both wandered the area, and the spell was not broken until Frank called me from across the clearing. I ran to him, expecting a few glowing coals or some kindling still smoldering in the grass. Instead, I found him knelt beside a burn mark on the ground that made my skin crawl from something more than the autumn wind cutting through my jacket.

I was grateful that Frank could still find his voice, for mine was lost beneath a knot as my mind struggled to absorb the presence of the human silhouette scorched into the earth.

"There's no way this can be natural. It's just not possible," my partner whispered to himself as his fingertips wandered to the ground. No sooner had his flesh made contact with the spot than the woods exploded in a cacophony around us.

The glowing eyes I had seen earlier rose to the air amidst a horde of singing shadows as the whippoorwills took flight. The dark forms of the birds circled above the clearing for several deafening moments before finally leaving only echoes in their wake.

Reaching for my partner's shoulder in amazement, I watched his empty clothing fall to the ground atop a pile of ash that now bore his shape alone. I had never screamed before that night, but I still shudder at the thought of what prey the birds had been waiting so patiently for, and what they actually captured as they chattered in triumph overhead.

◇◇◇◇◇◇◇◇◇◇◇◇◇◇◇◇◇◇

44. THE OFFERING
by R. Scott McCoy

G ather close, Troupe; I have one last story to tell around this old campfire. It was a story told to me by my Troupe leader, fifty years ago tonight in this same campsite. I miss that old man. He was brave and strong and could tell a tale better than anyone I've ever met.

Long ago this whole country was wild and untamed. There were a hundred different Native American tribes, all with different languages, traditions and gods.

You all know your history and we've visited Plymouth Rock. What you may not have heard are the legends of the Norsemen who visited these shores six hundred years before Columbus set sail. Those fierce warriors were the masters of the sea in their time, and they came to these lands searching for plunder.

They brought more than their ships, axes and swords. They also brought their gods. Like the fierce warriors that worshiped them, the Norse gods craved new lands and plunder.

The men and gods from across the sea were more powerful than the natives and more skilled in battle. The natives and their gods fell before them one tribe after another, until finally, the tribes united. The native gods were smaller and knew less of war, but they outnumbered the invaders ten to one. Odin, Thor, and even Loki joined forces to meet the onslaught, but in the end, none of the gods survived.

The few Vikings that were left sailed back toward home. The native tribes also went home to heal and morn the loss, shocked by the deaths of their deities.

The battlefield was littered with dead, and the animals of the forest came to feast. They ate from the flesh of the fallen gods and were changed by it. Soon, they craved no other flesh but that of the divine, and when the bodies were all gone, they turned on each other. A second battle ensued between the beasts and it raged for many years, until only a few were left. The smaller creatures fell first and in the end, only a wolf and a bear remained. Hunger drove them to a final battle, and while terribly wounded, the bear won and consumed the wolf.

Our Troupe leader told us this tale, then went on to tell of how the great wounded bear hibernates for fifty years at a time. He wakes only to feed, but there is no divine flesh left, so he grows weaker. The next closest food is people, though our small spark of a soul does not fill the void. Once every fifty years the bear must feed, and our Troupe master gave himself to the bear so that the beast would not fully wake and hunt the people in the surrounding area. Just as his grandfather had done and just as I will do this very night.

I've had a good life and will not give myself over easily. I will face the creature and try to slay it, and like the Norsemen believed, if I die I will do so with a sword in my hand in combat so I may cross the bridge to Asgard. I relish meeting death on my own terms. I watched my father die in a hospital bed drowning in his own spit. I prefer a better death.

That night fifty years ago, I followed the old man into the woods to a cave less than a mile from this spot and saw him do battle with the great bear. He fell and was consumed, but he marked the beast and I saw blood run down its face. The great bear weakens. Who knows, I may win and may yet die of old age. What a horrible thought.

◇◇◇◇◇◇◇◇◇◇◇◇◇◇◇◇◇◇

45. THE PLUMBER

by Matt Hults

I answered the door on the third ring of the bell, and the look on the plumber's face as he stood waiting in the falling snow said he'd been waiting for two rings too long.

"You Dick," the man said.

I gasped. "Excuse me?"

The plumber scoffed and shook his head with evident irritation. He looked like a gnarled hunk of gristle in overalls, stout and chunky, with a frown that seemed as permanent as a bent metal bar.

"Are you Dick Shelby?" he demanded, enunciating each word loud and slow in a heavy Maine accent. "I got a call about a busted pipe at this address."

"Yes," I quickly amended. "Oh, God, yes, I'm sorry. For a minute there I actually thought you were calling me a—

The plumber's eyes rolled under his single black eyebrow.

"It really doesn't matter. Yes, I'm Richard Shelby."

"Got a leak in the basement, huh?"

"A flood is more like it," I said as the man lumbered inside. "That's why I couldn't get to the door sooner."

"You got a sump?" the man asked.

I blinked at him, mentally scrambling to find the meaning of the word in the limited mechanical section of my vocabulary. "A sump?"

"I'll take that as a no," the plumber replied. "Drainage is crap in this area. It's all clay under the topsoil. You stick a basement in clay without a sump pump and you got yourself a swimming pool. This it?"

We'd crossed the main hall to the oak door at the back of the kitchen. I noticed the plumber hadn't bothered to wipe his shoes, leaving a trail of dirty wet footprints on the hardwood.

"I'd like to thank you again for coming out on a holiday," I said without mentioning the mess. "I really appreciate it."

"Urh," the man replied.

"Is your... family... celebrating the holidays?"

"I ain't got no family," the plumber grumbled. "And since when is Halloween a goddam holiday?"

I frowned. "Actually, quite a few cultures consider it a time of—"

"Are you going to show me this mess or are we going keep gabb'n all day?" he cut in.

"It's right this way," I whispered, having learned all I needed.

I opened the door, and when the rubber seal came away from the jamb, the stench from below blew over us like a rotten breath from a corpse.

"Jee-zus," the plumber howled.

The far wall of the room had collapsed, exposing tan clay and dark soil behind a pile of shattered cinderblocks. An eight-inch metal pipe ran parallel to the crumbled foundation, and a steady stream of foul black liquid spewed from a huge crack in its side. Already more than three quarters of the basement lay submerged in raw sewage.

"This ain't a water pipe problem, fella," the plumber said through a cough. "You got yourself a ruptured septic line."

But I wasn't interested in the pipes. While the plumber gaped at the sight below, I stepped back and planted my right foot at the base of the man's spine, shoving him off the staircase with a savage cry of consignment.

The plumber screamed, plunging into the black liquid and vanishing in a titanic splash. I prayed he'd stay under, that I wouldn't need to see what happened next, but then he burst into view again.

"Ahhh," he roared, wiping sludge from his face. "I'm gonna kill you for that, fella! I'm gonna—"

Then the tentacles seized him.

They snaked out of the ooze one at a time, three of them, each blood red and over half a foot thick. They coiled around him and cinched tight simultaneously, crushing him silent. The creature's malformed head arose from behind.

I shuddered at the sight.

The monster's single basketball-size eye looked up at me as it drew the plumber into the cavern of teeth that made up its mouth. A smile tugged at the corners of its lips.

I slammed the door shut before the thing bit into its meal, knowing I'd only bought myself another few days to figure out which spell would get rid of it before my greatest mistake got hungry again.

◇◇◇◇◇◇◇◇◇◇◇◇◇◇◇◇◇◇

46. THE TALE OF SIX

by Sheldon S. Higdon

Sixty-five years ago there was a cemetery called the Baxter Pet Cemetery. It was where Percival Proctor Baxter, who served as the Maine governor in the early nineteen hundreds, buried his six Rottweilers. It is said that when Percival himself passed away—years later—that he had his own body buried next to his protective dogs, rather than in the family plot next to his wife. And in nineteen-thirty-eight, all of the bodies were exhumed; Baxter was finally placed next to his wife, and the land was eventually sold...on which now sits this campsite.

But not many people know of the real story that haunts this campsite. About the graves that still remain here today. You see, only Governor Baxter's body was removed that day. Supposedly, they left all his Rottweilers behind!

Two years ago a group of students came up here on summer break from Boston College. They set up camp here. Referred by some locals, I guess. They intended to make the best of the time they had before the fall semester nipped at their heels. So they brought coolers of beer and food, and fishing gear. They hiked along the trails that follow Casco Bay, and when the tide came in, they cooled off in the salty waters of Maine.

From what I've heard, they only lasted three days.

During that first night—soon after nightfall—they began to hear low growls coming from the darkened woods that surrounded them. Their campfire gave them little light to see by, but they saw nothing...nothing until night three. One camper, Tim Reddenfield, is said to have heard the growls coming from all directions. Some, he said, were out deep in the pines and poplar, while others were so close that is seemed that they were right at his ear. They all slept with their eyes open that first night. Not even alcohol could induce sleep, relieving the awful sounds from their young minds.

On the evening of day two, while on a hike, the campers came to an open section in the woods where pine trees formed a circle, and within that circle, six deep holes were freshly dug. There were no signs that anyone else had been there: no shovels sticking into the dampened earth, no trash of any sort. It's said that whatever was in those holes clawed their way out, leaving claw marks around the edges of each hole and black and brown fur clumped in the dirt.

The campers immediately headed back to their campsite. They built a fire before darkness fell, drank beer and ate, conversing with one another about the newfound holes and the previous night's growls. They came to the conclusion that some farmer or hunter had lost his dogs and that that's what they had heard the night before. As for the holes, they never could rectify an answer. They slept shaken that second night.

The campers spent most of the last day swimming and fishing. They all settled down with mackerel in their bellies and beer on their breath. It's even said that one couple consummated their relationship on that last night. But all I can say is that—days later—their bodies were all found back at the deep holes in the circle of pines, mangled and dismembered. Some were buried. Others were only identified by their dental records.

A voice recorder was found at the bloodied campsite. On it, Tim Reddenfield's last words gave evidence of what the creatures were. Screams and panic filled the background as he said that six Rottweilers encircled them, standing at the edge of the camp. Their teeth gleamed in the firelight. Empty black sockets stared back at them. Their fur was matted down with earth, only to reveal bone as they moved toward the campers. On the recording, deep growls filled the air. Then Tim's scream.

So if you're awakened tonight by low, deep growls coming from outside your tent, draw the sleeping bag up over your head, because you won't want to see the six rotted Rottweilers that have encircled the camp, waiting with gleaming teeth to drag you away to their graves—and eat you!

◇◇◇◇◇◇◇◇◇◇◇◇◇◇◇◇◇◇

47. THE VIGIL ON THE BANKS

by Patrick Rutigliano

Some promises are easier to keep than others, and glancing over the side of French King Bridge through my window, I knew this vow would be more difficult to honor than most. The urn resting on the passenger seat of my car drained the beauty of the Connecticut River to ash, and the many blazing trees below dulled to a tone little more than sepia to my eyes. The place was already haunted for me, for somewhere beneath the bridge, the spot my father had chosen as his final resting place awaited his remains.

The only child of an only child many years a widower, the duty had fallen to me alone to carry out my parent's wishes. The memories of the many summers I had spent with my father, hiking the trails in the woods, felt ever more distant for the loss of his company as I traveled the remaining distance to the launch area. We had been here together at this place many times before, but never out of the warmer season, and the chill November air whispering through the leaves spoke of a world far more subdued than I remembered.

The birds had already abandoned the area in search of more temperate climes, and not so much as a squirrel remained to stir the boughs overhead. Despite the lack of a priest or proper casket, it felt as though the woods themselves were acknowledging a funeral. The urn gained a few extra pounds in my arms as I started down the path that would take me to the banks.

The river seemed an odd choice on my father's part. Ever since he had nearly drowned in the boating accident that had claimed my grandfather's life, he had been petrified of water, refusing to do so much as fish on the stretch where the incident occurred. Whether this final wish was in hopes of some of manner of reunion or a final dissipation of his fears I did not know, but I would do what I could to execute my duties. The sun had not yet begun to dip below the horizon when I found the area my father had described.

The place appeared quite placid, considering all the menace attributed to it. The gusts that had cut through my jacket earlier now abandoned the low-hanging branches to their natural stillness, and the current of the river offered no ripple or wake to confirm its existence. Only a single boat near the opposite shore provided any human element to the scene, and it was every bit as static as its surroundings.

I had hoped to pay my final respects in privacy, but I doubted that the vessel's occupant could even make out my actions. He was too distant for me to discern any feature beyond the black long coat that enveloped him, and although I somehow felt he faced me, I could not even be sure that he was looking in my direction as I knelt to offer my father's soul what prayers I could find.

I had not lowered my eyes from the water for more than a minute, but when I rose to scatter the contents of the urn, the boat floated only a few feet from where I stood.

A chill independent of the season stole across my body as I realized the source of my father's dread those many years ago. No motor or paddles rested on the boat, and the gap had expertly camouflaged the cloak draped upon its captain. Not a single ripple broke the surface of the water as the boatman stood and awaited the inevitable.

Reaching into my pocket, I retrieved two pennies and nestled them within my father's ashes. A moment later, both coins soundlessly struck the floor of the boat as the ferryman finally took his leave in pursuit of far more distant shores.

◇◇◇◇◇◇◇◇◇◇◇◇◇◇◇◇◇◇

48. TRUE LOVE
by Alex Moisi

I hated the new house. It was an ancient building with an historic plaque attesting that it had been completed in the 1800's, although it looked much older. Hidden among the trees of New Haven's historic district, its wooden facade looked rotten and decaying, and the front steps were collapsed beyond recognition. It gave me the chills, but of course Tim loved it.

"It'll look great after we renovate it." He grinned at me while pulling the U-Haul truck into the driveway. I knew this was his dream house, so I kept my bad feelings to myself and smiled back.

We were still unpacking the boxes that contained our life when he got a call from his editor. The newspaper wanted him to conduct an interview that evening. There was no way he could say no, so I sighed and gave in once more.

"I hope he loves me as much as I must love him," I murmured to myself as he drove away, leaving me alone in that dreadful house.

I continued unpacking, sorting through years of shared memories. A picture of our wedding, a CD we burned together, the list went on and on.

Still, I couldn't help a strange feeling of sadness as I looked at all those little things. Had we grown apart? Was he still in love with me?

I had just grabbed another box when I first noticed the smell. It was strong, reminding me of cinnamon. I began wondering if the movers broke my grandmother's collection of spices, and if that meant bad luck.

Before I could make up my mind, the floor downstairs creaked strangely. I ignored the sound, opening the box before me. Cinnamon filled the room, so strong it made me dizzy. I coughed, wondering what Tim would say if he came back to a haunted house filled with cinnamon dust.

I was laughing when I heard the creak again. This time I reached for the cell-phone and called Tim. Nervously, I started going downstairs.

"Hello," I tried, but there was no answer. I was half-way down the stairs, texting him, when I heard the sound again. But I was just imagining things. New Haven was a safe town; that's why we'd moved here. Despite my logic, I felt a ball of fear curl inside my stomach, letting me know nothing was all right.

The living room was empty, so I slowly approached the kitchen. Suddenly, the floor creaked under me. Before I could move, the wood under my feet slipped, breaking loose. Boards with rusted nails reached upwards, above my head, like a fist that was closing itself.

I stumbled to the side, escaping merely by accident. Behind me the boards came down with a deafening crash, and brown cinnamon dust floated into the room. I rushed away as more pieces of the floor followed inside the dark, widening hole. Brownish mud was slowly sliding, crawling from within this sudden pit. With bewildered eyes I watched as hands and faces formed in the dark earth, hungry grins of polished stones. I could see their eyes hunting for me.

I screamed, rushing towards the front door. Somehow it didn't surprise me to find it locked. Behind me, a sickening wet sound of half formed feet was closing in.

I crashed to the floor, crying and screaming. My voice covered the noise of the door breaking open. Wooden splinters framed Tim's figure as he looked at me with worried eyes. I glanced back towards the front room. It was as it always was, empty, save for the smell of cinnamon still lingering in the air.

* * *

Tim never believed my crazy story, but the cinnamon smell inside the living room made him nervous. He sold the house and we moved back to New York a week later. He even took a week of work and we went to all our favorite spots in the city. It was perfect; we were in love again. Later, I helped him unpack, carefully hiding the box with my grandmother's broken spice containers. My mother said those spices would save my marriage, but who have thought they could also spark my fantasy so easily?

◇◇◇◇◇◇◇◇◇◇◇◇◇◇◇◇◇◇◇

49. VERMONT IS FOR LOVERS

by John C. Caruso

Back when I was in high school, I spent one of my summer vacations working at the Vermont's Own processing plant just outside Montpelier. The pay sucked but it was a guaranteed job, since Vermont's Own Hearty Stew is one of the largest employers in the city. It's a huge operation, open 24/7 with people working three different shifts around the clock.

Let me tell you, in the summer months it got pretty dang hot in there with those giant 500-gallon cooking vats cranked up. But since I worked the 10 pm to 6 am slot, I was a little bit lucky in a couple regards. Not only was it a little cooler in there during the night—still hot, though not quite as awful as in the daytime—but I also got an extra thirty cents an hour over minimum wage.

The night shift was a motley crew of misfits and refugees, ex-cons and junkies, people who just weren't right in one way or another. There's a reason all the myths and legends have the nightmare creatures coming out at night. I tried to get along with people, but they all seemed a little off, damaged goods somehow, except for this one older guy named Blake who kind of made friends with me. I appreciated his friendliness since not only did he act more normal than most of the others, but he also spoke English, which wasn't exactly the norm there. He could be kind of racist sometimes, but I didn't get into it with him since he was also pretty critical of the people he called "white trash," which mostly seemed to consist of the smokers and the ones with tattoos. I figured he was maybe secretly a little afraid of them, and I guess I was too.

Blake was a big guy with a loud belly laugh and long square beard like something you'd imagine on a lumberjack or see in a picture of an old preacher man. He had a belly on him, and he wore big red suspenders to hold up his jeans.

Blake was always telling jokes, and he had a million of them. To tell you the truth, most of the jokes weren't that good, and he always laughed harder at them than I did, but I liked him telling them because it made the time pass while we were working those vats.

And then one night in August, the cops showed up and arrested Blake, led him away in cuffs and everything. It was weird too since Blake just kept making jokes the whole time they were arresting him. He never shut up once, even when they reminded him more than once that he had the right to remain silent. I asked one of the younger cops what Blake had done, and he told me it was a pretty sure thing that Blake had murdered his wife and her lover.

After the two lovers disappeared and got reported missing, the authorities found a bunch of bloodstains in the bedroom of Blake's house and in the bed of his Chevy truck. The only weird thing was they never could find the bodies. They dug up Blake's yard. They searched under his house. They combed a lot of the woodsy areas around the city, but they never could find anything.

Summer was coming to an end and school was starting up again soon, so I only worked there for another couple weeks after they arrested Blake. The other people who worked there had never been friendly, and now they avoided me even more since I'd been friends with the accused murderer. It sure was quiet without him there, and I missed his jokes—even the bad ones. I had a lot of time to think during those last two weeks working the nightshift at the plant, tending those giant stew vats, watching them churn away.

I had a lot of time to wonder what Blake might have done with the \

bodies.

I never could prove a thing.

But I also never did eat another can of Vermont's Own Hearty Stew.

◇◇◇◇◇◇◇◇◇◇◇◇◇◇◇◇◇◇◇

50. VOGO
by Ian Rogers

There's nothing to do in Calais on a Friday night. Ryan suggested jumping the border into Canada—he knew a girl in Burnt Hill who could hook us up with some weed—but Alex shook his head, which immediately nixed that idea. We were cruising in Alex's car, and even when we weren't, he was our unspoken leader.

"I'm not going to chance getting busted by the border pigs just for some shitty New Brunswick green."

"Then you pick something," Ryan groused.

"I will." Alex put one finger to his lip, like he was thinking deeply, and that made me spit out the beer I had just sipped. I had snagged us a couple six-packs of Bud Light from my old man's beer fridge. Alex looked over and stared at me thoughtfully. I thought he was going to punch me in the throat for spilling beer in his car, but he grinned instead.

"We're going to steal a boat."

We headed down to the docks and found a rowboat no one would miss for a few hours. After frigging with the knot for a few agonizing minutes, Alex cut the line with his Swiss Army Knife and told us to hop in.

Ryan and I each took an oar and used them to paddle us out into the lake. Alex sat back and barked orders at us. "Row, droogs! Row!" That's what he was calling us lately. He was on A Clockwork Orange kick. Said it was the funniest movie he'd ever seen.

By the time we reached the middle of the lake, Ryan was already whining about going back. "I don't like it out here," he said. "It's too dark!"

"Don't be such a nancy," Alex snapped. "What are you afraid of? Vogo?"

We laughed, perhaps a bit too hard. Everyone in town knew about Vogo, although I didn't know anyone who'd ever seen him. Sometimes a tourist passing through would take a picture of something he claimed to be Vogo, but it always turned out to be a log or an otter. There had been no major sightings since the 1950s. If there ever was a Vogo, he was long dead.

We sat in the middle of the lake for the next couple of hours, finishing the six-packs (Alex called them our "stores") and watching the moon make its way across the sky.

It's hard to describe what happened next. I want to say something came up out of the water, but that's not exactly what happened. Maybe it doesn't matter. One moment our boat was bobbing in the water, and the next a great silvery shape came rising up next to us. Breaching, I guess you would say, considering the size of the creature. It was as big as a whale, but that's where the similarity ended. I don't know what it was. I'd never seen anything like it.

It had a long, tapering neck, which I at first took to be a tentacle. Then it turned toward us. I wasn't sure what I was looking at, this long silvery appendage with two coal-black dots on the tip. Then they blinked and I realized they were eyes. I had never felt so small as I did at that moment, sitting in that boat, out in the middle of the lake, on that dark night. So very small.

The creature continued to rise out of the lake as if in slow motion, leaving the water long enough for us to see the fins on the sides of its luminescent body. Each one was as big as a man. Then it came back down, like a shimmering torpedo, and disappeared into the water.

That's not the strangest part, though.

Whatever it is that lives in Pyper Lake—Vogo, I guess—I don't think it's alive.

You see, the creature that rose up next to our boat never disturbed the water, not even a single ripple. And when it left the water, when it hung for

a moment in mid-air, I could see the moon.
I could see the moon through its body.

51. WINTER WONDERLAND

by J.C. Tabler

I went to law school in Boston in the late seventies, though I won't say which school or exactly when. Some degree of anonymity needs to be maintained.

I got my B.A. at a state university down South, scoring well enough that scholarship offers poured in. When I accepted an Ivy League offer, I had never seen snow that lingered well into spring, and was unprepared for New England winters. Biting cold and demanding classes had, by my final year, worn away any semblance of nerves.

In my final year, Boston was blanketed with several feet of freezing snow. Schools let out and children played along my street, where I kept an apartment among lower-income families, but law school didn't take snow days. So, after plows rumbled past, I bundled up and began the long walk to class in chilling weather.

Originally from a warmer climate, I wore several jackets along with a ski mask to protect my sensitive skin. Also, thanks to long classes and the high crime rate of my neighborhood, I carried a switchblade knife in my outermost pocket for protection on my walk home in darkness.

Dressed and armed, I left for class that day. What I found resembled more a tunnel than sidewalk. Snow had been piled, by both plow and shovel, on either side of the path. White walls at least six feet tall stood silent guard on either side, concealing pedestrians from the road or houses.

I don't remember much of that day, but nobody remembers routine occurrences, and classes were certainly routine. I remember walking home in darkness between those towering walls of snow. I recall passing an acquaintance from class, a pretty girl from my area of the world, a comforting accent in this harsh northern wasteland. After greeting her in the darkness of our accidental tunnel, I remember nothing except waking the next morning in a freezing apartment.

I couldn't find my switchblade when I dressed, or the jacket I had worn. According to the morning paper, the police couldn't find my classmate's pretty head, though they found the rest of her lying between two walls of snow on a sidewalk not far from the law school. I was shocked, as I remembered seeing her the night before, and considered calling the police before deciding to stay quiet. After all, exams were coming up and questioning would take time I could spend studying.

There was color in the picture on the front page, did I mention that? It had been taken from a distance, but you could see red splattered on the pristine snow walls.

I rummaged through my kitchen drawer to find a knife, slightly bigger than my switchblade, to carry for protection. Armed and wrapped in my jackets, minus one, I headed for class.

I couldn't find that knife the next day, or the jacket I had worn. The front page carried a story of another murder, grisly red on glistening white. I began to get scared, found another knife and wrapped myself up. I decided to walk a more trafficked route. The next day, that knife was gone, as was another jacket. I didn't look at the paper.

After three murders the walls of snow came down, opening the sidewalks to view. There were no more killings, and for a while that was the happiest winter of my life. I laughed and loved, had no worries until spring finals, and graduated with honors. I even found a job down South, near my hometown, where snow and cold are never seen.

After a few years of stress and heat, I decided Boston had been the happiest time of my life, even braving the winter cold. I sold my house, took a job with a northern firm, and moved back, finding a nice apartment within walking distance of my new office.

I'm still not completely happy. Something lingers in the back of my mind, refusing to rest. The days are getting shorter, though, and winter will be here soon. I look out my window and hope for the cold, for any memory of why I was so happy that winter. Above all, I hope there's lots of snow.

◇◇◇◇◇◇◇◇◇◇◇◇◇◇◇◇◇◇

52. THE CREATURE OF MOUNTAIN GATE

by Nate Kenyon

...A damn creepy story, that was. Now put a log on the fire, that's right. Let me tell you mine. It's a doozy, and it's all true.

There was a time when the three of us—this was Jackson, Steph and me—went up to the cabin at the foot of Mount Mansfield. This was before Steph and Jackson had their fling. Anyways, Steph had heard tell of this hidden graveyard along the Long Trail. Supposed to be the site of some worship back when Mansfield was still a town. There's been a good few disappearances along the Trail over the years. They say it's the monster of Mountain Gate Cemetery that gets 'em.

I didn't buy any of that, but Steph did, and I suppose Jackson went because he was sweet on her. I just went for the hike. It was a bit creepy seeing those cliffs and caves on the northeastern edge shrouded in fog, and the mountain looking like some sleeping giant. Indians say that in the days when the mountain was taller, the sick would go there to die. One day the old chief tried to reach the top, but his heart stopped halfway up, so the good Lord took that peak down and carved his face right into the mountain where he fell.

"The entrance to Mountain Gate is supposed to be guarded by this monster," Steph says, when we're getting out our gear. "If you see it, you know you're close."

"The only monster you're going to see is a moose," I says, "and they're dumb enough to pet."

Jackson laughed, but Steph didn't. She said her aunt's spiritual advisor told her all about Mountain Gate. Her aunt had just died, see, and the legend is if you find it, you get a glimpse of the afterlife, just like those Indians. Well, I didn't buy that either, and I don't put much stock in spiritual advisors. But Steph, you could tell she'd taken it hook, line and sinker.

It wasn't long before we were deep into the woods. The bugs were swarming and there was a drizzle, so there weren't many others on the trail. Steph seemed like she knew where she was going. Jackson, he was just behind me and probably staring at her ass.

I don't know how to explain the next part. The world just seemed to float away for a while, and the fog fell across the mountain until you could hardly tell if it was day or night. Before too long we heard a howl that echoed across the trail and through the woods. I stopped dead in my tracks and made a joke about a moose in heat, but Steph didn't even turn around. She was on a mission, and nobody was going to stop her.

At some point Jackson sort of shouldered me out of the way and took up the middle. That fog seemed like it had entered through my ears and took up residence in my head. Then Steph took this right turn into the woods, and Jackson followed. I saw that she'd picked up some kind of animal track or something. I ducked through the trees and climbed over a pile of rocks, more scared now to lose them than to keep going.

Steph stopped where the trail had entered a natural clearing. We were near the top now, I thought. There was a smell in the air, like something dead. I don't scare easily, but right then I just about soiled my drawers. It felt like we'd gone back in time, and there was nobody else in that world but us. But Steph, she didn't seem to be bothered one bit. She knelt in the middle, unzipped her pack, and pulled out this urn. Then she looked up, and across the clearing in the shadows stood this thing. It must have been nearly ten feet tall, and hairy, and I could see its eyes glint in the dark.

Steph stepped back and took Jackson's hand, and they stood there watching as the creature walked out into the clearing, picked up the urn, and disappeared back where he came.

Right then there was this blinding light through the trees, like the sun in midsummer. I guess that was the cemetery back there, and maybe if I had been a little closer I would have seen something special. But I wasn't, and before too long it was gone and the woods were silent.

On the way back to the car, I asked Steph about the urn. At first she wouldn't speak at all, but finally she told me it was her aunt's ashes. She'd wanted to get to Mount Mansfield but had passed before she could. Steph was fulfilling a deathbed promise.

Steph and Jackson got real close after that, and the three of us drifted apart. I went back to the mountain a year later, but never could find that trail again. But I had burns on my face for two weeks, and the look of that thing is seared into my memory forever. I figure maybe those disappearances along the Trail aren't accidents after all. Maybe they meant to go there, and it was their time. Maybe they never meant to make it home.

That's the truth, God as my witness. Now throw another log on the fire. Who's next? Tell us a good one...

◇◇◇◇◇◇◇◇◇◇◇◇◇◇◇◇◇◇◇

53. DOWN THE CELLAR
by Joseph Grant

L ike many people, it had been a dream of mine to find that jewel in the rough, a Craftsman-style house or an even earlier Victorian, restore her from the inside out and make that gem shine again. An avid home shows watcher and a very amateur carpenter on the side, I was always picking up tips when they'd renovate some Queen Anne, Italianate or a Second Empire style structure. For years, I had been taping and TiVo-ing shows, scouring real estate weeklies or surfing websites, so it was with a wonderful sense of optimism that I found the house in Bennington, Vermont where I currently live. But little did I know that to have my slice of heaven, there would be hell to pay first.

From the start, there were problems one expected with an old house. The insurance company threatened to take away my homeowner's insurance if I did not dispose of the antiquated asbestos-laden flooring and the decades-old lead-based paint that coated the interior and exterior of the house. The most interesting thing was that the real estate agent had mentioned nothing of these matters, and was only too happy for me to sign the papers and leave as promptly.

It made sense then, as the house was in a terrible state and rife with mold issues, as I was to find out later when the inspector came to visit. He was the one who pointed out the many troubles with the property. As a new homeowner, I wasn't used to such things. It was too bad he couldn't have pointed out the other troubles with the house—the cold drafts and other issues I was also unaware of—but they wouldn't remain that way for long.

As soon as the floors and walls were being stripped, strange occurrences started. Lights turned on and off seemingly by themselves, but with old wiring this was not uncommon. Workers angrily reported tools missing, only to find them later in places where they had not put them or could not have placed them, such as behind the walls they were tearing down. They also reported sounds of children running down the stairs when there were no children, and my wife had yet to join me at the time. Finally, beneath layers of wallpaper in one of the rooms were burnt, crudely painted pagan symbols and what appeared to be an inverted cross. This frightened some of the Mexican workers, but it wasn't anything I hadn't seen growing up listening to Ozzy. Lights also turned on and off seemingly by themselves but with old wiring this was not uncommon.

As I painted the hallway one night, I heard the sound of children laughing—not the innocent laughter of children at play, but almost an insidious laugh. It grew in volume until it made me stop and wonder if one of the workmen had left a small TV on in one of the rooms. When I removed my respirator to investigate, I started to smell smoke. What I saw turned my blood cold.

At the head of the stairs stood an elderly man with a frightened countenance, dressed in an old-style parson's robe, muttering in Latin. It scared the bejeezus out of me, but when I looked back, he was gone. I'm working too hard, I thought, but it certainly explained the peculiar paintings that lay behind the wallpaper for decades.

Research showed the house was originally built in 1890 as an orphanage. It had burned down; most of the children perished, having been tied to their beds by their tyrannical head master, Deacon Brown, a cruel man by all accounts.

While this did not bode well for a new home, I learned to live with the dead, but my wife would not. As the house was nearing completion, she moved in—and almost as quickly, moved out. What saved our marriage and sanity was a friend of her parents', a parish priest, Father Daley, who blessed our new home to rid it of any lingering spirits.

The only problem was that our cellar wasn't finished at that time and therefore, the priest had no access. Down the cellar was where the child with the burning red eyes resided.

◇◇◇◇◇◇◇◇◇◇◇◇◇◇◇◇◇◇◇◇

54. LOOKING BACK
by Steve Vernon

I t happened in the spring of 1971. First it was just animals disappearing from the farms around Devil's Washbowl - which is what they call the road around here, only it's too green and pretty a countryside for that old sinner to be sticking his snoot into.

Then a boy vanished, clean out of sight. Of course, he was a teenager and teenage boys are as like to run off as poorly trained dogs. But that didn't explain the missing animals or the creeping sounds folk heard in the bushes outside of town. Those, and the squealing. High and twisty, like someone jamming a live suckling pig into the mouth of a meat grinder.

Jed Perkins and myself figured we'd get to the bottom of things. You remember Jed, don't you? A tall fellow, lanky like corn that has seen too much rain. Old Jed set up on his back stoop with his two dogs—Panzer-breath and Mauser—and his shotgun.

"It's the devil's work," Jed decided. "But a blast or two of double-ought buck ought to consecrate old Nicky B. Scratch for wonderful certain."

Of course if old Jed was dealing himself in, then I was bound to be nowhere else but right beside him. We'd grown up together and had once kicked the jehosephat out of a bully who figured on one but hadn't counted on two. We beat that old boy black and blue and a few other colors until I looked in the boy's eyes and seen something like a dark mirror of myself looking back, so I told Jed he'd had enough.

The two of us sat there on the porch, listening to the dogs stink and worry at their fleas, the katydids and peepers squeaking in the night. Jed lit up a fresh coffin nail and was smoking thoughtfully when we heard something that sounded like rooting through his trash heap out back.

Mauser took off running. Too bad it was in the wrong direction.

Panzer-breath was built out of stronger stuff and headed straight towards the commotion.

"Get him, Panzer-breath," Jed called out, angling to his feet and cocking the shotgun as he stepped from the porch.

Old Panzer-breath lit into what ever was rooting through the trash — and then set up a terrible howling before taking off in the footsteps of old Mauser. Whatever it was, it was too tough for dogs.

"Come on," Jed hollered out to me, but right about then I was giving serious thought towards whatever lay on the better side of valour, figuring maybe Mauser was right in running. I settled for hitting the yard's flood-lights. They lit up the night like a miracle grin, and that's when Jed and I first saw the Pig Man.

He was standing there in the rubbish heap, with his snout buried in a can-opened tin of corned beef. It was almost like a man, only but a little taller, naked as bare feet, and covered in a thick pale thatch, like hog bristles.

His face was what got to me. There was nothing one bit human about that face, all pushed together and tumbled down like a pig's snout. I took one look into its eyes, dark and swimming with some kind of feeling that I couldn't quite hang a label on. Whatever it was it squealed like a pig, and old Jed tripped over his own panic and darned near shot his own foot off. I caught up to Jed while he was refixing his aim and I snatched the shotgun from him before he could let fire with intent.

"What'd you do that for?" Jed asked me angrily.

That Pig Thing kept running in a long loping gangle of a ground-crossing stretch, sort of like it was trying to cover too much ground in too little time. I looked at Jed and I could see the anger and I could see the boy I'd grown up with and I knew that simmering anger was going to blow over like a summer storm, if I let it.

So I did.

"I couldn't let you do it Jed," I told him, after he'd calmed down. "I took one look in that Pig Man's eyes and whatever I saw there, I just knew we couldn't ought to shoot it."

That wasn't quite true, of course. Darned few things are in this world. The truth is, what I'd seen there in the dark quiet pools of the Pig Man's eyes was a reflection of myself looking back at me.

That Pig Man is still out there, as far as I know. Some nights I hear him creeping in the darkness. Of course maybe it's just the wind or the trees gossiping with the hoot owls, but I believe the Pig Man is still out there listening in the darkness, and I hope he's grinning a miracle grin.

Can't you hear him now? Creeping up on us?

Just listen to him squeal.

Just don't look in his eyes, mind you, or you're bound to think twice.

◇◇◇◇◇◇◇◇◇◇◇◇◇◇◇◇◇◇

55. PUKWUDGIES: LITTLE MONSTERS OF NEW ENGLAND

by Pamela K. Kinney

I paused in my walking in some woods in Bristol County, Massachusetts, when a bright orb appeared to bounce up and down in front of me. Excited, I took out my digital camera to snap a picture of it, but it vanished, reappearing a few feet further up the trail. I took off after it. It gave me a merry chase, and before long I stopped as I realized it had lured me deeper into the woods.

Fear filled me. About to turn back, I froze when I saw it. No bigger than two feet tall, it was a little man. We stared at each other; then I bolted. I looked back over my shoulder to see the figure move back into the woods.

That wasn't the only time I saw the strange being. My wife and I had an experience of seeing a few, years later in a parking lot near the same forest. I saw the same figure standing behind my car in my rear view mirror. We had the radio on to listen to some music when suddenly, the car's engine roared to life and the music rose to wild screaming. I drove out of that parking lot, scared shitless, and didn't stop until we arrived back home. It took me a long time to get out of the car, as I sat behind the wheel, my hands shaking.

I learned later how I had gotten away with only seeing the little monster. Others who came into contact came down with a mysterious illness, and one woman suffered nasty scratches on her arms after following an orb.

What are the pukwudgies? Demons, trolls, fairies, monsters under the beds, whatever; they been in New England as far back as in the myths of the Wampanoag, especially with the creation giant, Maushop.

Beings with magic, they torment and manipulate humans and, it is claimed, are able to transform into other animals. They have been related to a tall, dark figure and are sometimes known as shadow people. Using orbs as Will-o-the-Wisps, they entice foolish mortals into the woods, to harm or kill them.

Whatever the case, I lay I bed at night, afraid to sleep. For with sleep comes nightmares and with the nightmares comes that damn pukwudgie. I know he waits until I sleep; then he'll finish what he wanted that first day, and kill me.

◇◇◇◇◇◇◇◇◇◇◇◇◇◇◇◇◇◇◇◇

56. RELIVING THE BATTERY

by Shadow Kain

I returned to the Battery Erasmus Keyes, the old military structure that sat on the cliff overlooking the cold Maine Atlantic waters, that one winter's night to try and recapture the emotions of my past. As a teenager, I had spent many nights there in the hollow bones of history, smiling with friends in the empty cement halls, listening to the crashing sea, our laughter keeping us warm from the cold winds that rode atop the waves below.

Attempting to relive those days of freedom, my steps into the old Battery had mirrored the years past, and had brought a smile across my chilled face and a warm tingle to the surface of my skin.

Until I saw him.

I was deep into one of the Battery's hallways, surrounded by black, rot-covered walls, standing on dead leaves and garbage that covered the floor in a horribly-scented rug. The moon behind him cast his silhouette in complete darkness as he stood at the entrance to the Battery, staring down the hall at me. His stillness unnerved me, his frame only a black mass that made his features invisible.

I was about to announce my presence, more to break the silent ice of the moment than for any attempt at conversation, when I realized it. The man standing and staring at me from the moonlit night was not breathing. There was no vaporous steam from his mouth or nostrils seeping into the winter's air.

I steadied my urge to run, the idea of speaking to him long ago discarded. For what seemed like ages I stood statuesque, praying that the shadows of the hallway kept my presence its secret.

A startled gasp involuntarily escaped my lips when the man ran at me. At full speed his legs swiftly carried him into the Battery, into the same shadows where I was hidden. As he was enveloped by the darkness, I lost all sight of him. His movement brought no sound; the heavy breathing resounding off the walls around me was my own, and only my own.

I braced for an attack, but it did not come. From deep within the old Battery I heard voices begin, the rushing sound of men scattering back and forth, yelling to each other.

"Man the guns!" a voice boomed through the halls.

Finally my legs obeyed my brain's command to run. I fell twice to my hands and knees, squishing my flesh into the slimy coating of the garbage underneath. Behind me, the halls still reverberated with the shouting of men at battle, excitement mixed with terror in their shaky voices.

"For the USS Maine!" a voice hollered.

As I emerged into the moonlit night, I could see the men atop the Battery, rushing back and forth, pointing out to sea. A blast knocked me over onto my backside, a shockwave passing through my bones that rattled me like branches caught in a violent breeze. I saw no fire, no smoke, no cannons, but the sound repeated in my ears, pierced my eardrums and caused them to ring.

Getting to my feet, I headed through the trees and bushes towards the parking lot, all the while a battle that had never been fought erupting behind me. Stealing a final glance at the Battery, I could see the men illuminated by the moon, watching my cowardly flight. Their glow was not of this world, their uniforms transparent, mixing with the distant ocean waters. Their eyes stared at me, a sadness inside them, perhaps a longing to join my retreat or disgust at my lack of bravery. Before two breaths they returned to their engagement, hurrying to reload invisible guns in an attempt to protect what to them was still a young nation.

That was the last time I ever saw the Battery Erasmus Keyes. I vowed, as my feet hit the pavement of the parking lot, my car within sight, to always concentrate on my future. Never forget the past but never try to relive it again. The past would continue on just fine without me.

◇◇◇◇◇◇◇◇◇◇◇◇◇◇◇◇◇◇◇

57. SELF EMPLOYED
by Sharon M. White

Last year, Bonnie came to stay with me after being evicted from her place. We'd both been without steady work for months and were starting to feel the pinch of fear that harasses the unemployed. We made the Rutland rounds and turned in applications for every position from dairy farm hands to ice cream parlor clerks. It seemed no one was hiring in lower Vermont. My savings was down to the bare bones, rent was due, and if I couldn't make the rent Friday, I was out.

Friday came and I didn't have a job or the rent money. Saturday morning, Bonnie and I went job hunting, and when we returned, my key didn't fit the locks. Trying to save our hundred dollars for food and the daily ration of The Rutland Herald, we slept in the car.

Bonnie suggested we go to the local witch for a fortune-telling session. Thinking it would be wasting twenty dollars and a half-tank of gas unless the old woman could show us the way to a buried treasure, I declined. After a while I agreed that going to Trudy Mae's house out by Patch Pond for a "reading" would be a much needed break from the stress of our situation.

Trudy was older than air, horrible to look at, and smelled like honey-roasted crap. Doing Bonnie's reading first, Trudy laid out cards, blew some smoke, waved her hands, and recited a bunch of hooey that didn't make a bit of sense. All the while, I sat on a dusty, musty sofa conjuring up new and interesting ways to make money.

Finally, it was my turn at the table. Again, Trudy laid out the cards, blew smoke, waved her hands, and then stopped short.

Leaning over the table and close to my face, her baggy skin and wrinkles framing her wide eyes, she informed me that I had a demon in me. I laughed when she told me she could get rid of it for fifty bucks.

Soon, she had Bonnie convinced that our luck would change if I'd agree to be rid of the possessing spirit. Bonnie thought fifty bucks would seem a small price later. After much consideration, I told Trudy to do it and gave her the money. She set to the ritual and there was a LOT of hand waving and smoke-blowing then.

During one of her wild trance dances, while chanting something about casting out the devil, she did just that. Something slammed me back on the couch and I couldn't move. A dark, smoky thing roared out of my mouth and nose, gathered in the center of the room where it swirled and took on an almost human form. Bonnie freaked and ran away. Trudy kept chanting until I passed out.

Sometime later I awoke. Standing in the doorway, twisting her rosary beads, Trudy watched me like a scared rabbit and sidled away as if I had something contagious when I silently walked out the door. My head felt like someone had cut it off, used it for a football, and jammed it back on the stump afterwards. I was weak for a long time and spent most of my days sleeping in the car, looking over the classified ads, or doing small odd jobs to make some cash.

As I scanned the Herald about a month later, I found an article that stated Trudy had been admitted to the Rutland Regional Medical Center's psychiatric ward after attacking a priest at Saint Peter Catholic Church out on Convent Road.

Being out on Merchants Row, only a few miles from the hospital, I decided to pay Trudy a visit that evening. I stepped into her room, shut the door, and smiled as she backed into a corner. I told her that for a hundred dollars I'd take my demon back—no ritual needed. Seems it was an offer she couldn't refuse.

I've not been late with the rent since. Seems there's no shortage of people around here willing to rid me of my demon—or to take my money for the service. And they're always willing to double my money if I'll take him back.

◇◇◇◇◇◇◇◇◇◇◇◇◇◇◇◇◇◇◇◇◇

58. TAKE THE EXIT
by Nathaniel Lambert

There's no better feeling, when a man finds himself with a head full of booze and a soul filled with regret, than opening up the throttle and letting it glide. You gotta grab hold of the beast on two wheels, take charge and make her skip across the slick pavement like a smooth rock against the surface of a placid lake. Baby, when you and her are idling at the crossroads of chaos and mayhem, where any minute she could spill you out onto the concrete, that's when things click. Adrenaline surges through your veins and your heart's running a marathon. You become fused with her steel and chrome and gasoline and all you wanna do is make her scream.

On that particular night, I was laying down a thick lawn of rubber and breathing in the fumes of a gasoline sin. I'd just merged onto The Spaulding Turnpike and headed for blacktop as straight as the Devil's spine. Roads like that, where you're all alone for miles, is where you can really let loose; bury the needle and let your Guardian Angel take the helm. It would've been a normal ride, a route I've taken a hundred times, until I heard the rumble of the engines.

They came out of nowhere and were on top of me before I even had time to react. And they were fast, real fast. There were twelve in all, decked out in crisp leather and stainless steel. Even above the mindblowing roar of the engines, I could hear the cool air whistling through the polished chrome. That wind cutting across all those perfect angles sounded like a bottle rocket going off in my muddled mind.

At first, they looked like any other band of brothers out for a similar nighttime joyride like myself. But once I was absorbed into the ranks, the similarities became few and far between.

I tried to stay upright as painted flames rose up off the gas tanks and flickered forked tongues of brilliant reds and oranges before my eyes. I felt the heat and it singed my exposed flesh. Even though it was dry out, plumes of steam rose up from all the steel and left a trail behind that choked the roadway of any visibility. They boxed me in and I feared all the horsepower would grind my carcass into the ground. But the motorcycles were the least of my worries; it's what piloted them that held the real fear.

All that leather began to melt away in thick, oily tendrils. Each rider shed its outer layer like skin from a snake and I screamed in horror at what was beneath. They were all bone with horns and tufts of wiry hair. Their mouths opened up wide enough to swallow me whole. Giant, slick tongues ran across a thousand jagged teeth and lapped at the air. Their eyes were no more than slits that glowed a crimson red. I couldn't help but stare, and what I saw reflected back made something snap within me. I saw mountains of burnt bodies stacked along a blood-drenched highway. The wreckage of twisted steel and shattered glass reached all the way to the sky. I closed my eyes and prayed for a quick end to it all.

They were minions from Hell, so help me God, and I was about to become a permanent member of their gang.

At the last moment, the point of no return, a bright light caught my attention. Off to the left, perched on top of an evangelical church, a neon cross glowed in stark contrast to the pitch black surroundings. Without hesitation, I torqued the handlebars towards the cross and braced for impact. I passed through those monsters as if they were made of smoke. They disappeared as quickly as they had arrived. I slammed on the brakes, skidded onto the shoulder, where I collapsed to the loose gravel. I got to my knees and thanked every saint ever imagined for putting up that obnoxious neon cross.

After that night, I never got back into the saddle. Who could've? And for damn sure, I never took the Spaulding Turnpike exit onto US16 again.

◇◇◇◇◇◇◇◇◇◇◇◇◇◇◇◇

59. THE WRITING ON THE CHALKBOARD

by John Lance

Growing up in Salem, Massachusetts, I heard all sorts of silly stories about witches, haunted houses, and ghosts. Well, now I'm going to tell you a real ghost story, a true one. And I know it's true 'cause it happened to me.

My freshman year of high school, there was an old science teacher named Mrs. Spirroni. If ever there was someone who looked the part of a witch, it was Mrs. Spirroni. It was as if the phrase "old crone" had been created for her. She had wild white hair, a hairy wart on her chin, and she cackled when she laughed. The only thing she was missing was the pointy black hat.

But if Mrs. Spirroni was a witch, it certainly didn't extend much beyond her looks. Every week she played the same numbers in the lottery, week in and week out, year after year. So if she did have a crystal ball tucked away somewhere, it wasn't very accurate.

Then, one week, she forgot to buy a ticket. Of course, that was the week that her numbers came up for the largest jackpot in the history of the lottery.

The shock and disappointment killed her stone dead. They even had to have a closed casket 'cause her eyes were all bugged out and the undertaker couldn't get her jaw to stay closed. Even when they tried to wire it shut, it still popped open, as if Mrs. Spirroni still couldn't believe her crummy luck.

Anyway, when I was young I have to admit I was a bit of a class clown, and as a result, periodically wound up being kept after school by teachers who had no sense of humor. I was there so much that the janitors used to get me to help out cleaning the rooms.

So one day I was all alone washing the desktops in the science classroom when I heard the distinctive squeaking of chalk on a blackboard. When I looked up I saw someone had written a one on the blackboard, kind of like this:

1

It was weird, 'cause I was the only one in the classroom and I had just wiped down the blackboard, but I did it again and then headed home.

Well, the next day I was after school again. I can't remember what I did but it was a week's worth of detention. Anyway, I was back in the science room, sweeping the floor, when I hear the squeaking again. On the blackboard I saw:

1 – 20 – 21

I thought someone was playing a prank on me and searched the room, but I couldn't find anyone. So I quickly erased the numbers and got the heck out of there.

On the way home the bus driver was playing his radio, and I heard the D.J. talk about the huge lottery drawing on Thursday.
Then it hit me. The science room I was cleaning was Mrs. Spirroni's room. She was reaching out from beyond the grave to give me the winning numbers she could never use!

I spent the next two days after school in that science room and sure enough, each day a few more numbers appeared. By the time Thursday rolled around I had a complete set:

1 – 20 – 21 – 29 – 31 – 41 - 51

After school I raced down to the local Mini-Mart and bought myself a lottery ticket. They were laxer in those days about enforcing the laws, and let kids get away with buying things like that.

Anyway, needless to say, I lost. It wasn't even close.

The next afternoon I was back in the science room and I heard the squeaking again.

I turned around and there were the numbers again, only this time the ghostly apparition of Spirroni was standing next to them. Her white hair floated around her head and her bugs eyes glared at me.

Slowly she pointed one of her skeletal fingers at the first number.

1

Her jaw creaked and squeaked, then in a ghostly whisper, she said, "That's a seven, you idiot."

Then she and the numbers disappeared.

And that's the closest I ever came to winning the lottery.

◇◇◇◇◇◇◇◇◇◇◇◇◇◇◇◇◇◇◇

60. ALONG COAL HOLLOW ROAD

by John Connors

I was twelve years old when it happened.

I am now twenty-seven, and yet what I saw on that summer night long ago still haunts me.

It was July 4 in Bedford, Maine. I was headed home from my Little League game, depressed. I had struck out four times and my season batting average dipped into negative territory. I loved the game, but boy, did I suck at it.

I walked along the road shoulder. Gravel crunched softly beneath my sneakers. I'd hooked my old mitt around the handle of my bat and rested it against my shoulder as I walked. I looked around. Lush, dark woods flanked the road on both sides. Except for the occasional insect chirp or the distant pop and sizzle of a bottle rocket, the night was still. Stars and a half moon hung high in the black dome above.

I stopped.

I had to pee.

From where I stood, I knew my house was still a good twenty minutes away. No way was I holding it for that long. I crossed the shoulder, jumped down into a shallow drainage ditch, and moved through the high weeds toward the nearest tree.

I leaned my bat against the trunk of an old maple and unzipped my fly. Sweat stung my eyes. Mosquitoes hovered all around me, sampling my young blood, but soon relief flowed through me, splashing loudly against the bark. I sighed happily, swiping at the summer pests with my free hand.

Leaves rustled behind me. I turned my head. Saw nothing. The wind had not stirred. Something had moved those leaves. But what? I shrugged and zipped up. Probably just a squirrel, I told myself. Nonetheless, my heart sped up.

Then it happened.

A Ford Mustang shot around the bend, swerving wildly. Tires squealed. Headlights stabbed the night, sweeping across my face. I squinted into them. The Mustang veered sharply into the far lane, onto the shoulder, bounced over the ditch and smashed into a tree. The headlights died. The engine sputtered. Smoke billowed up from its crumpled hood. Screams and shouts of terror poured from the car's interior.

Shocked, I stood there, waiting for it to explode like in the movies.

But it never did.

Instead, I heard a thunderous beating of wings overhead. I looked up...

And screamed as a monster descended from the night.

The treetops swayed and a warm breeze brushed against my cheeks. A rotten stench filled the air. I watched as the creature glided down on its massive black wings. It slammed onto the Mustang's roof, its enormous bulk buckling the metal with a loud crash. It squatted there like a man, breathing roughly, snorting, its wings folding inward like a bird.

I stopped breathing, froze.

The thing was huge. Its hairless, muscular body appeared a pale, sickly yellow in the moonlight. Its bald head turned slowly from side to side, its eyes two narrow slits of glistening silver scanning its surroundings.

It jumped down and tore the passenger door from its hinges, flinging it to the asphalt with a harsh clang. I heard the wet sounds of fangs tearing into flesh as the beast dived in and began its feeding. Those screams quickly turned to blood-choked gurgling.

The driver's door swung open. A young man stumbled out and up the road. He didn't get far. The creature stepped back from the car, its mouth and chest drenched in the blood from the passenger, and reached him in one long, impossible leap.

It made wet snarling sounds as it ate.

Then, my bat fell to the ground.

Crouched over his kill, the creature looked directly at me. It roared furiously, its mean, soulless glare boring into me like a drill. It definitely saw me. As food.

I pissed my jeans.

Then a second car zoomed past. Radio blaring.

The creature gave me one last hungry look, and flew off after the car.

Once it disappeared out of sight, I breathed.

I never saw it again. The events of that night remain unsolved. It is still out there somewhere. And to this day, I refuse to drive along Coal Hollow Road for fear of what may descend from the night.

◇◇◇◇◇◇◇◇◇◇◇◇◇◇◇◇◇◇◇◇

61. HOW BEST TO SEE AXQA

by Gene Stewart

I see you're new here, fresh across the water, your legs still in the boat, as we say, and headed up to see the Castle and its view of Lake Je, yes? May I offer a word or two of advice?

As you can see, the city and its bay are tucked behind the cliffs that wrap around from Mount Harxen, where the dire winds flow like water. This means you cannot see Biddeford, or any of Maine, from the city. We face the dawn, and have put the mainland behind us, as we say. Ah, but gaze inland on our island and be assured there are sights to rival any in New England's landlocked places.

It is said that only the blind can hear Axqa's songs, just as only the deaf can see clearly the hidden colors of the city. And of course it follows that the gourmands of Axqa delight their palates most who blind and deafen themselves, the better to focus on the layered savories to be found sizzling, crackling, or iced along the many side streets leading like a shattered maze to and from the market squares.

And above each shop catering to the truly dedicated enjoyers of Axqa's feast hangs, from black iron hooks, one of the city's notorious Bound Maidens, virgins who volunteer to starve themselves as they dangle above shop entrances blind, deaf, and unable to move. Further, once they have gone numb from lack of circulation and the ingestion of Qaxala weed distillations, they cannot feel anything, either. This sets free their imaginations to focus upon the world of sensory delight one among them each evening will experience.

Each week, monks in black robes, with green gloves, from one of the seven churches maintained by their order, choose one among the Bound Maidens using rites no one has witnessed and lived to describe. From one of their Churches of the Cauldron they creep, three with a net, one with a long sharp hook to harvest — that is their term — one of the dangling maids. How they always manage to choose a living one is not known, for not all of the maids survive to be harvested, as the stone troughs on either side of most streets attest. Each trough is liable to hold a dead Maiden as birds and animals, insects and time, render her gone. This is considered not a failure, nor yet an attainment, but merely a necessity among the Dangling Maiden Cultists.

Such a fate is not for the chosen one, though. As the head priest cuts her down, the others catch her in a net and carry her back to their church where, it is rumored, she will be cut from her bonds, bathed, dressed in finery, and given an entire night of sensory pleasures ranging from meals to sex to power and beyond. She will know all that Axqa can offer, so that her single night is a fulfillment beyond the most decadent dreams of even the oldest mendicant soothsayer. Her experiences, it is whispered, touch the very dreams of every inhabitant of the city.

And at dawn she herself will be touched, at the throat, by the priest's sharp hook, and as she sighs her last red sigh, she falls into their always-bubbling cauldron, there to simmer for a week as meat melts from bones and spices mingle to create the stew the monks sell in their shops for what ever passersby wish to pay.

And yes, the bones are used to construct their churches, each bone white elaboration a tribute to the maid who is, although nameless, forever memorialized.

So as you stroll among the sights, sounds, and scents of Axqa, remember if you will these weekly harvests, and stop for a bowl of delicious stew to fortify yourself for your stroll up Castle Hill. It is a long one, dizzying to most, but the view it offers of our city—which some say will one day grow to cover the whole island and perhaps spill into Maine and points south—is spectacular, and best understood by those who have fed upon its secrets.

◇◇◇◇◇◇◇◇◇◇◇◇◇◇◇◇◇◇◇

62. BABY GIRL
by Jeremy Kelly

While I was wandering up the coast a few years back looking for work, I stuck to the back roads to get a good view of the country on my way into Massachusetts, and I soon found myself lost by late afternoon. I drove well into the night without finding anywhere to stop, so my only choice was to keep driving until I came across a filling station or a motel. I found neither.

It had been hours since I'd seen another vehicle on the road, and my eyes started to get dry and heavy. I barely caught a glimpse of the blindfolded man shuffling alongside the road before I was almost on top of him. I swerved, just missed him, and barely stopped myself from running into the ditch.

I took a deep breath and peered in the rearview mirror and saw the man shuffling away from me at the same slow pace, as if he hadn't even heard the squealing tires. I leaned my head out the window and called out to him, asked him if he was all right. He was moaning. I called out to him again, but he ignored me and kept walking.

I threw the car in reverse, backed up, and then stopped beside him.

I rolled down the passenger side window and asked, "Hey mister. You okay?"

The man stopped crying and tilted his head up, as if he were trying to make out the direction of my voice. He stumbled over to the car and bent over so I could see his bandaged face.

"Baby Girl?" he muttered.

I thought that maybe he had been in some kind of car accident. At the sound of my voice, he stuck his head inside the window and raised a hand to fumble with the blindfold. I saw that his fingertips were stained with blood.

"Baby Girl," he cried. "Listen. I'm sorry. So sorry I did that to you! But you left me no choice... You were bad! So bad! You... I take it back, baby girl. I'm so ashamed. I can't even look at myself in the mirror anymore!" He tore the bandage away from his face and revealed fresh bleeding wounds in the sockets where his eyes used to be. I was so frightened at that point, I didn't know whether to jump out of the car and help him, or slam on the gas.

Then I saw the little girl.

She was walking on the side of the road towards the blind man and the car, wearing a dirty white dress that was soaking wet. Her matted hair, tangled with seaweed, fell entirely in her face, hiding it from view. Barnacles grew on her arms and ankles—she looked as if she had been dug up from the bottom of the ocean.

The man stopped talking and tilted his head to the sound of her wet flapping feet as she plodded along the asphalt towards him. He began to whimper as he quickly stood up and shuffled away from the car on down the road. The little girl followed him, taking no notice of me as she passed the car.

I slammed on the gas pedal.

Two miles later I hit the coastline. I headed north to the nearest town and stopped at the sheriff's station to report what I had seen.

"That's the ghost of old Tom Jeffries," the sheriff growled. "He had a hell of a temper. Never let his daughter out of his sight until the day she asked him if she could go to the neighbor's to play. He took her to the coast and threw her in the sea. We never found her. Couldn't stand himself for what he did, so he went home, gouged his own eyes out in front of a mirror, and hung himself. Folks see his ghost all the time up there. And they see his dead daughter too, following him home.

"Once you get up here in New England," the old sheriff said as he winked at me "you're better off sticking to the highways."

◇◇◇◇◇◇◇◇◇◇◇◇◇◇◇◇◇◇◇◇◇

63. BAG OF GUTS
by Robert Masterson

This is a true story and it happened in a town near here and it wasn't that long ago. My friend's cousin told it to him, he told it to me, and I'm telling it to you and it is totally true.

There was this kid named Tommy or Timmy Guttman or Tony Guttbaum or Guttfreid or Gutt-some-goddamn-thing-or-another. The important thing is that this kid's last name started with Gutt. Maybe his family was from Germany or something. Whatever it was, his name started with Gutt and he was fat. I mean this kid was really fat. A complete pig. Enormous. Huge. Fat.

So, naturally, when this kid started school, the other kids, the normal-sized kids, sort of latched on to him and started teasing him about being so fat. It was one of these really small towns with only one school, so everybody knew each other from kindergarten until senior year. They started teasing Tommy or Tony or Timmy. Probably even some of the other fat kids at school teased him because, standing there next to Gutt-whatever, they didn't look so fat anymore. It was practically fate or destiny that the other kids teased him, picked on him, and made up names for him.

He'd been born for it. They called him "Jelly Belly," "Porky Pig," "Fatso," "Blimp," and whatever popped into their heads.

By third grade, though, everyone had pretty much settled on calling him "Bag of Guts" because of his last name. And that's the way it stayed until even some of the teachers thought of this kid as "Bag of Guts" like it was his real name. Hardly anyone remembered what his first name was, that he even had a real name besides "Bag of Guts."

By the time he got to high school, Bag of Guts weighed in around 400, maybe 500 pounds, and his life was hell. He had taken so much shit for so long that it was pretty clear what the rest of his life was going to be like. He could barely make it to school anyway, could barely walk, so he just sort of dropped out and nobody — no guidance counselors or truant officers—came by the Bag of Guts' house looking to get him to come back or anything. It made everyone's lives a little easier to just not have him around. A few of the meanest, the most sadistic kids really did miss him, but they just shifted their attention to the next weakest kids and made their lives miserable instead. And some of those kids really, really missed the old Bag of Guts.

A year passes, maybe two years, and everyone is getting ready to graduate. Some kids are going off to college, some kids are going off to the army, some kids are just going to get a job, get pregnant, settle down, and settle in. The usual shit. Somebody spray-painted "Class of 19-whatever Rules" on some rocks. Graduation, caps and gowns, pomp and circumstance, best friends forever, don't ever change, blah blah blah.

There was one big party on the night of graduation, a bonfire out at the end of a dirt road into the woods, woods just like these, and about half the newly graduated seniors were out there going "woo hoo" and playing music on car stereos, drinking beer and wine coolers and peppermint schnapps.

All I know, all anyone knows, is that no one came home from that party. When the cops went out there the next morning to check, the fire was still smoldering and the cars were still there, maybe just running out of batteries and still playing party music. What the cops did find out there in the woods, woods just like these, and what freaked everyone out so badly, was a huge burlap sack that someone had made by taking regular size burlap sacks and sewing them all together, an enormous burlap bag stuffed full of teenaged hearts and livers and intestines. One big, gigantic bag of guts—and nobody has seen that Guttman, Guttbaum, Guttfreid kid since.

◇◇◇◇◇◇◇◇◇◇◇◇◇◇◇◇◇◇◇

64. CAT'S CRADLE
by Roger Lord Zeck

Still smug from finding all my camping gear earlier that week in a thrift shop, I ended my afternoon Baxter State Park hike near a stream and pitched my tent.

The guy ropes were extraordinarily long; I had to drive in the pegs a stupid distance out. Fortunately, I knew about hanging white bags off them: save me tripping in the dark.

I got the bags and, when I turned... was it my imagination, or had I really arranged the ropes like that? Like some crazy cat's-cradle?

Wind suddenly rustled the autumn leaves, and I heard fat raindrops plopping.

Working fast, but not fast enough to stay dry, I tied bags to each corner rope. By the time I'd finished, water was trickling down my spine.

I dove inside the tent. Zipping that entrance made one of the most satisfying sounds I'd ever heard.

Daylight fading, I suddenly realised I was starving. But with the rain, I had no way to heat food. I assumed it would be dangerous to light my ancient stove inside the tent. So, what were my options?

I rummaged inside my rucksack.

A can of beans—cold. Better than nothing.

They were sweet and sticky, but I hadn't eaten for five hours, and I scraped the can to extract every last drop.

The rain was hurling itself at my tent now, making it rattle like a drum.

You'll be lucky to get any sleep in this, I thought. I looked for somewhere to put the can.

Not daring to open the flaps, I placed it in a corner, then wriggled into my sleeping bag, got out a book and my wind-up torch. It extinguished almost immediately.

Cursing, I wound for ages, then turned it back on and read.

One paragraph later, the torch faded again.

I swore, closed the book, zipped up my bag and settled down.

At least, I thought, *you're not in that rain. This sleeping bag stinks, though. Pity there wasn't time for Mom to wash it.*

I drifted off.

When I awoke, the rain had ceased, the tent was flooded with moonlight, and everything felt tight around me.

Must have gotten twisted round while I was dreaming.

I was hot anyway.

I tried to pull the bag down to cool off.

The bag wouldn't unzip.

The top, gripping my neck, wouldn't loosen either.

And—was it my imagination, or was the bag actually starting to squeeze harder?

Suddenly, I realised I'd no feeling from the knees down. Panic turned to full-throttle dread in about two seconds!

My circulation, cut off! I hate that!

I drew up my knees and kicked.

In response, the sleeping bag arched, flicked into the air, threw me to the ground, and knocked the wind out of me.

Astonished, I rolled onto my side, recovered my breath, and again brought up my legs.

The sleeping bag immediately responded by solidifying around them like a plaster cast.

Get out this bag now! I thought. But how?

The can! I'd left the jagged lid sticking up. If I could grasp it through the bag...

I wriggled round, used my head to manoeuvre it halfway down the tent, then grabbed; it was like wearing some giant oven mitt. I hacked at the fabric.

The bag tightened around my neck in retaliation, choking me. Knowing I'd black out quickly, I slashed faster.

In seconds a hand was free: I took the can and cut the bag all the way up to my neck.

It went limp, fell away. I lay gasping for breath.

Then, creaking, the tent collapsed over me; the cat's-cradle of ropes tightened, trapping me.

I heard hissing as air got sucked from the tent. I began suffocating.

I gripped the can.

'No tent's eating me!'

I started slashing.

Guy-ropes immediately encircled my wrist, pulling it down.

I flexed, pulled back.

For long moments it was stalemate, while my lungs screamed "Air!"

I was lucky. Rain-softened soil gave, and with it, the pegs. My arm was loose.

I hacked, got out, and ran.

Some people say it was nothing. Coincidence.

But I know what happened. I think it would have eaten me, like an anaconda.

I don't go camping anymore.

◇◇◇◇◇◇◇◇◇◇◇◇◇◇◇◇◇◇◇◇

65. COVENTRY GREENS

by Jason M. Tucker

Until I was twelve years old, I lived in the quiet little town of Coventry and spent most weekends hanging out with Hooper Johns, my best friend.

I'll never forget what I did to him.

Hooper came over to the house on a cold Saturday afternoon in October. Being twelve, we soon found ourselves bored. We weren't at the age yet where we thought chasing girls or sneaking booze would be any fun, so instead we decided to see if we could find the Greenies.

Everyone had tales about the Greenies, inbred folk from the backcountry. People said they were deformed and their skin was green like a witch's. Stories like that were gold for kids our age.

Anyway, Hooper and I grabbed our bikes and told my mother we were heading into town to grab some pizza at Marco Polo's. Instead, we pedaled in the opposite direction and down Harkney Hill Road until we finally came to a little dirt road that led towards Johnson Pond.

The road became a footpath, and we ditched our bikes. Hooper – poor Hooper – said it was getting dark and that we should just forget it. I told him he was a pussy – just about the worst thing one twelve-year-old boy could call another. His shoulders slumped and he nodded.

We walked another quarter mile into the woods until the trail vanished among the weeds and briars.

Then we heard it, a high-pitched whooping sound. I hoped that maybe it was a loon – they make some awful noises – but deep down Hooper and I knew it wasn't birds.

We turned to leave and saw one of them about fifty yards away. It darted into the trees. The remaining sunlight bounced off its twisted, deep green flesh.

Another whoop erupted from the woods behind us, then two more from the front. The Greenies were hunting.

Well, Hooper must have lost it because he took off running and screaming, arms flailing. I did the same. The trail became a blur, and I was strangely aware I had to piss. Then something smashed into the side of my head and I hit the ground hard.

When I awoke, it took a moment for the scene to focus. I was in the corner of what looked and smelled like a slaughter shack, the kind where my father used to butcher deer. The only light came from lanterns hanging from the ceiling. Dried blood spattered the walls.

I heard Hooper whimpering and saw him splayed out on a wooden table. Two Greenies pinned him down as he writhed and tried to get away. Another Greenie, a woman, stood over him. She was chanting unintelligibly and holding something bright green that wriggled in her hand. It looked like a giant worm or grub, one end filled with gnashing teeth.

The woman lowered the worm-thing toward Hooper, and it started to burrow its way inside through his Thundercats t-shirt and into his chest. He started screaming. I must have started screaming too because the Greenies turned toward me. Their eyes were pure white. One let go of Hooper and scrambled toward me. I lashed out with a kick that caught his deformed face and stunned him.

Then I was up and running. Screaming, I ran past the other Greenies and out of the shack. I left Hooper, but caught his frightened eyes on the way out. I never stopped; I never looked back. I left my best friend there with those things, and I never forgave myself.

***

They never found Hooper, and by the time they got to the slaughter shack, the Greenies were gone, probably headed deeper into the wilderness. They searched for months and found nothing. We moved away to Warren the next summer.

I did see Hooper again though. It was just last week, when I took the boys out fishing on Black Pond.

Hooper hid in the bushes across the pond, eyeing me. He was still wearing his Thundercats t-shirt, now faded, torn, and many sizes too small. His limbs were twisted and his skin was green. His eyes were pure white and angry.

I got a bad feeling I might see him again soon.

◇◇◇◇◇◇◇◇◇◇◇◇◇◇◇◇◇◇

66. CRANBERRY FOG

by Stephen D. Rogers

I always thought walking the cranberry bogs was safer than walking along Route 28. I was dead wrong.

The traffic on 28 might be heavy at times, the street poorly lit, the sidewalks non-existent, but I'd rather stagger along the dark and uneven shoulder of the highway than run screaming through the woods.

A twisted ankle was definitely the lesser of the two evils.

That night, my flashlight couldn't cut through the ground fog. Reflected. Refracted. But I'd walked these paths a thousand times. What could be different?

I don't know if I asked that question aloud, so I don't know if that was my mistake, tempting fate.

Tempting ... something.

I never saw what it was that came out of the bog.

I only felt it brush against my ankle. Jumped back but it was clutching at me before I landed.

I kicked blindly, danced, hopped from foot to foot.

And then bolted.

No matter how fast I ran, I couldn't get away from it, the thing grasping at one ankle and then the other.

How could it move so quickly?

Why? Why? Why?

At some point I started screaming. Perhaps I needed to vent the fear. Perhaps I thought I might scare it away. I don't know.

I screamed and I ran and I felt it brushing against me, all but entwining my legs.

Up ahead, the crazy Cape Verdean stood waving a torch.

I now knew what had happened to him all those years ago.

"Run!" He swung the torch and threw it past me.

The thing shrieked.

Pulled away from my legs.

Stayed away.

The creature was gone.

I dropped to my knees, panting, my throat raw and nerves shattered.

Sobbing with relief.

But alive.

◇◇◇◇◇◇◇◇◇◇◇◇◇◇◇◇◇◇

67. THE WHISTLER
by Dana Pearson

When I was a child, my parents would take me camping not too far from here. I look back at it as a really wonderful time in my life. We would fish, hike, and swim. My mother would make s'mores by the campfire and we'd sit around and talk about our day. The week we spent together enjoying the great outdoors was my favorite time of the year. But all that changed one night when I finally asked my father about the Whistler.

Every year as we were driving along the back roads, heading to our camping spot, we would pass a skinny old man hiking along the shoulder of the road. He was never in the same spot twice, and he wasn't always heading in the same direction, but he always wore the exact same clothes - khaki shorts, a plain white t-shirt, and black army boots. And he'd be whistling. Always whistling.

I never really thought much about it, but on the night that I brought it up, my father's eyes grew wide, very wide. I could tell that he knew something about the Whistler. I'd hit a nerve. Before beginning, he looked to my mother and she gave him a simple nod of her head. I was twelve then.

I was old enough to know.

He told me that the old man had been sent home from the war and, because of his wounds, was never expected to walk again.

No one knew his name. He never spoke. It's said that his medical records were lost and his dog tags never recovered. The Veterans Hospital over in Manchester simply referred to him as John Doe.

When he was lucid enough to understand, they gave him the bad news. He was paralyzed from the waist down. His legs were useless.

He didn't take the news well and had to be given a sedative to calm him down. It took three orderlies to restrain him. They say he lost his mind that day, that the shock was just too much for him.

The next morning when they went to check on him, he was gone.

They paged his doctor but, as it turned out, his doctor never showed up for work that day. When they tried to call him at home, his wife answered the phone in hysterics. She'd just found the doctor dead in the garage. His legs were missing.

Everyone suspected it was the missing soldier who murdered the doctor and took his legs, but there was never any evidence. Still, the police searched high and low for him, but he was never found.

But it doesn't end there. Eventually, the Whistler's body began to reject his new legs. The doctor died for nothing. This meant that, once again, the Whistler had to find replacements. From time to time you hear stories of bodies found in the woods with their legs removed. The local newspapers have a field day whenever a new victim is discovered. This kind of thing really sells papers. There have been reports of such corpses found from Keene to the Kancamagus Highway and as far north as the Canadian border.

When I asked my father why he thought the Whistler whistles all the time, he paused for a moment, and then said that it's because he's happy. After being told that he would never walk again, he's happy to be walking. And so he walks. And walks. And walks.

The police have never stopped looking for him, but he always seems to be one step ahead of them.

These days, of course, he travels just beyond the tree line - out of sight, out of mind. Completely out of his mind.

It's been a while since he's been spotted but, late at night as the wind works its way through the trees, if you listen hard enough, you can sometimes hear a whistle.

Shhhhhh….. Did you hear something?

◇◇◇◇◇◇◇◇◇◇◇◇◇◇◇◇◇◇◇

68. DREAM CATCHER

by M.G. Ellington

The Captain didn't rest at Massacre Pond.

His body was buried there and a monument erected, memorializing the tragic day the good Captain and his valiant men were culled from this earth by my people, the Micmac.

Yet still he roams.

Some say he lost his wife and child to a raid. Others say his widow married twice after. Whatever the reason, it is certain that he spent much of his life killing Indians, innocent or otherwise. He once decapitated a man and left his head on a spike as a warning to the other savages. That warning proved an invitation to his murder. He lingers there now.

Sightings of the gangly settler covered in blood surfaced every few years. His notoriety was renewed by the ghost buzz each Halloween. The most recent tale featured an evil specter hoisting the blinking head of his last victim. A local firefighter encountered the Captain at the edge of his 300 year old residence, now the local tavern.

Ghost stories were not told at our dinner table. Mom warned that discussing the dead would open a doorway into our home. In the case of the Captain, it would be sending an engraved invitation to the worst that hell could offer. Just the same, his legend was known in my household. His haunts were personal, not random. He was more than folklore for the descendants of his executioners. I knew something the townspeople didn't.

He still hunts us, the savages.

I was twelve when I first encountered the Captain. He stood there in plain sight. His tattered clothing touted stains from the blood of his victims. The red grime seemed to gleam as if freshly showered on his person. There was old blood as well, the black kind that looked more like mechanic's grease, smeared on his arms and neck. The reality of him was much worse than any fable circling the town.

I saw him from a short distance as dusk settled on the marsh. He was bold. He counted on my recognition. His appearance was intentionally hideous, a wretched sight. The snowy egret drew my eyes to his as it took flight. I couldn't look away. Something passed between us even at that distance. My body shuddered without warning, suspension of disbelief. His gruesome countenance compelled everything in my being to run. Fight or flight; no, just flight. In shocked protest at my hesitation, my jelly legs faltered and then failed, spilling me to the ground.

His sneer was triumphant. His pitch eyes and black hole mouth gaped at me. He was closer now. The edge of the marsh contained him. My parking lot seemed a false sanctuary as I reached for mom's car door. Hurry! Oh please hurry. She saw nothing. I am not sure which was more frightening, his appearance or her indifference.

I said nothing to her. How could I? She didn't see him. She looked right through him. I spent the ride home trembling and praying to the Creator for protection. I also watched the horizon behind us with diligence for the bloody hunter.

In my dreams, he chased me through the Scarborough Salt Marsh, screaming and howling that he would end my life. I woke in a sweat, terrorized and sore, ragged when my mom saw me. She was concerned. "He got to you; didn't he?" She knew the answer. She had seen him. She reached around her neck. With a white face and trembling hands, she passed her necklace to me: a small dream catcher. "He has been chasing our family for centuries. There is no Micmac tribesman in Maine safe from this vengeful monster." We sat facing. She rested her hands on my arm after fastening the catch. "We wear these to protect us from more than bad dreams. You can't leave it over your bed. You must wear it at all times."

I didn't speak. For once, I just listened. She told his familiar tale. "He waits until we see him, until he connects. He uses our dreams to extinguish us. You will see him. He is here. He remains. He can't touch you, though. Not if you wear this. You must wear your dream catcher."

◇◇◇◇◇◇◇◇◇◇◇◇◇◇◇◇◇◇◇

69. GHOSTLY TREATS

by Bobbie Metevier

This lake has always been a lake, but this place... this campsite used to be different. Over toward that tree... well, you have to squint to see it in this light, but there used to be a bakery.

Yeah, I know what you're thinking—a bakery, here in the middle of nowhere?

That's the thing... this didn't used to be the middle of nowhere. Hell, back in the '50s there were cottages—summer folks. They came from all over Maine just to get a taste of this bakery's cakes and turnovers. It was nothing but a mom and pop shop, you understand—rundown, shack-like and barely there. But the treats were addictive. Some folks stayed the summer just to have turnovers with their morning coffee.

Yeah, I know what you're thinking now, too. There isn't a treat in the world worthy of this kind of travel and stay. There's not a chance in hell that a bakery could stay in business out here, either.

That's what I thought too.

Then I came across this story. Maybe you heard a little something about it. Maybe it was before your time.

Either way... his name was Tobe Gardener and he was the first to make the discovery.

What discovery, you might be wondering?

You just stay with me and listen; this is where it gets interesting.

Now, Tobe had heard about the rare treats served up at this bakery, but had never tasted. So on the eve of Memorial Day weekend, 1953, just before the opening of summer season, he decided to set out on his bicycle.

Tobe was a local—well, as local as you could get back then. You see, in the '50s, the area outside this campsite was nothing but woods—a few ponds and wildlife thrown in for good measure.

It was a long trek, but he arrived just a few hours before the start of the season. He walked this very campground backward and forward. And do you know what he found?

Nothing.

There were no summer cabins. There wasn't a bakery. Hell, there weren't even any outhouses.

Tobe held vigil regardless. I suspect he knew the travel trailers would be arriving shortly. I imagine he was wondering what these summer folks would make of the missing bakery and rental cottages.

Then, according to Tobe, about five minutes before the official noon— opening day to the summer folks—something started to happen.

Shadows.

The outline of a small dwelling appeared over by that tree, that one right over there. Like I said, you have to squint to see it in this light.

Tobe said it was like watching someone turn up the contrast and color knobs on a television. At first, he could see right through the thing. I imagine it was like watching a cartoon strip projected on the horizon. Pretty soon the cottages followed suit.

When all these mirages became solid and truly there... that's when the first motor home pulled into the dirt lot.

A woman stepped out of the bakery to greet this first group of summer folks. She was dressed in an old fashioned apron. According to Tobe, the thing about that day that frightened him the most... not cottages and bakeries seeming to create themselves. It was something else. The woman.

Though Tobe was hunkered down in the bushes, she turned to him as if she knew he was there all the time. She winked at him.

Why a bakery, you might wonder?

Why not?

If a ghost wants to lure companions, I can think of far worse enticements.

Say... there's one more thing. Some seasons — not every season, now — but every couple summers people still report seeing the mirage of this bakery out here.

Did I mention the bakery used to be over by that tree? You might have to squint to see it in this light...

◇◇◇◇◇◇◇◇◇◇◇◇◇◇◇◇◇◇◇◇

70. GRAVEYARD SHIFT
by Adam J. Whitlatch

I was seventeen when I came to work the graveyard shift for Jeremiah Winters, the only mortician left in Salem. Not many people will work with Old Man Winters. They think he's a creepy old bastard. And they'd be right, but a seventeen-year-old kid facing college can put up with all kinds of creepy for eight-fifty an hour.

The work was simple, some janitorial work and general "gofering." Nothing too strenuous. Of course Winters was too old to do any heavy lifting, so that left the chore of hefting bodies onto tables and into coffins to me. But, hey, I was Salem High's star linebacker. I was used to moving bodies around, just not ones so cold and clammy.

Other than that I hardly ever had to help with the patients, but occasionally the old man would need an extra pair of hands. That's right, I said "patients." I told you old Jeremiah was an odd duck, but I learned to put up with it. I even learned to put up with it when he started talking to them.

But that's not really so odd. I mean, morticians talk to the deceased all the time, right? Staves off boredom, helps pass the time, keeps you sane. It helps you forget that you're playing with a dead body like a damn Barbie doll; doing their makeup, styling their hair, dressing them up in fancy clothes. No, what bothered me was when the patients started talking back to him.

At first it was just a moan here, a groan there. Winters explained to me that it was just the natural processes. Since I started working for the old man I've heard dead bodies groan, wheeze, even fart. I once saw a body sit bolt upright on the embalming table. Ol' Jeremiah laughed himself silly while I ran up the stairs like an Olympic gold medalist on speed.

So at first we just passed it off as natural processes, but after a while even the old man couldn't deny it anymore. Mr. Lieuziki from down the street was the first to come back. He laid there on the table for over thirty minutes just talking about the weather while the old man continued the autopsy. You'd have thought the old guy was getting a shave and a haircut instead of having his internal organs inventoried.

Even more shocking was when Ol' Jeremiah pulled out a .22 pistol and said, "Sorry, George. Time to go back to sleep. Don't need you upsetting the bereaved."

There wasn't any blood. You need a pulse for that. Thanks to the old man's skill with mortician's wax and some artistic hair styling, no one at George Lieuziki's funeral was ever the wiser. At first I was really disturbed by the whole experience, but the old man gave me a dollar raise to stay and keep my mouth shut. Hey, like I said, I can put up with all kinds of creepy for eight-fifty an hour. And I did, for about a year and a half until things went sour.

Last week while I was scrubbing down the body of Mrs. Brown, the late organist at First Baptist, I suddenly realized she was watching me with those dull, cloudy blue eyes. I damn near pissed myself when she sat up on the table and began licking her pale, wrinkled lips at me suggestively. To this day the image of that withered old crone groping herself and calling out to me in her wheezy, croaking voice still haunts my nightmares.

This behavior was just been too much for Old Man Winters. He simply would not stand for such lewdness in his mortuary, and he told Mrs. Brown this... right before she bit his index finger off at the second knuckle. I had to put her down myself with a crowbar.

So, as you can imagine, we're a little short staffed at the moment with Old Man Winters gone. Poor guy's heart gave out when Mrs. Brown started gnawing on his finger. So what do you say? Think the embalming business is right for you?

Oh, hell. Hand me that shovel, will you? Old Man Winters is getting back up.

◇◇◇◇◇◇◇◇◇◇◇◇◇◇◇◇◇◇◇

71. JUG MEDLEY
by Brandon Layng

We were driving on Route 3 to Laconia when I urgently motioned for Kenneth to pull over. My husband was shocked, slammed on the brakes, and we skidded. My brother, vibrantly snoring in the backseat, pounded into the front seats.

"What the-" Ralphie belched.

"A yard sale." I pointed to a cluttered driveway.

"We almost had an accident!" Kenneth said, exasperated. "Yard sales are full of crap, honey. We'll miss the race."

Kenneth loves motorcycles like Southerners love NASCAR, and Laconia was the biggest event close to home. I flashed my pretty eyes and because he loves me more, he pulled the truck over.

"What about the race?" Ralphie asked, ruby nose poking over the seats.

God bless Kenneth for his patience. He put up with my brother for my sake. My bleeding heart felt sorry for him and Kenneth pretended the same.

"You never know, Ralphie," he said. "Might be a bottle you take a shinin' to."

"I only like them full," Ralphie said, breath beer-soured.

I couldn't help muttering, "We know."

We all got out, Ralphie slugging his gut between the protesting seats, and we looked around. The driveway and a good portion of lawn were scattered with paintings of New Hampshire by local artists, antique farm equipment, piles of books with sailboat covers, mismatched dinnerware sets, and assorted bric-a-brac. To others it was detritus. To me: history. A rusting saber caused wonder about the bodies it had skewered in a bygone era.

Purple finches flitted through the lilacs in front of the house. Traffic rushed back at the road.

Ralphie's delighted exclamation pulled me from my imaginations. I turned to see his discovery, hoping it was sobriety—and wouldn't you know it, the boozehound had found a half-filled jug of dark amber fluid that resembled rum. I could see shadows in the liquid that unsettled me; I swear they were screaming faces. I couldn't resist its pull. The jug itself had piqued my curiosity.

I examined the impression in the glass. It bore the New Hampshire name, yet the pine tree and upright fish on either side of a bundle of arrows was wrong for the state seal.

"Only you, Ralphie," Kenneth said with a shake of his head.

"It's a fake," I said, half amused.

"It's not," said a gravelly voice belonging to an old man coming from the garage. He was nigh on eighty and walked hunched over a cane. "That was the first seal created in 1775. The frigate Raleigh one and its many versions didn't come about until 1784. The current seal's just over fifty years old."

"This jug is over two hundred years old," I said, astounded. "I thought they made the rum jars out of fired clay back then?"

"This one and four others were commissioned by the five counties that made up New Hampshire in 1775. Only three still exist."

Ralphie clued in. "Two-hundred year old rum?"

Sorrow fell on the man. "No, that's new."

"How much?" Ralphie asked, licking his lips.

"Five bucks, will do." The old man shrugged. "I think you deserve it."

"Deal," Ralphie said, and fished in his pocket. The old man stuffed away the crumpled bill and walked lightly into the shade of the garage.

In the truck, Kenneth had his eyes on the road, wanting to make the end of the race. Watching Ralphie guzzling the rum gave me chills. He asked if I wanted the jug when he was done, but the suffering moan caused by his breath over the glass mouth froze my tongue and blood. I wanted to tell him stop, drinking was going to kill him. I couldn't. He smiled, tilting the jug to get the last drop, and I shuddered, watching his mouth twist into silent screams. The jug had begun to...

* * *

It sits on the fireplace mantle now, next to the urn with Ralphie's ashes. I figure he would want to be close to them. I keep a cork in the jug because I can't stand the song of his tortured soul. Coroner pronounced him dead from consumption. That's the truth of it.

I only wonder where the other two jugs are though.

◇◇◇◇◇◇◇◇◇◇◇◇◇◇◇◇◇

72. LEFT HAND WAY
by Frida Westford

Sunset was turning the autumn sugar maples a bloodier red. I was not allowed to be here in the arboretum alone, especially after dark. My small New Hampshire boarding school was big on rules to protect us students. If I were seen returning late to the campus proper, I'd be "grounded" for a week. Just then, I was too furious to care. There was another reason not to linger: these woods were said to be haunted. That's why I stayed.

This is a large wood, much of it wild, with a big pond at the center. The treetops glowed then in the fading sunlight, but by twilight it would be easy to get lost.

It was the ghost of Mother Carvey, who was said to haunt the place. She was supposed to be a witch who lived on a nearby farm. According to legend, her neighbors were too scared to accuse her openly, but they finally drove her out. She died about 1700, but no one knows how. They say she was buried somewhere in these woods.

I wanted to meet her ghost. It sounds crazy, but I had been planning this for weeks. I was curious why a strong, smart woman would choose the left-hand way. Now that I was angry, I thought I knew.

"Donna, are you there?" Amy, my one-time best friend, had followed me. She was gorgeous and could have had any boy. The night before I had seen her in a clinch with Ted, the only boy I wanted.

I took a candle and matches from my pocket. According to local legend, the way to call Mother Carvey was to light a black candle and say certain words. It took me three tries to keep it lit, using my shaking hand as a shield against a sudden breeze.

"Donna, please answer me. I have to talk to you. And we're going to be in a lot of trouble if we're late."

I called loudly: "Mother Carvey, come to me, your student I will be." I was supposed to say "servant," but I didn't want to be in her power. I wanted to learn her power and use it for myself. To make Amy pay, for a start.

"Please, Donna. I didn't mean for Ted to kiss me. I told him off and sent him away. I've been trying to explain, but you won't listen."

I called a second time, louder. The leaves rustled in the wind and, when I moved, those that carpeted the ground crunched under my feet. A cracking twig startled me. Amy was getting closer. I could hear her crying.

I shrieked the final repetition, putting all my fury into it. The black candle flared.

Suddenly, Amy screamed, and then there was silence. Even the breeze died. Frightened now, I blew out the candle, dropped it and ran toward where her voice had come from. "Amy, are you okay?" I tore my jeans on the branches and my hands were bleeding by the time I got through the underbrush to the reedy edge of the pond.

Amy lay crumpled on the ground. I yelled her name again, but she didn't move or answer. I touched her and there was no pulse. Now I felt like crying. I might have given her warts or something, but not this.

The wind that whipped my hair became a laugh. I saw then that the black area behind Amy was not just the shadow of the yew tree. It was a black-cloaked woman older than anyone I had ever seen before. "Come," she croaked. "You were foolish to think you could get power without cost. I will teach you what you have asked to learn. You have paid the tuition." I heard crackling behind me and whirled to see a tree red now with flames, then another and another.

I screamed.

◇◇◇◇◇◇◇◇◇◇◇◇◇◇◇◇◇◇

73. NIGHT SCARES

by Joel Jacobs

I was in the Old Colony Tap in Provincetown, having a scotch after my shift. Ice cubes clanging in a glass caught my attention. I turned. The customer next to me was shaking so hard that his whisky was splashing his shirt. I said, "Are you okay, buddy?"

He looked at me sideways and said, "I'll be fine as soon as I get this down."

"Maybe a straw would help," I suggested. "You wouldn't need to use your hands."

He grinned, put the tumbler to his lips, drained it and plopped it down on to the coaster. I signaled the bartender to get him another.

He inhaled, tilted his head back and blew the air out toward the ceiling. He shrugged as if he had made a decision, grasped the fresh drink, nodded at me, and said, "Thanks."

"You in trouble? The wife driving you crazy? Work getting to you?" I was curious.

"No, none of that, but I've been having terrible nightmares the last couple of weeks. So when it starts to get dark, I become nervous, jumpy."

"What kind of nightmares?"

"Well, it's the same one. It repeats. Are you sure you want to know?"

"Yeah, tell me."

"It's scary," he warned, raising an index finger and waving it back and forth.

"Go ahead,"

"Okay, you asked." His eyes rolled up in their sockets as he began. "I'm climbing a set of stairs in a dilapidated building. Coming up after me is a huge African lion. I can hear the thumping of its footpads reverberating throughout the hollow stairwell and its claws scraping on the metal steps. It's snarling and growling."

He stopped, shivered at the memory and looked wide-eyed at me.

"Go on," I urged.

"My heart is thumping. My legs are cramping. I'm short of breath and running out of floors."

"Creepy," I said.

He shook his head and gulped at the liquid in his glass. "But that's not all," he said. He leaned toward me, exuding the smell of spirits. "There's a door at the top. I push through it into a small room with one window. It's open. The old paint on the frame around it is flaking. I look out. It's about twenty stories down to a wide concrete sidewalk. Just then, the big cat enters. He glares at me and roars. The sound is deafening. I realize that I'm going to have to make a choice, the lion or the drop."

"That's awful. What happens next?"

"I wake up."

"That's good."

"No, it isn't."

"Why?"

"Each night the lion gets closer and I edge nearer to the window sill. Last night I could smell his rancid breath and feel his rough paws on my leg as I was about to jump."

"But you woke up?"

"Yeah, except . . . well, look." He pulled his pant leg up to his knee and pushed down his sock. On his left calf were a series of ribbon-like scabs, behind which was the tell-tale red swelling of infection.

I grimaced and said, "Have you seen a doctor for those?"

"Not yet, but I'm glad you asked me about my nightmares."

"Why, does it make you feel better to talk about them?"

"Well, I didn't start having them until I asked some guy about his. I saw him the next day. He said he slept through the night."

"Great, you're hexing me. I'm outta here, pal." I turned, finished my drink, left a tip and split.

That was three weeks ago.

I'm one of those people who don't dream, ever. The docs say everybody does. You couldn't convince me.

This morning in the shower, I was brushing white paint chips from under my fingernails, when I felt a stinging sensation as the water hit my shoulders. I got out, and looked backwards into the bathroom mirror. Four open scrapes swerved down my back. Blood coursed from them in scarlet rivulets and dripped onto the tile floor. My breakfast surged in my stomach as my mind flashed to the stranger with the terrifying slashes on his leg.

That's why I had to tell... you.

Maybe now, it won't happen to me anymore.

Sleep tight.

◇◇◇◇◇◇◇◇◇◇◇◇◇◇◇◇◇◇◇◇

74. CREEPY CRAWLEYS

by Mary Rajotte

A familiar smell greeted me that first morning I came down to break-fast in the quaint little Colonial house near Gloucester Harbor. "I thought your Granny's recipe would make this feel more like home," John said, ushering me to the table where our plates were piled high with golden griddle cakes. "And we can top them off... with this!"

Side-stepping unpacked boxes, he deftly popped the lid off a small jar of homemade strawberry preserves and dolloped a healthy spoonful in the middle of the stack on my plate. "There were a bunch of these in a basket on the porch this morning with a note. "Welcome to The Bay State. Your neighbors, The Crawleys."

"Isn't that nice!" Instantly brightening at the kind gesture, I cut a por-tion from the stack, slathered it with preserves, and took a bite. Nodding and raising my eyebrows in delight, John took a cue from my approval, and picked up the jar.

As I lifted another forkful to my mouth, he suddenly swatted it out of my hand, sending it skidding in a crimson streak across the floor.

"John! What the hell!"

"Look!" He shoved the jar under my nose, jabbing his finger towards a brown spider floating at a spot near the surface. Two large eyes in the center of its head looked like glossy pellets of caviar that seemed to be dilating, focusing, until suddenly, its legs spasmed all at once as it stirred and tried to pull itself free from the gloop.

"Oh god! Oh no!" I clutched at my somersaulting stomach with one hand, gripping the edge of the table with the other. When I looked up, John had already resealed the jar and flung it into the basket.

"I'm going over there right now!" he barked as he stomped up the hallway.

By the time I staggered outside, he had already hopped the crooked fence separating our property from the Crawleys', and was banging on their front door.

"John!" I hissed at him, cursing under my breath as I followed him.

"I don't give a shit! What they did is fucking unsanitary. What if they're poisonous?"

"Maybe they just... crawled in there and died."

He looked at me incredulously. "Into a sealed jar?!"

"What is all this racket? Why are you thumping on my door?" Mrs. Crawley squinted out at us from behind lace curtains.

John held up the jar. "This! This is why we're thumping on your door!"

The door creaked open slowly, revealing a silvery coif like spun cotton candy. "You don't like strawberry? Something different next time, then."

She nodded matter-of-factly, then moved to close the door, but John butted it wide open with his fist. He bounded into the foyer, and as I followed after him, Mrs. Crawley moved into the living room, where an older gentleman was sitting in a wheelchair with a wool blanket across his lap.

"We like strawberry just fine. It's the fucking spiders we don't like. What the hell's wrong with you?!" John shook the basket at her, but she stood there, unmoving, so he flung it to the floor.

"Tsk-tsk! Such rudeness! Thumbing one's nose at the healthful benefits of spiders." She patted Mr. Crawley's hand, reaching for a jar of preserves that sat on the table beside him. "In my day, one welcomed them."

"What are you talking about?" I scowled, watching as she began to feed Mr. Crawley overflowing tablespoons of the strawberry concoction.

"It is a gift that these little insects give. Warding off fever, staving off infection." A river of strawberries and saliva now dribbled down Mr. Crawley's chin. She smiled at him broadly, her web of hair pulsating and shifting as she spoke. "All it takes is but a few spoonfuls to help the medicine go down. Isn't that right, Edward?"

I could see the swollen bodies of more tiny spiders as they tried to pull their sickeningly disjointed legs free from the sticky syrup. And when Mrs. Crawley turned to smile at me, there were spiders slowly crawling out of her hair, and teeming over her face, and creeping into her eyes.

◇◇◇◇◇◇◇◇◇◇◇◇◇◇◇◇◇◇◇

75. PASSION PLAY
by Michael Josef

I heard about the house as a little kid, we all did. It had been sold a few times since sixty-five, but no one ever stayed there for long. I suppose all towns have their ghost houses, especially in New Hampshire, but this is the real deal.

Anyhow, like I was saying, I always heard the stories about how Mr. Thompson killed his wife and then himself. And certainly, I knew how he had over fifty thousand dollars hidden in the house that nobody has ever seen. But hell, I pretty much figured those were urban legends.

So when Joey told me he wanted to break in and look around, I said no. Of course, a six-pack later, he and I were jimmying open the back door with a rusty crowbar.

At this point, the house had been empty going on twelve years. We entered through the kitchen, armed with only our small flashlights and another six-pack.

There was a door separating the kitchen and dining area from the rest of the house. Joey had already gotten to it and went through, closing it behind him. He was the one holding the beer, so I had no intention of him getting too far ahead. I turned the handle and pushed. It felt like he was holding it closed from the other side, being the jerk he was. I mustered up some strength and shoved hard.

The door opened fast and I nearly fell over on myself. I expected to see Joey standing there pointing and laughing; instead I saw a fully furnished family room, complete with a roaring fireplace.

I turned around fast to leave and realized that the empty kitchen I'd stood in a second ago was now completely different. There were curtains on the windows and dishes in the sink. Hell, I could even smell the roast beef that had been dinner probably only a few minutes ago.

I turned back to the living room and stepped inside. My heart stopped as a man entered into the room at the same time I did. He was muttering to himself and didn't seem to notice me at all. I got closer to the back of the couch to see what he was doing.

He had knelt down to the fire and was emptying the contents of a bag into the fire. I could tell from where I was that it was money, lots of it. I could also see that behind the man lay the body of a young woman, her throat cut. Blood pooled out and there were bloody footprints that were made as he walked past the body.

When he finished with his chore, he left the room again. I have never been so scared in my life. I wanted so badly to be outside that house, out of that nightmare.

I crept around the couch and tried to see if he was on his way back. I didn't see him, so I crept over to where the woman lay on the floor and tried to find a pulse. She was colder than I expected, and it sent a chill down my spine. I went over to the fireplace to see if I could salvage some of the cash. Sadly, it was burned past all hope.

I turned back from the fire and was face to face with the man. In his hand was a pistol. I gasped, and told him to take it easy. He didn't see or hear me at all. He sat down on the couch directly across from me, put the barrel of the gun in his mouth, and pulled the trigger. The sound of the gun was deafening. He slumped down on the couch.

I ran like hell back through the kitchen door, knocking Joey and his open beer onto the floor. He was laughing and cursing at me. The room was now empty of furniture, dishes, and dinner. I went back into the family room; it was now dark and empty.

After I calmed down, I told Joey everything that happened, especially to the money. He didn't believe me 'til later, when he noticed the dried blood on my sneakers.

◇◇◇◇◇◇◇◇◇◇◇◇◇◇◇◇◇

76. PEMAQUID POINT

by Michael J. Hultquist

I flew into Boston and drove up the coast toward Bar Harbor for a lobster vacation, but the plane landed late and traffic was horrendous driving out of Logan. I stopped in a town at the edge of the water in Maine called Pemaquid Point, got a hotel down the street from the famous lighthouse. The stop was semi-planned. I wanted to experience the ocean view and get a head start on the food.

I pulled in early evening. There was just enough glow to make out the water over the coastline. I hit a local restaurant, had my first lobster of the trip with extra butter, and washed it down with a Harbor Lighthouse Ale.

I stumbled back to the hotel and nearly fell asleep to the sounds of the ocean crashing on the shores. It was so rhythmic.

That's when I heard the wail.

It was low, sort of a distant moan. Something about it made my skin crawl. When I heard it again I stepped off the porch and cocked my ear. I could hear it just over the waves, almost trying to mix in. The night was black. I could only make out vague shapes by the crescent moon.

I followed the road down the West Strand Loop, toward the sound. The crashing of the waves was so close off to the left. I passed odd-looking homes on the right, some abandoned and overgrown with weeds, some with faint lights glowing from television sets.

"Help me." I heard it clearly. It was the voice of a young woman, soft, almost inviting.

I passed a thicket of bushes and came to a path that led down toward the water. I couldn't see the rocks. I'd always imagined the oceanfront as being soft and sandy, but I learned the hard way that isn't true.

"Come down here." Her voice was clear as day, directed right at me. I could see her down there, just a silhouette.

I stepped onto the path, but didn't see the pitch, and tumbled down about five feet. I'm sure I looked like an idiot, but I almost kept my balance until I wedged my ankle between two boulders and smacked my right shin onto the rocks. It wasn't broken, but it hurt like hell.

The girl on the rocks came toward me, nothing but a form really. She had to be about 16, maybe a little younger, with dark hair. She looked bluish in the dark. Everything about her looked blue.

"Are you all right?" she asked.

I told her I thought I'd busted my leg, but she didn't seem to listen.

"Can you help me?"

I rubbed my shin and asked if she needed help getting up off the rocks.

She leaned closer and that's when I smelled her. It was like rot, like something died inside of her. She had no eyes, just empty sockets with black tendrils of skin flapping inside of them.

"Help me find her!" she screamed.

I didn't feel the pain in my leg anymore. I didn't feel anything. I don't know how I did it, but I was up and off those rocks and back on the West Strand Loop before I knew it. I didn't look back.

The next morning I told the lady at the front desk what happened. I thought she'd have a good laugh, but she just said, "Where?"

I told her it was dark, but she said she insisted I show her. We headed down the West Strand Loop, past the houses and bushes, and now I could see clearly where I fell. This lady climbed down onto the rocks and started searching for something. There was no way I was going down there.

Near the water between two boulders, she suddenly pulled out a toy doll. It was an old one, a baby doll with ragged, matted hair. She climbed down, stopped at the water's edge, and tossed the doll in.

The doll bobbed along a minute or two. And then suddenly it was gone. It just sank like a stone. Or maybe somebody grabbed it from underneath.

◇◇◇◇◇◇◇◇◇◇◇◇◇◇◇◇◇◇

77. THE PUKWUDGIE

by Linda L. Donahue

I stood atop the Ledge, having hiked the wooded trails of Freetown State Forest in Massachusetts.

Staring into the former quarry, an overwhelming darkness filled my heart. Never had I been suicidal. Never. I had a wonderful job and a beautiful house in New Bedford. Life was good.

Yet something urged me to jump. I believed that by finding perfect happiness, life could only worsen. I scooted nearer the edge, losing the internal argument as to why I shouldn't end it all. The distant, calm lake would be my last sight.

Then I spied a shadow, its unnatural darkness making me shiver.

A black-haired, troll-like creature stared at me. Bulbous eyes glared. A hooked nose overhung snarling lips. Its gut hung to its knees, its naked skin smooth and grey. The creature reeked of malevolence.

I almost plunged to my death trying to run away.

For hours I wandered lost until a park ranger found me on Bell Rock

Road. Scratches I didn't remember getting covered my arms.

Still afraid, I babbled about the creature.

The park ranger drove me to my car, saying, "Local natives call it a Pukwudgie. We've had nine jumpers in six months."

I half-listened, seeing two-foot tall creatures peering around boulders and trees or clinging to wooden signs. Even in my car I wasn't safe. When I glimpsed an evil 'troll' in my rearview mirror, horror film images pervaded my thoughts.

For weeks, I saw shadows sneaking around corners. Footsteps creaked on the stairs. At night they watched me through my bedroom window.

Sleep brought nightmares of committing suicide. While awake, I found myself pouring rat poison in my tea or teetering atop the stairs, remembering the Ledge while vile whispers urged me to jump. When sharp fingernails stabbed my legs through my jeans, I ran from the house.

I sped down Route 79, thinking about ending the madness. I could swerve into oncoming traffic. Or turn around and drive until I hit the ocean. By nightfall, I reached the state park and imagined myself crashing into a tree.

The car scraped against a roadside sign, knocking off the side mirror, restoring my senses. I struggled to stay on the road, fighting un-seen hands at the steering wheel. When I grew too weary to struggle, I hit the brakes.

The car skidded to a halt outside the Wampanoag Reservation. Had fate interceded, taking me to who best understood the nature of these evil homunculi?

While crossing gravel, I heard a truck engine roar, drowning out the crunching beneath my feet. All I need do was run onto the road. It'd be quick. Maybe painless. But the ceaseless whispers would end.

I tensed, resisting. With greater determination, I approached the reservation. I pounded on the longhouse doors.

"I need help!"

An old man with braided hair and wearing Native buckskins under a checked shirt answered. "Come back tomorrow."

"I might kill myself before then."

"There's no outrunning Pukwudgies," he said.

"Then I'm dead."

"I didn't say that." He waved for me to follow him to another cabin.

Bottles, animal-skin bags, and variously shaped skulls cluttered shelves. He mixed strong-smelling powders in a medicine bag, chanted, blew smoke, and shook a rattle. To the bag he added a feather, some dirt he said had come from beneath Profile Rock, a fish scale, and a splinter of charred wood, these four things symbols of nature's elements.

He hung the charm around my neck, saying, "Wear this at all times to protect you from Pukwudgie influence."

"This will get rid of them?"

"Once, my people could have banished evil from the land, but now—" He hung his head almost shamefully. "May the Spirits keep you safe."

As I drove, the self-destructive urges vanished, along with the vile whisperings. Yet oncoming headlights seemed like hateful, glaring eyes. Roadside shadows were hunched, dwarfish shapes. Scratching came from the back seat.

I drove, clutching the medicine bag, recalling the shaman's chant, its rhythmic sound comforting.

I parked in my driveway, then hurried to the covered stoop.

A voice, not inside my head but coming from the darkness, said, "You will slip up. When you forget to wear the charm, I'll be there."

◇◇◇◇◇◇◇◇◇◇◇◇◇◇◇◇◇◇

78. BLACK TOM
by Stephen Mark Rainey

Five people, in three separate incidents, had disappeared while hunting for Black Tom.

That was the geocache's name. It was hidden in the woods east of Providence—in Massachusetts, actually, along the Palmer River. For a time, rumors and speculation ran rampant through the geocaching community, but inevitably, new news replaced the old, and memories of the lost cachers faded like the Narragansett mist at midmorning. Still, for three years afterward, no one ever went looking for that cache.

Having taken up geocaching as a hobby about a year earlier, I decided to change that situation when I went to Providence on a business trip. Geocaching was a sport something akin to high-tech treasure hunting: a person hid a container full of trinkets in the woods; recorded the latitude and longitude coordinates with a GPS device; and then listed the cache, with an appropriate title, on the geocaching Web site. Cache hunters used their GPS devices to go to those coordinates and try to find the container, which was usually well hidden to prevent accidental discovery. The contents themselves were mostly irrelevant. The thrill was in the hunt.

According to his online profile, Black Tom's owner—who went by the name Messor—had never placed or even found any other caches. It all seemed a bit suspicious, and I wondered whether the Massachusetts State Police might have paid this individual some special attention during their investigations. Still, diverting a dedicated geocacher from his purpose usually takes an extreme act of God, and over the past year, I had become very dedicated.

The area in question was a pocket of exceedingly old, very dense woods. I couldn't find a trail, so I parked at the end of a little side road and bushwhacked in. I had been comfortable roaming deep woods since I was old enough to wear shoes, but knowing that several people had vanished from this very spot, I felt an uncustomary edginess beneath the dark canopy. My GPS indicated that my target was less than a quarter-mile away, so I made a beeline straight for it, hoping to find it, sign the logbook, and get out of there before the approaching nightfall.

On the Web site, Messor had written that his cache was named Black Tom after the infamous pirate Tom Grimm, who plundered merchant ships in the waters from Maine to Delaware during the late 17th century. On the order of Massachusetts governor William Phips—the same governor who had overseen the Salem witch trials—Black Tom had been hunted down and killed, supposedly in these very woods.

I didn't find it difficult to envision a bloodthirsty pirate and his crew using these ancient woods as their hideout. It was uncommonly quiet out here; no sounds of birds or other animals—except that, now and again, I heard a peculiar, deep croaking sound, which I didn't think was a frog. In fact, in all my years in the woods, I had never heard anything quite like it.

Soon enough, I came to a particularly dense thicket, and my GPS indicated I was only a few feet from the cache. This was definitely a target-rich environment, full of tangled brush, fallen trees, and rotting stumps. Then, behind a latticework of branches, I spied a stump with a gaping cavity in one side. Inside it, I saw a hard, straight edge: the corner of some kind of container.

Black Tom.

Exhilarated at having found it so readily, I started forward, only to halt in my tracks as a shadow, like a thick, black liquid, began to ooze from the stump—straight toward me. Its leading edge coalesced into a vaguely human-looking form, and in its midst, one glaring blue eye opened to stare at me with unambiguous malice.

I didn't wait around to see what Black Tom actually looked like.

Those others, the ones who had disappeared, must have hesitated a second or two too long.

* * *

Recently, I discovered that Black Tom's woods have been purchased for development by a firm called the Messor Corporation. They plan to build a new subdivision of luxury homes.

That should be interesting.

◇◇◇◇◇◇◇◇◇◇◇◇◇◇◇◇◇◇◇◇

79. SIGN OF THE BEAR

by BV Lawson

We'd seen signs of the bear—the prints, the scat, the mangled trash cans and garbage with scraps half-eaten. Not too unusual at a rural Vermont camp for girls in late summer. The bear usually came around at night, when the girls were in their cabins, sleeping. My husband and I kept the .44 Magnum loaded, just in case.

Then we noticed kitchen knives had gone missing from the lodge. The cook didn't catch it at first since hot dogs and French fries didn't need much in the way of chopping. It wasn't until the delivery of watermelons from Biehlman's grocery over in Swanton that the cook realized her largest, sharpest knives couldn't be found. But bears don't usually steal knives, and the routine "contraband inspection" of the cabins came up empty.

Maybe we'd miscounted before summer began; maybe one of the locals had helped himself while the camp was closed over the winter. We weren't sure. I added knives to my list of items to buy on our next trip to town, and put it out of my head.

Our newest counselor in training was the kind of girl you'd not ordinarily associate with a camp—a fondness for designer shorts, the latest Croc shoes on her unusually tiny feet, and bright nail polish, but we were a little desperate for help this year, so we hired her. Jennifer Gaintree was her name, and she also had a problem with insomnia. One night she came pounding on our door, yelling like she was trying to wake the dead, which we had been—or at least I'd felt as much, too disoriented at first to make sense out of what she was saying.

"I had to use the toilets and on the way back, I saw it! It was the most hideous, evil-smelling thing. I was frozen at first but then I ran here as fast as I could."

I tried to soothe her fears. "It's just a bear, Jennifer. We'll set a few traps."

"But bears don't have red eyes, do they?"

"Red eyes?"

"This thing had red eyes and it was walking upright."

I'd seen bears haul themselves up on their hind legs before, and the moonlight sometimes played strange tricks on you. I assured her that was all it had been, and sent her back to her cabin.

The next day started off well, with lots of sunshine and the usual shrieks of children swimming in the lake or playing badminton. During the afternoon, storm clouds rolled in and by suppertime, the rain was like a waterfall from the sky, with lightning so close, the thunder was almost as loud as sonic booms.

We settled for watching movies in the lodge, but even "The Parent Trap" couldn't lighten the moods of the campers and counselors. We tucked them in with hopes for a brighter day ahead, not knowing how wrong we were.

That night we were awakened by pounding on our door and shouts of "Let me in, it happened again!"

This time we took flashlights and walked with Jennifer along the path she'd taken from her cabin to the outhouse, but the only thing we spotted in the deep mud near the softball field were more bear tracks. Jennifer was almost hysterical, but being a CIT, she needed to be with her group, so we made her return to her assigned cabin.

Back in our own house, we hadn't even had time to take off our shoes, when we heard a drawn-out scream. I'd never known what bloodcurdling meant until I heard that sound, cutting off as suddenly as it began.

My husband picked up the Magnum and we headed for the lake, then stopped dead at the edge of the dock. There was blood all over the wooden planks. No bear tracks this time, just a few footprints outlined in red—left behind by small Croc shoes.

The Sheriff later found a bloodied knife under the dock, but I don't think they ever found prints. Or at least, no human prints. They dragged the lake, but Jennifer's body was never found. We shuttered the camp for good that year. I doubt we'll ever sell it.

◇◇◇◇◇◇◇◇◇◇◇◇◇◇◇◇◇◇◇◇◇

80. SNIP AND RIP
by William T. Vandemark

My flashlight clattered down the stairs, one step at a time, each clunk louder than the previous. The beam bounced crazily in the dark, and shadows raced about the hallway.

"Holy hell," Tommy called out. His own light waved below.

"Sorry," I said.

"Sorry and a cup of bleach won't clean my shorts."

"Just get up here."

Tommy shrugged off his bandolier of wire, picked up my flashlight, and cursed his way up the stairs. At the top, he poked me in the stomach; I took my flashlight and pointed at a doorway.

Within, dark ate the light.

Tommy hesitated.

To be fair, abandoned houses can be kind of creepy. And after Millinocket's paper mill closed, creep was plentiful.

Cavities, Tommy called the houses. Cavities that were rotting the town inside out.

Till then, I'd never really given it much thought. You see, with snip and rip jobs, you get in, punch lath, yank wires, get out. No time to think. At least not till you cash in at a scrap yard.

But sometimes, abandoned houses aren't abandoned after all. That's what I was trying to show Tommy as I steered him ahead, my hand on his shoulder.

In the room, an apparition fluttered.

Tommy jerked and let out a yell. He choked it off and laughed. "It's a curtain, you idiot. The window pane's broken."

As if listening, the tattered gauze lifted. It waved once, then settled.

"No, not that." I swung my flashlight until its beam fell across a woman in a rocking chair. With her head bowed, pale golden hair covered her face. It flowed down to her lap, where withered hands grasped knitting needles. A scarf hung off the needles. It draped to the floor and snaked across the room.

"Goddamn," Tommy said. He stepped to the woman and let out a soft whistle. "Her hair, all that hair—she's knitted it into a scarf. How god-damn freaky is that?"

"She's dead?"

"Dead as dust." He tapped his forehead with his forefinger, a gesture he used when weighing the risk-reward of a job. Then he pulled wire cut-ters out of his pocket.

"What are you doing?"

"Souvenir for a chilly night."

"Don't," I said.

"Why not?"

Now everyone knows that messing with the dead isn't the best of ideas. But I guess to Tommy, defiling a corpse wasn't much different than pluck-ing innards from an abandoned house.

"Well?" he asked, impatient.

"Hair grows," I blurted out, knowing how crazy this was going to sound. "Even after you die."

Tommy blinked several times.

"Maybe she's not done knitting," I explained.

"And maybe you've grabbed too many live wires and done shorted out your brain." He turned, snipped the scarf from the knitting needles, and with a flourish, wrapped the end about his neck. "See," he said. "No oogie boogies."

Then things happened fast.

The woman, relieved of the weight of the scarf, rocked backwards. Her head came up, and her trimmed hair parted. From a mummified face, teeth grinned.

With a start, Tommy lurched away. As he did so, the woman rocked forward with her needles, and Tommy let out a shriek, the quality of which I'd never heard before. It froze me, even though I knew everything was all right, because that kind of sound—when it comes from a place that deep down—makes you wonder if everything's not all right after all. If you follow.

By the time I'd recovered my wits, Tommy was at the door stumbling, twisting, running—the scarf still wrapped around his neck. At his exit the window curtains lifted, as if waving farewell, and a gust of wind slammed the door.

The tail of the scarf caught at the jam.

From without came a strangled squawk, then a thud, heavier than a flashlight.

"Tommy?" I ran and opened the door. The scarf slid free and a second thud followed.

At the bottom of the stairs, Tommy lay flat on his stomach, the scarf wrapped neatly about his neck. He was looking straight up and smiling. For a moment I thought he had just been clowning.

Then I realized the impossibility of his position.

"Tommy?" I called again, my voice small.

Behind me, a rocking chair creaked. Knitting needles ticked. A door blew shut.

◇◇◇◇◇◇◇◇◇◇◇◇◇◇◇◇◇◇◇

81. THE DARE
by Jason A Lavertue

"Come on, Jimmy, or are you chicken?"

Dale Davenport had been busting my balls since I moved to New Hampshire in the second grade. After six years, I'd had enough.

My best friends, Sarah and Steve, had come to support me, and I was grateful to them.

"Just go down, dude, and prove the chump wrong," Steve urged.

We stood at the wood line looking at St. Paul's Church. Beyond it, thousands of grey headstones marked two centuries of the town's history. The autumn sun was falling away and a chill nipped the air.

My gaze was focused on the basement window. Obscured by remnants of mowed summer grass and dirt, I tried to see through it into the abyss. See if all the stories were true. Were there dead bodies of ancient church parishioners stored down there? Or were there young children chained to the walls awaiting the arrival of perverted church elders? No, it was just a church basement, I knew that. Filled with old chairs and dusty religious ornaments. Yet....

"Are you going to wimp out on me, Brodeur?"

I took a step forward. Sarah grabbed my arm.

"You don't have to do this. No one will think less of you."

Sarah's lips moved, but my mother's voice was what I heard. Ultimately, this was what spurred me on. What teenage boy takes his mother's advice?

The crisp fall leaves crunched underfoot. My heart pounded harder with each step. When I was half way there, I stopped and looked back. My three companions eagerly watched me. Dale smirked. Fear of ridicule prevented my feet from doing what my brain wanted them to do: run right past the church and not stop until I hit Washington Street. But manhood awaited me. I would become a legend. That was, if I survived.

I reached the window and knelt down to wipe the grime off the panes. I fished a flashlight out of my pocket and held my breath as I flooded the cellar with light. To my relief, it was exactly what I knew it would be. Nothing but discarded furniture and boxes. I was filled with bravado. Though things could be hiding in the dark recesses or something most undesirable could be waiting in one of the boxes, I pushed the thoughts from my mind and worked my fingers in-between the window frame and concrete to loosen it for removal. It twisted sharply, evading my grasp. I grimaced in anticipation of the impending crash. To my surprise, the window landed in a box of rags.

I rolled onto my stomach and slid my feet in first. I dropped to the dirty wooden floor, and I knew as soon as I touched down I was a made man. James Ryan Brodeur was the shit.

I stood by the window, basking in my newfound glory. I looked at my watch. Five minutes would be plenty long enough to seal my celebrity status. Then I heard it: Sarah's high pitched yelp, which was quickly muffled. I stayed out of sight, too afraid to look outside. I listened as someone trampled across the dead leaves several times from the forest to the church and back again.

I waited. There were heavy footsteps above me. A latch jangled. The door opened and a dull light crept in. Then a series of thuds reverberated down the stairs, followed by another set, then another. My friends' bloodied bodies came to rest at the foot of the staircase.

I stifled a scream. The door slammed shut. As if a dinner bell rang, something in the shadows sniffed the air. A wicked, guttural moan echoed within the pitch black cellar.

With a leap and a pull, I was out the window. I stood up to run but was compelled to check my friends. I bent over and illuminated the room with my flashlight. A pair of sinister red eyes reflected back at me.

I sprang to my feet and ran, but no matter how far away I got, even

after all these years, those eyes are etched eternally into my brain—as are the screams of pain-riddled anguish of my friends.

◇◇◇◇◇◇◇◇◇◇◇◇◇◇◇◇◇◇◇◇

82. THE EXCHANGE
by Michael Stone

The soft plash of wood on water brought to mind a quote. "There is nothing, absolutely nothing, half so much worth doing as simply messing about in boats." My fake English accent stirred Grace to sit up in the bow.

"*Wind in the Willows*, Daddy?"

"You betcha, honey."

She flashed an impish grin, her pale face dappled by the sunlight on the water. I inhaled the tang of leaf that carried from the wooded shoreline. Spring in the northern Appalachians was never less than glorious.

A cold wind came out of nowhere to tease spume from the glittering wavelets. I reached over to secure Grace's lifejacket. She batted my hand away.

"Bad child!" I tweaked her chin playfully and she giggled.

"I can see the moon." I followed her pointing finger, ready to argue that she was mistaken. But the moon was there all right, round and chalky in the daytime sky. It was a strange sight.

A louring cloud moved across the sun.

A large black bird beat its wings overhead.

The stirring of the peach-fuzz hairs on the back of my neck had nothing to do with the plummeting temperature. I laughed off my sudden nervousness.

It was my grandmother's fault. Every Sunday afternoon she sat me down and told me New England legends of hobgoblins and changelings, of werebeasts and ghosts that prowled the woods and shorelines, devouring humans too stupid to realize they'd strayed over otherworldly borders.

I was a rational man; nevertheless, I turned the boat to shore.

"Daddy?"

"Not now," I said sharply. "Let Daddy concentrate." Her brow creased. I forced a smile. "You wanted to tell me something?"

She pointed to the water at the side of the boat. "I saw something down there."

I flicked my gaze to the dark depths and for a second saw something inchoate and white. "The moon's reflection," I said without conviction.

Grace leaned over the gunwale.

"Sit back!"

Something thumped the underside of the boat. My daughter's eyes widened.

"Driftwood," I spat through gritted teeth.

She was still resting her hands on the gunwale. I stopped rowing to rub a sleeve over my brow. "Grace, I asked you to sit—"

She wasn't there.

I blinked stupidly and scanned the wooden seats as though she was playing hide-and-seek.

Her lifejacket bobbed on the water.

"GRACE!" I stood up and the boat rocked dangerously.

I removed my lifejacket, took a deep breath, and jumped in.

The water was colder than I could have imagined. I forced my eyes open and the world was bottle green, giving way to blackness as my clothes dragged me down.

My feet touched the bottom of the lake. I sank to the ankles in soft silt. In the darkness I swept my hands like a blind man.

Please, God! I was haunted by her face, dappled by sunlight and framed by auburn curls.

My tortured lungs rebelled. Silver bubbles erupted from my mouth. I peered upwards, where the hull of the boat was a stark black shape against a bright, unattainable ceiling. I knew I would die down here.

Then Grace was above me. She grabbed my collar and pulled.

My head broke the surface. My marvellous Grace looped a lifejacket around my shoulders and struck out for the shore. Together we scrambled onto a spit of shingle jutting into the lake. A young man ran toward us.

I dropped to my knees and puked up green water.

The guy squatted and regarded me with concern. "You okay, mister?"

I rolled onto my back. A child looked down on me. She wore Grace's sodden clothes and smiled Grace's impish smile.

"Are you OK, Daddy?"

She even had Grace's voice.

"There is nothing," I whispered, "absolutely nothing, half so much worth doing as simply messing about in boats."

I waited for her answer.

She arched her eyebrows. "If you say so."

The young man mistook my tears for relief and clapped me on the shoulder. I rose to my knees and the fey child hugged me. I could not bring myself to hug her back. Her hair reeked of silt and weed and fish rot. I gazed over her shoulder, weeping uncontrollably for my daughter among the waves.

◇◇◇◇◇◇◇◇◇◇◇◇◇◇◇◇◇◇

83. THE HUNT
by Lee Anne Carlson

I don't go out on patrol anymore. My days of walking the beat are long over. Now I'm considered the ears and eyes of the Salem Police Department. I see everything that goes on in the station. After all, I have a great vantage point.

* * *

I ran, blind in the night. They were fast on my heels. Men, jeeps, and ugly dogs. Even now I heard their yelps ricochet off each black tree trunk, echoing in my ears along with the panicked pounding of my heart.

They were coming for me.

I had veered from the trail some time ago, had taken to the misty woods and the lesser known thickets that hemmed in the town. But my shrunken legs were no match for a man's stride, and I floundered through the brush like an ATV, noisy and noticeable.

They would be on me in a minute.

I tried to think back to the evening now, the usual dinner I ate with my wife and bickering kids in our stereotypical suburban home. It had been a long day of traffic tickets, capped off by a single DUI. I had an early morning the next day, what with the department holding its annual opening day. When I went out on porch for a smoke I didn't even notice the neighbor's sprinkler click off, or the haze that crowded about the streetlamp.

She came for me then.

That fat broad I had pulled over three days ago in a stolen vehicle. The one who was stupid enough to run from the Salem PD and then crazy enough to pull a gun on me and my partner.

I didn't want to shoot her.

In the end, she fell flat on the highway, blood spilling from her distended belly. My bullet had nicked an artery. She was dead before the ambulance got there.

I sat in my sergeant's office that afternoon, shaken but too damn stoic to show it. Strange how something like that can unsettle a cop, or perhaps I knew then that the woman wasn't like other perps, with her sly smile and chicken bone fingers.

She came for me three days later while I stood on my lawn, venom slithering into her green eyes as she chanted her hex. And my bones broke. And my nose grew. And I was no longer the man I had once been.

After three hundred years, there were still witches in Salem, Massachusetts, except now they jacked sports cars instead of broomsticks and wore dirty Red Sox caps.

Now my feet were shredded by midnight, sticky crimson matting the fur between my clawed toes. Foam coated the back of my throat, along with putrid bile and blood. I gagged and felt as though my lungs would rupture if I ran any further.

The dogs howled, throaty moans stretching far into the fog. I heard the blaring horn of a jeep. The hunters were loading their guns.

They had me trapped in a clearing with only few bushes and a skinny, sapling oak.

Clever. That witch was disgustingly clever in the way she worked her spells, in the way she mixed meaning and irony into her revenge.

I would be killed by my own friends, the boys I went hunting with on weekends. And I would be torn asunder by the lazy dogs I had let sleep on my living rug.

My wife and kids would probably think I'd skipped out on them.

The hounds burst into the clearing and I felt the first of many rotten jaws close about my body. They took their time tearing fur from skin, gnawing off my ears and tail.

The final blow came when razor teeth punctured my neck. Blood surged against my remaining flesh, cutting off the last scream of pain that rose in my throat.

* * *

They stuffed and mounted my head on the wall above the sergeant's desk. The plaque below me reads "Wild Fox." I'll have to take their word for it. I've never seen my reflection.

No, I don't do much patrolling these days and my squad car has been given to some rookie. But I'm the eyes and ears of the police department, thanks to the last witch in Salem.

◇◇◇◇◇◇◇◇◇◇◇◇◇◇◇◇

84. THE LOST KING OF ATLANTIS
by Dawn Allison

I grew up in Salem, where they burned the witches, or maybe hung them. I'm not real sure. We don't talk about it a whole lot since it was a bazillion years ago and they probably weren't even real witches anyhow.

My dad was a fisherman who worked on one of the big commercial ships. He spent a good deal of time, when he was home, sharing his tall tales of the sea. Mermaids, sirens, the Bermuda Triangle, pirates, sunken treasure, and sea monsters that would have eaten the ship in one swallow if they weren't deadly scared of the surface. Most of the time, though, he was gone. Out at sea.

I don't know if it was because he was gone so much and I worried about him, or just the stories he told, but I was terrible afraid of the water and I never went down to shore, even if the seafood festival was in full swing. Dad warned me that the seawater had a way of getting into your heart and your mind, and that once it was there you couldn't get it out again, you could only obey the call of the waves. Even though I avoided it, the seawater must have got to me somehow, because I heard the call and my feet wouldn't listen when I told them to stay put.

It woke me up from a dead sleep. It was raining out, drizzly and miserable. I could see the glow of the lighthouse from my window. It used to give me comfort, but not that night. I thought I saw a silhouette, the figure of a man, blotting out some of the light. I thought I saw the shadow beckon to me. Then I heard it call my name. Not like a sound coming in through the closed window or anything, but like it came from inside my own head, only it didn't.

I stumbled through the dark house and put on my galoshes and raincoat before I went out the door, through the cold rain into the gray fog that settled on top of the water. That early in the fall it was still a fair bit warmer than the air.

I walked straight to the lighthouse. My father lounged at the base of the building, leaning against it, dripping wet. His skin shone silver in the moonlight, like he'd grown his own scales.

"What are you doing?" I asked.

"Saying goodbye, if I must," my dad said.

"You're supposed to be out to sea."

"I am." There was a glitter in his eyes that matched his skin. "My God, boy, I know I've spun some tall ones, but I've really gone and found it this time!"

"Found what?" The more I looked at him, the more he didn't look like himself. His cheeks puffed in and out like it was an effort for him to breathe.

"Atlantis, my boy! And wouldn't you know it, but the mermaids took me there themselves. I told them to keep an eye out for you. Thought maybe you'd want to see it for yourself someday. If you come, they said they would take you for their king. Howdy-do! Wouldn't you like that? It's a beautiful place, I tell you, a real community down beneath the surface." He looked longingly at the water. I followed his gaze and thought I saw two shimmering faces with full lips and gills. But it was dark, so I wasn't sure.

"I can't stay," Dad said. "You come see me whenever you're ready, though. No shame in being the father of a king, you know it?" He loped off down the beach and splashed into the water. I thought I saw webbing between his bare toes. I could be wrong, though.

When I got back home and slipped into bed, two angelic voices sang me to sleep, like the slap of waves on the hull that my dad swore he couldn't sleep without. Sirens.

He hasn't come back yet, and each day that he doesn't return I think about what he said. Soon, I think, I'm going to go. I've heard the call.

◇◇◇◇◇◇◇◇◇◇◇◇◇◇◇◇◇◇◇◇

85. THE RESTORATION OF PURPLE CURTAINS & OTHER THINGS
by Catherine J. Gardner

It was one of those accidental resurrections. Beatrice Drake was an old lady who lived in Fitzwilliam, New Hampshire. She was a member of the local historical society and had invited a bunch of us over to help restore some old curtains. Foul-smelling things – all dust and mothballs – but adding a few stitches and patching a few holes would earn us the all-important extra credit.

Classical music was playing in the background: a dull piece that sounded as if someone was slamming his or her fists down on a piano. I think it was an amateur effort.   Mrs. Drake had opened the window to let in some good autumn air; a couple of dry leaves had blown against and caught in the net curtains.

I'd pricked my finger for the eighteenth time when I heard a thud. We all looked at each other, counted heads, and then lifted the curtain.

Mrs. Drake had slipped off her chair and wasn't moving. A few of us giggled. One of us screamed. I think I may have been that one.

We all dropped the curtain. It bunched around her body like a shroud. Chairs scraped back. At the window, the net curtains lifted and rose as if the wind was rushing in to give breath to dead Mrs. Drake.

Ed Borovac kicked a corner of the curtain. When she didn't move his shoulders slumped. Someone needed to check her pulse. I was that someone.

Grey hair swirled at her temple as my panicked breath leaned in. There was no pulse at her neck and I didn't need a mirror to know there was no breath left in her body. I stepped away.

Everyone looked at me as if I would have an answer for them as to who we should call or what we should do.

"We should finish restoring the curtain," I said. "She would want that."

I won't deny I was concerned about not getting the extra credit.

No one spoke as we patched up the old curtains. Our stitches were erratic, but then they hadn't been that straight before old Mrs. Drake slipped underneath. As my foot jittered nervously, I felt her cold ankle beside my foot. Ed, seated by the head, looked afraid to move. We finished the curtains and dropped them with a collective sigh.

Beneath her shroud, Beatrice Drake flinched.

Ed Borovac was first out of the door. I was last. The old woman let out a terrible death wheeze, only it was in reverse. This was breath returning to. The old woman shivered and pulled the purple curtains around her thin body. I could see in her eyes that she knew she had died. Tears glistened at the corners of her eyes and I couldn't tell if she was happy or sad. She pulled the old curtains to her face and breathed in and when she looked at me… I shivered and ran.

She's still breathing, old Beatrice Drake. Children chase after her and tell her she smells – and she does – but not of typical old lady things like cat pee and sweat. Beatrice Drake smells of dust and mothballs. It's a scent you never want to find on your skin. It has become an omen for death around Fitzwilliam.

The smell hung around Ed Borovac for a week before he died. His parents received a note scrawled on purple paper on the day of his funeral. The paper had an odd perfume and they couldn't get the scent out of their noses. You can guess the rest.

◇◇◇◇◇◇◇◇◇◇◇◇◇◇◇◇◇◇◇

86. THE STRAND
by Gina Ranalli

Lucy and I had been bumming around historic Quincy Center, window shopping mostly, when we decided to walk over to Chestnut and the old Strand theatre to see what was on the marquee.

Sweating in the sun, both of us in cut-offs and T's, we strolled leisurely, just two teenage girls enjoying the summer.

"I hope they're playing a horror flick," Lucy said.

"Me too," I replied, though I kind of doubted it. The Strand only had one screen and it seldom played any current movies. I supposed we might luck out and get to see Hitchcock, but I was pretty sure it would be some lame romantic comedy.

When we hit Chestnut, we could clearly see the Strand from the corner. The place was huge. Ancient. Built some time in the twenties, I guessed. It had a balcony and a "cry room," things you never saw anymore, not even in 1982, the year Lucy and I went there for the last time.

The marquee, in enormous red letters, announced the playing feature as Humongous, something we'd never heard of, but by then we were desperate to escape from the heat.

We bought our tickets, stopped and grabbed a few cheap goodies from the snack bar, and then found our way into the theater. It was dark and cool, draped in maroon and black. With the scrolled woodwork and curtained walls, it was like stepping back in time, and it was easy to imagine that people had once flooded the place to watch Tracy and Hepburn, Leigh and Gable, from high up in that mysterious balcony that we were never allowed access to.

Our arrival had been perfect timing, with the movie only minutes from starting. Even luckier, we had the entire place, which seemed more like a coliseum to us than a theater, all to ourselves.

The lights dimmed, the curtains slid back to reveal the screen, and the feature began. Lucy and I snuggled down in our seats, munching popcorn and Raisinets, sharing the same soda.

We'd been giggling that the title Humongous sounded like a porn flick, but exchanged a glance when the word Horrendous splashed across the screen, stark black letters on vacant white.

The scene was instantly eerie: we were looking at the inside of a movie theater that bore a startling resemblance to the Strand itself. The camera focused on the seats, apparently filming the audience's reactions.

But only two people composed the theater-goers. The camera zoomed in on a lone woman, smiling happily, perhaps watching a particularly amusing movie. Completely immersed in the film, she didn't notice the man creep stealthily along the row behind her until he suddenly wrapped some kind of cord around her neck, yanking her head backwards as her eyes bulged in surprise and terror.

Beside me, Lucy gasped. My mouth hung opened stupidly as the scene abruptly changed. A young mother in the cry room smothered an infant in her lap with a scarf, seemingly oblivious to what she was doing. Her eyes stared forward, presumably trying to watch whatever movie it was she'd come to see.

The next scene: the theater, again mostly abandoned. Several shadowy figures appeared to be hitting a young man with sticks, until another camera zoom clearly showed that they were not wielding sticks at all. They were plunging knives into the young man, whose face had already gone slack, his eyes glazed.

Scene after scene, until we finally ran from that building (never to return), we bore witness to countless horrific events that had happened in what was now obviously the very theater we were in. Through decades, through time and space, the violence perpetrated within that historic structure came back like ruptured veins of memory, forcing us to watch and learn that places, like people, can be defiled and forever damaged.

And sometimes, also like people, those places will wake up screaming.

◇◇◇◇◇◇◇◇◇◇◇◇◇◇◇◇◇◇◇◇◇◇◇

87. THE T'ANGLE
by Rio Youers

Only when it's raining, and the old-timers say the wind has to be blowing just so. They never tell you from which direction, or how fast. All they say is "just so," as if this will explain everything. But some things can't be explained.

There's a magic at work, you see. Might be Abenaki magic, or some residue from the witching years of the 17th century. Whatever force moves there … it is powerful, and it is real. It can brighten your soul, and it can also be cruel. I've seen it with my own eyes, and I swear it has brought me to my knees. Tears and pain.

My wife, God bless her, used to tell me that my head was wayward. "You're like two people sometimes," she would say, trying to add the appropriate humor to her voice, but I would always catch an undertone of seriousness. Two people, and she would laugh like it was the funniest thing. But I know what I saw.

They call it the T'angle. It's a clearing in the woods just off I-93, not far from the town of Campton. It's triangle-shaped. The sides are equal. Nothing ever grows there. The old-timers say that if you step into the

T'angle when it's raining, and if the wind is blowing just so, that you will be visited by the ghost of a loved one. They will appear in the center, as real as if they were still living. You can talk with them, hold them. You can say goodbye.

We lost our son, Tyler, last November. Seven years old and all the heaven you could hold in your arms. There were five children murdered in Grafton County last year, and Tyler was the last of them. His eyes were as bluc as Lake Winnipesaukee when the sun lays its flat, warm hand upon it. His skin was always so soft.

They never found his killer.

The T'angle, with a cold spring rain filling the sky and the wind gusting in strange eddies: circles of energy, ghosts in themselves. My wife and I—accompanied by the other mourning parents—walked through the forest and came upon that little clearing. We wanted to say goodbye to our children. We wanted magic.

Tyler appeared first. My wife fell to her knees and sobbed. Her shoulders hitched and all the beauty drained from her face. The other parents helped her up. She staggered and fell again. She wiped away her tears and threw out her arms. Our dead son walked into them and held her.

"I love you, baby," she said.

"I love you, Momma."

Tyler looked at me. His eyes were still blue.

"Daddy?"

The wind swirled. His ghost faded, and then reappeared.

"Who did this, baby?" my wife asked. The other parents were crying now, gazing through the swirls of wind for their lost children. I stood rock-still. My heart was static. "Baby … who did this to you?"

Other children appeared. I could see them all now, their faces as blank as paper plates. Small hands.

"I'm scared, Momma."

"Just tell me who did it. Just tell Momma."

"But … he's here."

They entered the T'angle. Weeping, trembling, and disbelieving. I stood on the outside and looked into my son's eyes. He was afraid. Crying. Even death couldn't stop his tears.

My wife used to say that I have a wayward head. "You're like two people sometimes," she would say.

Two people.

I stood at the edge of the T'angle and counted the tears.

"He's here," my son said, and pointed at me.

◇◇◇◇◇◇◇◇◇◇◇◇◇◇◇◇

88. TOOTH FAIRY

by Stephen D. Rogers

I remember when we used to spend a week of summer vacation in Maine. I don't know where the cabin we rented was exactly, only that my father couldn't wait to get away from civilization, the Boston traffic he tolerated every gawdamned day.

That was when my brother was still alive.

We didn't go back afterwards.

The week in Maine was mostly an adventure to me and Jimmy. Because there were so few cars on the road, we were actually allowed to walk to the general store every morning, Jimmy with two dollars and me with three.

We bought balsa airplanes that never lasted the day, always veering towards the nearest pine tree.

We bought handfuls of candy that were gone by the time we reached the cabin and always left us aching.

We bought our freedom from the toothless woman who blocked the screened door as soon as we entered the store.

She only had about four teeth, so it was easy to understand why she wanted a quarter rather than the sweets we'd just bought.

I was happy to give her the money and be done with it. But Jimmy, he couldn't seem to get her out of his mind, and he kept glancing over his shoulders as we walked home each morning with our treasures.

The day before we were scheduled to leave, Jimmy went crazy. Instead of handing her his quarter, he ducked under her arm and scooted out the screened door.

Bang, bang. Bang.

The toothless woman lowered her face until I could count every hair sticking out of her nose.

"Know why I'm missing so many teeth?"

I shook my head.

"Whenever a child tries to cheat me, a tooth goes loose. Then it falls out the day the kid dies."

I handed her my quarter. Jimmy. I offered her everything I had.

"You can't buy back the boy's life." She coughed, and then spat a tooth into her open hand. "It's much too late for that."

The sound of her cackle followed me as I ran out of the store, down the street, and into the cabin.

Jimmy wasn't there.

We searched high and low for him until dark, when my parents called the police.

I stayed up until midnight, and when the day finally ended, I knew I'd never see my poor brother again.

◇◇◇◇◇◇◇◇◇◇◇◇◇◇◇◇

89. WHEN THE DEAD CARRY US AWAY

by Barry Napier

Dale Wilson passed away in 1951 at the age of seventy-seven. He had survived heart attacks and blood pressure problems for twenty years or so, but it was cancer that finally took him down.

But I was there when he passed away, and I don't think cancer had much to do with it.

See, in Dale's younger days, in the late 1800s, there was this movement in Salem and the surrounding towns. There was this shadow organization that met in secret. They were self-proclaimed men of God that did everything they could to revive the fabled witch hunts that had once flourished in Salem. Poor old Dale was born into this culture, watching his father and grandpa capture women who were supposedly practicing witchcraft.

Later in life, Dale became more active in the group. He captured several of the accused and, at the age of thirty-five, burned a "witch" at the stake with his father.

Dale told this story to a few visitors that had come by his house to say their farewells. I'm not sure if he was boasting or trying to finally unburden his heart, but he told the tale to anyone who would listen.

It just so happened that I was one of those people. And before you judge me, rest assured that I never participated in those bogus witch hunts with the Wilson men. But I had known Dale since childhood. So when I got the call from Emily, his daughter, saying that the doctor didn't expect Dale to make it through the night, I went to him.

I sat by his side and we talked about his family's vineyards, our youth, and Dale's deceased wife. Seventy-seven years old, and that was the first time I'd ever seen him cry. He told me he felt certain that God would turn him away and deny him a reunion with his wife.

I asked him why he felt this way.

"I burned that poor woman," he said. "I knew she was innocent, but we burned her. And when the flames licked at her feet and her skin started burning, she prayed to God. When I heard her speak His name, I knew I was damned for what I was doing. But I just kept helping Daddy and threw more wood on the fire."

I had nothing to say. What do you say to something like that?

What he said next was worse.

"I heard her screaming last night in my sleep." He wanted to say more, but his voice was weak and I could see in his eyes that he was fading fast.

He looked away from me as a tear coursed down his cheek. Ashamed, he cast his eyes to the window.

And gasped.

He whimpered and reached out for my hand. "She's here," he said in a trembling breath. "She's come for me."

"Who?"

I looked to the window, wondering if Dale's cancer was making him see things that weren't there. But what I saw at the window nearly made me scream.

There was a woman standing there. She wore a white dress that seemed to have been charred. Her face was in a similar condition, her features blistered and burned. But through the cracked pain of her face, there was the faintest sign of a smile.

"I'm sorry," Dale moaned.

The smile dropped from the girl's face as she reached up to the glass with a mangled, burned hand.

Dale whimpered once more and then expelled his final breath. And as this breath dissipated, so did the woman at the window.

I stood up from the chair, trying to gather my wits. I called for Emily, wanting to tell her about what I had seen. But I was already trying to convince myself that I hadn't really seen it.

So in the end, all I said was, "He's gone."

We covered him with a sheet, and Emily prayed over him as we waited for the coroner to arrive. As we left the room, I looked back to the window.

Sometimes, in my dreams, I can still see what remained on the glass after leaving that room: a delicate handprint, smudged with ash.

◇◇◇◇◇◇◇◇◇◇◇◇◇◇◇◇◇◇◇◇

90. WHERE SPIRITS DWELL
by Brendan P. Myers

One summer, my mother sent me to visit an uncle in southeast Massachusetts. I cried and said I didn't want to go. She smiled and said he lived on a lake and the outdoor air would do me good. On a Saturday, she kissed me goodbye and told me to be good, then put me on a bus.

My uncle greeted me at the other end. On the way to his house, he tried to be nice. He said he worked nights and we probably wouldn't get in each other's way, except on weekends.

We turned off the highway onto a road that cut through deep woods. A few miles later, we turned onto a dirt road that went up a steep hill, and I saw the house. It was more like a cottage, made of white clapboard and peeling paint. The lake beyond was about a half mile across and surrounded by thick woods.

He showed me my bedroom and then the kitchen. There were cereal and canned beans in the cabinet. He winked and said he hoped I liked beans.

Down on the beach, there was a small boat pulled up on the sand. He asked me if I fished and I answered no. He said he'd remedy that.

We settled into a routine. I explored the woods during the day, sometimes waded knee deep in water. At night, I fell asleep in the empty house.

One night, I dreamed I was being chased through the woods. My feet became tangled up in something. I began to struggle. When I opened my eyes I saw moonlight streaming through tattered brown curtains. My legs were tied up in my sheets.

Drenched in sweat, I pulled hard to free my legs and was about to smile at my own foolishness when I heard a thud. Pulling my blanket tighter, I heard it again and shivered. It had followed me from my dreams.

I realized it was coming from the roof. I took a deep breath and tried to reason it out. I'd been sleeping, and in my dreams I heard a thud. But the thud was real, like when you dream a phone rings and then the phone rings. It was nothing more than that. Calming myself, I sat up and listened more intently.

Above my head came a rustling sound, like a huge flag whipping in the wind. That was followed by a sweeping, brushing sound. The roof creaked from the weight and then a pattern emerged: creaks of heavy movement followed by a tap-tap-tapping followed by more creaks and then the rustling.

Feeling silly, I sat up and threw off my covers. As soon as my feet hit the floor, there was a scream. Bloodcurdling and otherworldly, it shook the house. Something fell off a desk across the room and crashed to the floor. I froze.

More rustling and creaking followed the scream — if that's what it was — and then came something new, something my mind said was impossible, but what I knew to be the flapping of gigantic wings. I turned my eyes toward the bedroom window. There was more flapping and then the room went dark. I closed my eyes for I don't know how long. When all I could hear was the beating of my own heart, I opened them again.

Silvery wisps of moonlight again streamed through the window. Whatever was big enough to block out moonlight was gone.

I walked to the window and looked out. The moon was at about two o'clock. It was a few hours before it would set behind the impenetrable forest on the other side of the lake. And up in the star-filled sky flew an enormous bird. It flapped its batlike wings and flew higher, floating on the wind, soaring across the lake. I watched until it disappeared into the trees on the other side.

I never told my uncle. It never happened again.

Many years later, I heard of a place the Wampanoag Indians called Hockomock, where lived their Thunderbird of legend. To them, it was a sacred place. The place where spirits dwell.

◇◇◇◇◇◇◇◇◇◇◇◇◇◇◇◇◇

91. SOME THINGS I'VE LEARNED ABOUT THREE-FINGERED WILLIE

by James S. Dorr

You've heard the legend about Frye's Leap? You know, that big rock formation on Sebago Lake where Captain Frye was chased by Indians—I guess nowadays you say "Native Americans." Anyway, it's a 60-foot drop and he had to jump. But he landed in a snow drift at the base where the lake had iced over, and managed to make his escape to Frye Island.

That's how I heard it.

There're other legends in this part of Maine, like Three-Fingered Willie. And it has to do with Frye's Leap too. He's supposed to be sort of like "Jason" in those movies on TV. But I've learned some things since.

Willie — William — had left his car at the top of the Leap, where there used to be a sort of dirt road, just to drink some beer and enjoy the sun setting over the lake. A group of Boy Scouts had been hiking around there — this was more than fifty years back when even the island was mostly all woods, and not the summer resort that's there now — and a couple of boys started messing with his car. Willie chased them away, then got in his car to leave, but that was when they still had manual gear shifts and he was so mad he accidentally put it in first instead of reverse. And he drove off the cliff.

He, too, survived to escape to the island, but smashing the glass to get through his car's window, he lost two fingers the index and middle ones on his left hand. That's how he got his name.

And now he hated boys.

There used to be a camp on Frye Island, so he was sort of the local boogeyman — you know, the kind the counselors use to scare the kids to keep them in line? But one thing I've learned since: Willie is real.

I know because one fall, after the camp was closed for the winter, I'd had a friend drop me off on Frye Island to do some hunting. Deer sometimes swim there across the lake. So anyhow, I was loaded with buckshot, kind of remembering the legend myself and maybe chuckling a little about it, when all of a sudden I heard a branch break. I thought it might have been a deer, so I sniffed the wind — but it wasn't a deer smell that hit my nose, but something rank.

That's when, with another cracking of branches, a figure reared up before me. Instinctively, I fired with both barrels.

That's when I realized I'd just shot a man. A big man, a bearded man, caked in mud and maybe a few rags left of clothing, and two fingers missing from his left hand.

I knelt down to help — even if, with two rounds of buckshot fired point-blank in his chest, he should have been already dead. Except he wasn't, and that's another thing that I learned. Three-Fingered Willie was not just a man. There was something more to him — some kind of pure evil.

His left hand caught my wrist, twisting it. Pulling. As if all his strength was in just those three fingers. I fainted from the pain, dreaming crazily about the stories, how Three-Fingered Willie tore boys apart whenever he caught them. Limb from limb, eating the pieces. How he once even killed a bear, using just his teeth and those fingers.

When I came to, there was only a hollow where Willie had lain. Some bones and some dirt. I felt waves of hatred take over my being, and now I knew. That it wasn't just boys that inspired this hatred.

A bitter old man, Willie'd hated everyone.

And one last thing I learned, as I gazed at my own hand, the two bloody stubs where there had been fingers: If, as an old man, after plunging sixty feet into the lake, Willie had still been able to swim across to Frye Island, how much easier it would be for a younger version, like me, to swim back.

◇◇◇◇◇◇◇◇◇◇◇◇◇◇◇◇◇◇◇◇

92. A YETI IN GREEN

by John Weagly

Some people would say that the perfect heist takes a team. The problem is, after the robbery the team splits the money, everyone taking their piece of the pie.

I walked into the Union Bank of Jeffersonville, Vermont by myself. I handed the teller a note listing my demands by myself. I walked out of the bank with a duffle bag full of money by myself.

And the whole pie was mine.

My getaway wasn't elaborate; I just got away. I hopped in my car and drove seven miles to Smuggler's Notch, a family-friendly resort at the base of the Green Mountains. Smuggler's Notch features an entrance to The Long Trail, one of four major trails you can hike to get to the summit of Mount Mansfield. I didn't plan on going to the top of the mountain. I just wanted to climb high enough to hide out while the heat died down.

It was fall. The leaves were changing, an explosion of color on every tree. The mountain was at its most beautiful. Families strolled everywhere with cameras and children and picnic baskets. The air was crisp without being too cold and the sun was out: perfect hiking weather.

I carried my duffel bag and walked up the trail. I could smell the pine trees and, under the sounds of tourists clomping about, I could hear chipmunks chittering. After a little while, the sounds of sightseers faded. I left the trail, walked a little while longer and, underneath an imposing sycamore tree, I found a rock without too much moss covering it. I sat down to count my money.

I took a deep, relaxing breath and noticed a new smell in the air, something spicy and unpleasant. I thought about finding a different spot, but I really wanted to see how much money I'd stolen.

Then the noises of the forest died down.

And I heard a twig snap behind me.

I jumped up from my rock, holding onto the duffel bag, and turned around. I expected to see a bear, a bobcat or, even worse, a representative of the Lamoille County Sheriff's Department.

Instead I saw an urban legend.

He stood over seven feet tall and was covered with matted gray fur. He had two long fangs hanging out of his mouth, like a saber-toothed tiger, but other than that his face was made up of human features. The new odor I'd noticed was coming from him.

My first reaction was confusion. I'd heard stories about Bigfoot living in the Rocky Mountains and Yetis living in the Himalayas, but I'd never heard anything about a beast haunting the mountains of my own backyard.

Then I realized I was alone in the woods with a savage creature that was built like a professional wrestler, and my confusion turned to fear.

Like with any other wild animal, I figured my best course of action was stillness. If the Yeti didn't perceive me as a threat, he'd probably travel on his way.

We stared at each other. After a moment, he lumbered toward me.

Sweat trickled down the back of my neck, but I stuck to my plan and didn't move.

He came closer and closer until we stood face to chest.

He smelled the top of my head a couple of times. He poked me in the shoulder with his massive hand. Then he reached down toward my duffel bag.

I tightened my grip on the handle and said gently, "No."

He moved forward, bumping my face with his chest and grunting.

I said, "No!"

He put his hand on the duffel bag and bumped me again. Then he started growling.

Not knowing what else to do, I let go of the bag.

The Yeti lifted my treasure up to his face and smelled it. He seemed to like the scent. Then he looked down at me and grunted.

I tried one more time. "No?"

He turned and walked into the woods.

I watched him go, carrying my fortune. He disappeared in a stand of spruce and silver birch, and I came down from the mountain empty-handed.

That hairy bastard took my whole pie.

◇◇◇◇◇◇◇◇◇◇◇◇◇◇◇◇◇◇◇

93. COYOTE DATE
by Christa M. Miller

The werewolf seduced me on my last night of shore leave. It had been a night of bar hopping and hard drinking—the kind everyone does in Portsmouth, NH—and all I cared about was getting laid one last time before we shipped out.

I guess I got laid. I don't remember. At 0300 I woke suddenly, for no good reason. My head started to throb right away, and that was when I noticed my left arm was doing the same. It was on fucking pins and needles and my first thought was Shit, it's a heart attack, but I'm too young to have a heart attack.

It wasn't a heart attack. It was her. She lay with her back to me, her head pillowed in the crook of my elbow, her dark hair fanned out all around. Under the sheets was a bulk that looked like it could snap me in half. My fingers felt about ten times their regular size.

Coyote date. I'd heard the term before, but until then, I'd never believed it possible that you could meet a girl so ugly that you might actually consider chewing your own arm off to get away from her.

Joke's on you, sailor. Start chewin'.

My arm moved when I tugged on it. So did the girl. She made a sound in the back of her throat, almost a growl, and I froze. All I could think of was that she'd wake up, realize I was leaving and start to cry. Or, worse, try to trade names and numbers.

I started to tug again. Had to fight real hard against the urge to make one massive yank, just pull my arm out straight like the tablecloth in that magic trick I'd never been able to do. Something like a klaxon was going off in my head and I just had this instinct that I needed to get out of there. Right. The fuck. Now.

She rolled onto her back as soon as my elbow was clear, her head right back where we'd started.

We'd gotten a room with drapes that wouldn't close all the way. I remembered that. They were open a couple of inches right in the middle of the window. I could hear the roar of traffic close by and thought I also remembered driving through the Portsmouth Traffic Circle. The orange glow of a sodium lamp streamed into the room. Her face was right in the light.

I swore it looked like it was changing. Even if the dark rings around her eyes were the result of a bad makeup job, the ridge in her nose was unmistakable. The deep creases in her brow made her look worried, as if she was concerned about waking before she was ready.

I started to smell something, a heavy musky odor like the woods. My old man had been a hunter, and I'd loved the way he smelled when he came home—all campfire and pine sap and sweat—but this wasn't a comforting smell. It was—Jesus, it was almost pheromonal, so primal and wild. I tried to shut my sinuses and only breathe from my mouth, but it was so strong I could taste it. I gagged. The alcohol burned back up my throat.

I didn't want to look at her face again, but I had to. This time there was no mistaking the changes. Her lips curled away from her teeth, which had sharpened like vampire fangs. Her breath sounded like soft snarls. The lines in her face had deepened.

Then her eyelids snapped open. Yellow eyes stared up at the ceiling, unfocused. She panted a little. Then, with the softest growl, she rolled over once more so that her snout rested on my shoulder.
She began to chew my arm off.

Once it was free I bolted. She never even seemed to notice. Guess sailor bicep was enough to satisfy her.

I never did return to base. Just ran, kept heading north. The arm socket healed nicely, and the arm itself grew back on the next full moon. I was glad about that. Made it a lot easier to pick up women in bars.

◇◇◇◇◇◇◇◇◇◇◇◇◇◇◇◇◇◇

94. OLD BASSLER HOUSE

by Kevin Lucia

I wish we'd never gone into that old house near my parent's Maine summer cabin in Harrington. We were only going to stay on the porch,
until Joel called Andy pussy.

I should've kicked Joel's ass.

Something felt wrong when I followed Andy through the window into
that musty room. Wallpaper peeled everywhere; junk littered the floor, a
door stood open in the corner.

"What's in there?" Andy asked.

"Don't know," Joel quipped. "You scared?"

"Idiot," I muttered.

Joel - eloquent, as always – replied, "Bite me."

Andy ignored us, approaching the door. When he froze and whispered,
"Holy crap," I joined him and stared at a huge brick pentagram, planted on
the floor in a near-perfect circle.

"Whoa," I breathed.

Joel propped the window with a branch and followed. "What's up?" He stopped, riveted. "Damn."

Of course, we inspected it. We didn't see the flies until we got closer and choked on the rotten stench. Something had died there. Recently.

We clustered by the second floor stairway. "This is messed up," I whispered.

Andy nodded but eyed Joel. "Did you know about this?"

Joel was unnerved, which wasn't cool. He was often an ass, but not a coward. "No way."

After a few minutes, we figured some idiot Goth kids probably made the pentagram. Relaxed, inspiration struck. Joel proposed, "Let's trash it."

Andy frowned. "You mean...."

"Sure. Chuck the bricks; screw up this little Goth-Satanist party." He smirked. "Scared?"

"Fine," Andy deferred, "after you."

Joel's eyes narrowed. I thought he'd pass, but he grinned, ran and grabbed a brick. He threw it, shattering the window.

What happened next is... fuzzy.

We threw bricks through the window; a whirlwind of arms. We grabbed, threw – our faces twisted, howling – as if in pain – eyes flashing weirdly. Minutes later we panted, soaked, though it wasn't hot.

Joel clapped his hands. "Let's go upstairs."

Suddenly, Bassler House was just an old house that needed exploring, so we did. Ten minutes later, we hadn't found much, because the rooms were mostly empty.

I don't know how we missed it, but the smell hit us at the bottom step.

"What the hell ..." Joel breathed.

The pentagram was back, untouched. Flies buzzed, louder than before.

"The window's not broken," Andy croaked.

I pointed to the other room. "Where we came in – it's closed!"

We fled...but found ourselves standing around the pentagram instead, frozen. That's when we heard something sliding down the hallway – something slick dragging near.

Joel grated, "The pentagram... wreck it!"

The spell vanished. We attacked the pentagram; grabbed, threw bricks again. When done, Joel clapped. "Upstairs?"

We ascended and descended. Again, the stench assaulted us. "What the hell?"

"The window's not broken."

"Where we came in is closed. It was open!"

We tried to run, but found ourselves around the pentagram again, while something slid closer.

We struggled, grinding teeth. Joel finally blurted, "Wreck… it."

Again we did, but inevitably found ourselves around the pentagram, the sliding closer. After the same fight, Joel choked, "Wreck…"

"No!" Andy shouted.

Joel stared. "We have to! It's doing this!"

Andy's head jerked. "No…it's a trap!"

I felt sick; stomach lurching. "How do we break it?"

"Leave," Andy gasped. "Leave…. forget!"

The pressure disappeared. The sliding, however…was there.

"Go!"   We sprinted towards the window, which was open, but the sliding filled the room. Hot breath warmed our necks.

Joel was fastest; he made it through first, turned and screamed, "It's coming!"

I was next; Andy last. He grabbed the windowsill and stopped. I saw it in his eyes - he wanted to see it, for some reason — needed to.

He turned.

Joel and I pulled him through the window and we slammed to the rotten porch. The window banged shut, the air silent.

It was over.

"We should go," I managed. "Dad'll have the grill hot by now."

Everyone nodded. We stood, walked away from Bassler House, never told anyone….

….but it wasn't over.

Every night when I sleep, it slides towards my room. The guys never say anything, but I think they hear it too. Something followed us home. Every night, it gets closer…and every night, I pray it's not my last; that the sliding doesn't get me.

◇◇◇◇◇◇◇◇◇◇◇◇◇◇◇◇◇◇

95. THE PACK
by Patrick Rutigliano

Hiking experience and a good sense of direction are prerequisites for any outdoor photographer. They had proven their worth to me countless times, in both warm and winter weather, but I now found myself at a loss.

There had been no haze overhead when I had begun the climb up the Hanging Hills that morning, nor any forecast with which to anticipate its arrival. So gradual was the encroachment on the sky that I missed it entirely as I took shot after shot of the landscape around me.

I knew the place to be ancient. Earthquakes and volcanic activity had birthed the hills shadowing the town of Meriden eons ago, and the evidence of their violence had left behind oddities that drew the eyes of geologists and campers alike.

Rocks pockmarked by escaping gas and shards of obsidian punctuated the route to the panoramas awaiting me above. The place had spawned folklore ranging from black dogs to specters; I could not help but be distracted from the obvious given my environment.

Observing a nearby ledge, a particularly odd formation of rocks drew me from the trail. By the time I had completed the journey to their resting place and taken a few photographs incorporating them into the view, the snow had already begun to fall.

The peaks seemed to attract the flakes as static electricity would gather dust, for hardly a particle of ice seemed inclined to melt. The route I had taken to the outcropping had been arduous, and a descent down the same way I had climbed proved impossible as the soles of my boots slid upon a frost that had manifested within minutes. My situation suddenly desperate, I surveyed my surroundings in search of an alternative.

At first glance, I thought the man another rock, for every aspect of his attire from boots to scarf was black and the large pack he wore upon his shoulders nearly doubled his bulk. He sat at the base of the nearby tree so silently that I started as he revealed himself with a tone mingling amusement and disdain.

"You picked a really lousy time to get lost."

I felt myself brighten despite the mocking character of the man's voice. He seemed unconcerned by the situation, and that confidence suggested possession of the knowledge that would ensure my survival.

The man did not give me the opportunity to speak before he rose and beckoned me to follow him through the grove of naked trees. Perhaps it was foolish to accept, but it is not difficult to find trust when the ground is disappearing beneath your feet.

For what was at least three miles, I echoed the man's footprints through the rising snow. The banks had grown tall enough to obscure all but the peaks of the rocks, and I had begun to wonder just how far refuge might be, when my guide abruptly collapsed to his hands and knees in front of me. I thought the weight on his back the sure source of his exhaustion, and rushed to free him of it so that he might collect himself. I was no more than a foot behind him when I realized that one hand was rising to his face.

I paused as I watched the scarf fall to the layer of powder blanketing the ground. The man's digits plunged into the snow a moment later, and again, the hand came to his mouth, but this time I could detect the motion of his jaws. What turned towards me then was the visage of a frozen corpse.

Water dripped from between thing's frostbitten lips as they formed a caricature of a human smile.

"We have traveled far enough for the sake of certainty. I shall provide you shelter when you are still."

Glancing back as I ran, I felt myself grow faint as he leisurely drew the leftovers of his last meal from the pack and began to eat.

◇◇◇◇◇◇◇◇◇◇◇◇◇◇◇◇◇◇

96. THE STORY
by William Miller

The three of us had come out to the Rhode Island coast to spend the weekend doing everything and nothing, and we had. We'd gone for a swim in Narragansett Bay, eaten lunch at a little inn in Westerly, then spent the afternoon watching horror movies till our eyes and brains were numb.

It was 10 p.m. Saturday night. When Dellamorte, Dellamore was over, Jim got up to turn off the TV. Then he squatted and poked the fire. Joy was half-asleep on the couch.

I rose from my old rag-tag chair, picked my way over the half-dozen Molson bottles piled at my feet, and went to the stereo, switching off the few lights that had remained on during the video barrage. "I have a tape I want to play."

"What is it?"

"*Koyanosquatsi*. The soundtrack. My brother taped it off the TV."

As the eerie music began to drift across the room, Joy stirred. "What is this?" She sounded nervous enough for me to have a little fun with her.

"It's the Devil's music, Joy." I said it low.

"Now don't start. You know that evil stuff scares the shit out of me."

"As it should." I could tell Jim had read my cue perfectly. "But Joy, it's just a movie soundtrack. It only means what you think it means." He paused. "But it really is the Devil's soundtrack."

I laughed. Joy didn't. "That's enough. I don't want to hear any more." She turned a light on, marched over to the tape deck and turned the mood music off. It was just like in Evil Dead. "Jim, you know Grandma said this house isn't blessed. Remember that dream she had when she stayed here?"

I couldn't pass that up. It was much too promising. "Back up a minute. Blessing houses? Nightmares?"

Jim motioned at Joy. "Grandma had a bad nightmare that weekend she stayed up here," she began, her face pinched with reluctance. "She said she dreamed about a man with an axe. It was so real that when she woke, she really thought a man with an axe was here in the house. She was so scared, she said she'd never come here again until the house was blessed."

Jim picked up the ball. "Joy, which one of us do you think would have the axe?"

She never even hesitated. "You!"

"Me? Wait." Jim held up his hand. "My brother Bobby. Maybe it's him."

"Yeah, he's pissed at your grandparents, right?" I asked. "And both of the outboard motors were sabotaged."

Joy was practically hyperventilating. "Grandma said she thinks this is a negative place, and that the people who come here are negative, or become negative. Like The Shining." Jim got up and sat in a chair, his back to the wall. "Remember how we were saying this trip seemed to be full of bad omens?"

"Like your dog shitting on the floor this afternoon?" I said.

"Well maybe it wasn't Simba. Remember that goat with the weird eyes where we ate lunch? The one we insulted the hell out of? Maybe the goat got here before we did. Maybe it was Evil in one of its multiple forms, and it left calling cards."

Perhaps it was even still out there, together with a man biding his time, axe in hand.

I went into the bedroom I was using to get my notebook and pen. This all would make a great story. I joined my friends in the living room, and we settled down in front of yet another movie.

Before long, Jim and Joy were asleep while I scribbled my story. It was the best way I knew how to face my fears: to fictionalize them. I had to wonder, though, whether writing them down gave those fears a physical form that maybe they shouldn't have.

I finished the story after midnight. I put the Koyanosquatsi soundtrack back on, low so as not to wake anyone. I knelt in front of the fireplace to stir the few remaining glowing cinders. Then I picked up the small dull hatchet near the mantel and hacked both Jim and Joy to death.

I thought I heard the goat laugh.

◇◇◇◇◇◇◇◇◇◇◇◇◇◇◇◇

97. THE FORT WILLIAMS SOUL-SNATCHER

by Lachlan Paige

My son used to love visiting Fort Williams State Park up in Cape Elizabeth. He probably still would, except I won't take him up there anymore. Something evil lives there.

We all heard the stories when I was a kid. Most of the old batteries are open for the tourists to walk around, but there's one not many people know about because it's been overgrown by vines and brush. Legend has it that something stayed behind when the old fort closed for the last time. Some say it's the ghost of a psychopathic soldier. Others say it's a demon. Most agree that if you go into that battery, you won't come out the same. It steals your soul.

I saw it happen. A bunch of my friends and I took beer into the fort one late afternoon and stayed past closing, hiding in the brush out behind the commander's mansion. After dusk, already drunk, we set out for the battery. Our friend Destinee thought she'd found it the previous weekend as she walked her dog. It was set into the hillside near the old guard house, under another structure's foundation.

The old iron door stood open a crack, just wide enough for a skinny teen to squeeze through. I wondered why it hadn't been welded shut like the others. Destinee stumbled up to it. "Yah," she announced. "This is it."

Our friend Kyle shouldered her out of the way. "Move it, Dee. What's in there? Just another room? Dude, let's get some sticks and build a fire." He grabbed the door with both hands and pulled. It didn't budge. He shrugged. "Oh well. Guess Dee has to stay out here."

Destinee looked hurt. I tried to put my arm around her but she shrugged me off and went after him. "Kyle? I don't think you should go in there alone. Kyle?" She wedged her body into the crack. She fit. Barely.

"Kyle, where are you?" we heard her ask. And that was it for another five minutes. Or maybe ten. All I know is that we all stood around with our beers, drinking and shivering and not talking, until Kyle came out. Alone.

"Fucked her and left her," one of the guys muttered. Someone shushed him.

"Destinee?" her friend Candice called, without getting too close to the door. "Dee? You okay?"

"She's dead, bitch," said Kyle, and it was his voice but it wasn't his voice, so that Candice screamed a little and jumped back.

"Don't be a tool, Candy." Kyle moved off into the dark. "Or I'll kill you, too."

Candice choked back a sob. The rest of us didn't know what to do. No one had a flashlight and we were all too drunk to make decisions. Eventually we all just left, though not the same way Kyle went, and none of us straying too far from the group.

We never saw him again. Destinee's body was found a few weeks later, when a dog broke free of its leash and followed its nose. She'd been strangled, her head bashed in with a rock.

I'd done my best to forget—and never return to the fort, either—but then my son was born and my wife refused to keep him from what, for her, were fond memories of kite-flying and picnicking. And so we'd taken him there a few times a year, without incident.

Until this past summer. The weekend after he turned six, we took him to visit his favorite spots: the lighthouse, the playground. I'd even gotten over my fears enough to park in the lot near the old battery. Of course Brandon ran off just as we were about to head home.

I panicked. All I could think of was Destinee and how she'd died. I ran straight to the battery, just like the dog who'd found her. There stood Brandon, facing the iron doors, his little face quizzical.

I think I got to him in time. But sometimes, especially when he's angry and lashing out at me with fists and feet still small enough to catch, his little fact twisted with rage... I'm not so sure.

◇◇◇◇◇◇◇◇◇◇◇◇◇◇◇◇◇◇◇

98. THE SEASIDE PARK ZOMBIE

by Christa M. Miller

I know how it must look to see a Bridgeport gangbanger in the New Hampshire north woods. Cops look at me the way they used to back in the city and I know they think I'm bringing business here. I wish I could tell them that's the last thing I want to do.

Three months ago my *jefe,* Fury, came up with a crazy idea. None of us took it seriously and we gave him a ton of shit for it, but he gave us that look, the one that says he'll cut your nuts off and make you eat 'em—he's done it, too—and we shut up. We should have taken him out then.

This was the idea. He followed some guy on the way home one night, he was going to hit him. The guy was dressed all in white, looked rich. Easy mark, right? Well five minutes after Fury started following him, he turned around and called him out. Right there in the middle of the sidewalk on Colorado Avenue.

What was Fury going to do? He couldn't jump him and he couldn't jet. So he had his nine and walked up to the guy, pointed his nine right between the guy's eyes.

And all the guy did was invite him to come with him. I don't know if that's the truth, it definitely don't add up and anyway I know Fury was lying by the way his eyes kept shifting around. They do that a lot. But he went with the guy, all the way out to Holly Street on the east side, to this little brown house shut up tight as a meth lab.

He didn't say what went down in that house. Said it didn't matter. This was what mattered: there was something called Santeria, like voodoo, and the people in that house made shit that was stronger than crank, stronger than chiva. You could turn a person into a zombie, make him do whatever you wanted. Think about that, he said. Whatever we want. Sell drugs without stealing money. Scope out the competition. Kill cops. Fight our wars.

Except he fucked it up. Spent a month hanging out with this weird guy he should've just shot, cooking shit in his lab. Maybe that was problem. Too much crank got into the potion or whatever the fuck he was making.

He made a zombie, all right. Blew his shit in the face of some homeless guy sleeping in the old burned-out bath house down in Seaside Park. But he didn't make a Santeria voodoo zombie like he thought. He made a fuckin' Dawn of the Dead flesh-eating zombie.

The homeless guy went after him first. Natch. No one else was around except me and Cholo, and we booked as soon as the guy bit Fury. Cholo went home to his baby mama and her grandma. Me, I jacked a white guy's Volkswagen and came straight up here. I seen those movies, man. And I seen the news just last week. Bridgeport's in lockdown. No one knows what's going on, but I do. Here's where we got to be, telling anyone who'll listen: make it hot enough. Get guns, get food, get moving. Cause it's gonna be a long winter, man.

◇◇◇◇◇◇◇◇◇◇◇◇◇◇◇◇◇◇

99. THE ROUTE 102 VAMPIRE

by Lachlan Paige

I've never believed in vampires. Let's get that straight up front. When I bought *Rhode Island's Vampire Road* as a housewarming present for my best friend Jill and her new husband Larry, it was because I knew she'd get a kick out of the legends. Not because I thought they were true.

Larry's parents had given them a great little log cabin off Route 102 just outside Exeter. Jay and I drove down to visit them about a month after they moved in. Jill laughed when she saw the book, which I'd found at a secondhand bookstore near our apartment in Dover, New Hampshire. "Perfect! I can't wait to read it." She left it on the kitchen counter. It sat in my line of sight all throughout dinner. I didn't know why it should hold my attention. I hadn't even cracked it. Just saw the title and grabbed it.

After dinner, as we sat talking in the living room, was when I felt it: the close prickle of being watched. It was so strong that I turned in my chair and looked out the window. Of course I saw nothing. What did I expect? Red glowing eyes? But I got up and drew the blinds, even though the living room faced the woods.

The next morning I looked briefly at the book, glancing over the stories of Mercy Brown and Sarah Tillinghast before I closed the cover. The prickle was gone and I felt normal again.

Until that night, when we left for home later than planned — after dusk. As I carried my bags outside, the feeling came back stronger than before. I thought I saw a figure standing near the shed. I was just as glad to get in the car and leave.

Except that the feeling stuck with me all the way up Route 102, around 495 and up 95 too. I had the image of a massive bat-like thing swooping low above the trees beside the roads. I turned my face from the window.

We got home around midnight. As Jay fumbled with his keys I looked into the inky sky, saw the flat faint disc that was the new moon's surface.

Then something bigger and blacker filled my field of vision, like someone on the rooftop had flung a giant black curtain down over me. I couldn't run. I could only watch, paralyzed, anticipating and dreading.

But it vanished. I blinked a few times. The moon slumbered on above me.

I hustled after Jay, heard the door's solid click and wanted to relax. But I couldn't shake the feeling: I was still being watched.

* * *

A few nights later, my nerves frayed by that constant prickle — so strong it had become more like a pressure draped around my shoulders — I sat alone in a nearby coffee shop. Jay was off with friends and I refused to be alone. I sat hunched in a corner, sipping decaf green tea, my back to a window so I could watch the other patrons. None of them seemed interested in me.

Until a young woman walked into the shop. The bell above the door didn't jingle for her. As she passed my table I couldn't take my eyes off her. She was dark and light, hot and cold, fear and comfort. I wanted to know her, and I wanted to run from her.

She caught my eye at the last second and smiled. It reached her eyes. Then they swallowed it, consumed it behind a hungry fire, and that was when I noticed the girl's pointed teeth.

I screamed. Everyone looked. Someone dropped a mug. And the girl vanished. For just a second I thought I saw something like a black cloth spread itself on the air, but it was gone before I stopped screaming.

I've gotten used to that prickle, that pressure. I know she's still with me, waiting. I look for her everywhere I go, see her in everyone. I keep thinking if I can just get back down Route 102, she'll go home, but somehow I don't think so. I think what she really wants is a companion. I just have to work up the nerve.

◇◇◇◇◇◇◇◇◇◇◇◇◇◇◇◇◇◇◇

100. BLACK LAKE

By Jake Burrows

Slaid Cleaves sings a mournful tune, called "Below," about a small village in Maine that was flooded by the Maine Power and Electric Company in 1950 when they built a hydroelectric plant on the Dead River.

The village was Flagstaff, with a population of about 4000 in Somerset County near the town of Eustis—about 20 miles north of Rangeley. Although the town was reportedly abandoned and dismantled to allow construction of the dam, very few people know that just outside of the village proper, the State had recently built and populated a transition camp at the base of Jim Eaton Hill to house 300 patients from the Maine Insane Asylum in Augusta.

Slaid doesn't sing about this part.

The Asylum had burned to the ground the month prior, and the Governor of Maine ordered the Asylum Director to distribute his patients around the state so as not to burden any one township with the entire Asylum population, which numbered in the thousands.

Flagstaff, whether by ill fortune or dark providence, took in the residents of Housing Unit D, the Criminally Insane Unit—a terrifying mob of murderers, serial killers, and arsonists absent of any conscience and alien to human compassion.

On a fog laden morning in March 1950, just before Maine Power and Electric closed the last floodgate on their brand new damn, most of Flagstaff lay silent—save a cluster of ramshackle buildings at the base of Jim Eaton Hill. In those buildings 300 unwary madmen stood manacled to each other by several hundred feet of solid Bath Iron Works' chain. The key to those massive iron locks had long since been discretely disposed of by the camp supervisor.

None would ever claim responsibility for the deadly gaffe that resulted in the mass drowning of Maine's most psychotic denizens, and the whole thing was later quietly relegated to a "clerical error."

I only know these details because I had the ill fortune of bearing witness to the supernatural consequence of this massive loss of life.

Two years ago I joined a group of friends for a camping trip on the banks of an obscure little body of water called "Black Lake." In truth, Black Lake was a bloated section of the Dead River created from the springtime run-off of the surrounding hills. It was an uncharacteristically hot afternoon that began to give way to a muggy, bug filled night. There were six of us—three couples and longtime friends, and we were well into our second bottle of Bushmills when we decided to shed our clothes and take a plunge.

We were all caught up in the moment—drunk on Irish whiskey and filled with the euphoria of good friends and star-punctuated skies. In my stupor, I tried to impress Jenny, my then-girlfriend, by executing a clumsy butterfly stroke towards the deepest part of the lake. A few minutes later I stopped and looked back towards Jenny only to see that she had not even been paying attention. Instead, she was wading back to shore with our friends, racing towards the cooler and the bug spray.

It was then that I realized how far I actually was from land and that no one even saw that I was gone. More importantly, I was exhausted from the swim. I did my best not to panic and began to slowly make my way back to shore.

I suddenly noticed a steady stream of bubbles breaking on the surface to my right. Then, another stream of bubbles appeared to my left; and to my front. I was quickly becoming surrounded by several submerged entities.

I knew that the lake held nothing more dangerous than a snapping turtle, but the bubbling black water completely unnerved me. I began to swim vigorously towards my friends.

As I kicked at the water, my ankles were violently grabbed in the ice-cold clutch of some unseen being. Its grip was hard and painful and began to effortlessly pull me under the dark water. I tried to scream out, but water filled my mouth. All I could do is fight to stay above the surface; and I did—with all of my will.

The water had a dank, fetid taste, like rotting garbage smelled. I spat it out and struggled to breath, the whole while I tried to reach the shore.

I fought as I had never fought for anything before. I did not only fear the possibility of drowning, but I began to consider it an inevitability—a terror that was compounded by the strong iron grasp that dragged at me.

It lasted like this for several minutes when, to my absolute joy, I saw that I was getting closer to shore. My heart leaped when I could see that my friends had taking notice of my situation and were running into the water to help. Yet still, an unseen creature clawed mercilessly at my ankles.

They met me in the water and dragged me to shore, my legs useless to me. As we all collapsed on a heap on the sand, I sucked in the sweet night air and silently thanked God for not drowning me.

Jenny noticed it first. She stood up and pointed towards my feet, a look of abject terror in her eyes. We all followed her gaze.

A pair of heavy antique shackles were secured firmly to my ankles, held in place by an old padlock—locked firmly.

Even in the dim firelight we could make out the letters in relief on the rusty iron chain that held my legs:

Bath Iron Works.

◇◇◇◇◇◇◇◇◇◇◇◇◇◇◇◇◇◇◇◇

www.ingramcontent.com/pod-product-compliance
Lightning Source LLC
Chambersburg PA
CBHW051130030726
47504CB00004B/796